Rebecca Harrington is a twenty-six-year-old writer living in New York City. She has worked at *The Huffington Post* and studied history and literature at Harvard and journalism at Columbia. *Penelope* is her first novel.

Penelope

REBECCA HARRINGTON

virago

VIRAGO

First published in Great Britain in 2013 by Virago Press

First publishing in the United States in 2012 by Vintage books,
a division of Random House, Inc., New York

Copyright © Rebecca Harrington 2012

The moral right of the author has been asserted.

*All characters and events in this publication, other than those
clearly in the public domain, are fictitious and any resemblance
to real persons, living or dead, is purely coincidental.*

All rights reserved.
No part of this publication may be reproduced, stored in a
retrieval system, or transmitted, in any form, or by any means, without
the prior permission in writing of the publisher, nor be otherwise circulated
in any form of binding or cover other than that in which it is published
and without a similar condition including this condition
being imposed on the subsequent purchaser.

A CIP catalogue record for this book
is available from the British Library.

HB ISBN 978-1-84408-926-0
TPB ISBN 978-1-84408-864-5

Typeset in Fairfield by M Rules
Printed and bound in Great Britain by
Clays Ltd, St Ives plc

Papers used by Virago are from well-managed forests
and other responsible sources.

For my beloved grandfather. Without his generous support, brilliance and extraordinarily dry sense of humor I could have never written this book.

And that, thought Reginald, is the last essential quality of the millionaire. Knowing when to say, 'Sorry, but I've got to go now.'

— A. A. MILNE

CONTENTS

I.

Letters of Note

In the July before school started, Penelope Davis O'Shaunessy, an incoming Harvard freshman of average height and lank hair, filled out a survey about what type of roommate she was looking for. She felt she had accurately represented herself as someone who was not too messy while, at the same time, not too clean. Hopefully, she would end up with people who answered the same description.

In August, the Harvard Admissions Office sent Penelope a brief note with the names of her future roommates and their contact information. One roommate, Emma Green, was from New York City, and the other, Lan Wu, was from Palo Alto, California. Penelope hesitated, unsure of whether to contact either of them. Luckily both contacted her before she could decide what to do about the matter.

The first missive was from Emma, the resident of New York City:

Hi, Penelope and Lan,
I wanted to get the ball rolling on introductions, so I figured
I'd tell you guys a bit about myself. My name is Emma and
I'm from New York City. I can't believe I'm going to be
missing out on New York pizza and dry cleaning for a whole
four years! I graduated from Spence and am thinking about
concentrating in history, with maybe an eye toward law
school. I am incredibly committed to my extracurricular
activities and am especially interested in joining student
government or the Institute of Politics. Go Schumer! Of
course, I like to have a good time, if I ever get time to have it.
Also I hear we are living in the worst building on campus.
My mother is complaining.

Emma

Penelope was just about to wonder how it was possible to miss dry cleaning in any particular region when she received an e-mail from Lan of Palo Alto, California:

Dear everyone,
Yes, I am a smoker.

Love,
Lan

Apart from this correspondence, Penelope's summer was much like any other summer. She worked at an ice cream shop. She went to the beach. Occasionally, she pretended she was Julia Child and talked in a funny voice while cooking beef bouillon. Penelope was normal and typical in many respects. Thus she looked forward to college with a certain amount of pleasant apprehension and dread.

When the day finally arrived, Penelope loaded all her possessions into the car and tumbled in next to her mother. Uncharacteristically, Penelope's mother was silent for a while, but as soon as they got onto the highway, her eyes started filling up with tears. Then she said, 'Oh my God, I can't believe this is happening. I just can't. Doesn't it seem like two seconds ago that you were in high school?'

'Yes, it does,' said Penelope.

'I can't believe it. It's sad, but so exciting for you. I bet you will meet the best people.'

'Probably tons of famous scientists,' volunteered Penelope.

'Probably,' said her mother. There was a bit of a silence.

'So what are you going to do once you are up there?' asked Penelope's mother. She said this very casually, which made Penelope nervous.

'How do you mean?' asked Penelope.

'What I mean is, do you have any strategies for making friends at Harvard? How are you going to make a good impression? How will you introduce yourself?'

'I don't know,' said Penelope. 'I was thinking I would strike a balance between friendliness and intelligent raillery.'

'Um, OK,' said Penelope's mother. 'I mean, you can be friendly, but not too friendly. Sometimes silence is best. Especially in the beginning.'

'I suppose,' said Penelope hesitantly.

'It doesn't do anyone good to be too enthusiastic, you know, because that can put people off. Just be friendly. Friendly and aloof.'

'OK,' said Penelope. *A reconciliation of opposites,* she thought.

'So let's go through this. What are you going to say to people when you meet them?'

'Hello.'

'Penelope, seriously. Because, you know, I have heard you say some things that might put people off and you really have to be careful of that.'

'What kinds of things? I don't think I say anything weird,' said Penelope.

'Penelope, I know what I'm talking about.'

'See, I don't,' said Penelope.

'The car seat thing, for example. Whenever you bring that up, it is totally bizarre.'

'What do you mean?' asked Penelope. 'What car seat?'

'Penelope, you know which car seat.'

'You mean the car seat I sat in until I was in fourth grade? That's an interesting anecdote. It is like something Noël Coward would say at a party.'

'What?' said her mother. 'It really isn't.'

'Fine,' said Penelope.

'And you never even had scoliosis.'

'But I was spiritually in a brace,' said Penelope. Her mother ignored her.

'Why don't you promote yourself? Why don't you say that you are a National Merit Scholar?'

'Who would want to know about that?' said Penelope sulkily.

'Lots of people,' said her mother.

'Not any famous scientists!' said Penelope. 'They would find that very boring information. What do you want me to say? Hello, I am Penelope, I am a National Merit Scholar?'

'No, you are missing the point of what I am saying,' said Penelope's mother.

'OK, except I am not,' said Penelope. They were silent until they got to Harvard.

*

Penelope was duly awed. Harvard stretched languidly and impressively into the rest of Cambridge like a redbrick monopoly. It was larger and more obliquely Federalist than Penelope remembered and, if she thought about it, she was intimidated. To her right she saw a large clock tower; to her left she saw a tobacco shop filled with antique pipes. In the center she saw a gigantic Au Bon Pain.

'Wow,' she observed to her mother.

'I know,' said her mother. 'I have never seen that big of an Au Bon Pain before either.'

Penelope and her mother parked the car on a small cobblestone side street and followed several signs emblazoned with arrows and the word 'Registration' in crimson filagree lettering. Eventually they arrived at a small table in the middle of Harvard Yard, the large field around which all the freshmen were going to live. The Yard was very impressive, a wide expanse of perfectly manicured lawns and pathways, surrounded by old brick dormitories. Penelope remembered Harvard Yard from her admissions brochure, specifically a picture of it where Abercrombie models were playing touch football in Harvard sweatshirts and disheveled cashmere bow ties. She was excited to live there. In her fantasies, Penelope pictured herself advocating for Title IX while attractively tackling several men at once.

Two men were sitting at the registration table. Both were about twenty and one had a ponytail. They were laughing at something.

'I know, man,' said one of them. 'What would we do without old Fermat kicking us in the balls?'

'Hello?' said Penelope.

'Oh, hi,' said the ponytail while the first one recovered himself. 'What can we do for you?'

'I'm here to register. I'm a freshman. Penelope O'Shaunessy?'

'O'Shaunessy, O'Shaunessy, ahh, here we are. You have two roommates, as you must already know by now, and you live in Pennypacker, which you also probably know. Here is your key. You live on the third floor . . .'

'Um, where is Pennypacker?' asked Penelope. 'Is it that one?' She pointed to a large brick building with a neoclassical stone porch. A handsome man with chin-length blond hair was walking past it. He was wearing a three-piece khaki linen suit and laughing into a cell phone, like the regent of a tiny, unpronounceable European principality. Penelope wondered if he was drifting toward the registration desk. It seemed as though he was going to.

'Oh, no, it's actually down past the library, across the street,' Ponytail said, pointing to an unseen building. Penelope craned her neck, but she was distracted by the blond man, who really was heading toward the registration desk.

'But I thought all the freshmen lived here,' Penelope said.

'Most all of them do,' Ponytail said. 'You, on the other hand, live in a converted apartment building above a radio station.'

'Oh,' said Penelope. She was disappointed but tried to hide it. The blond man was now within earshot.

'The radio station is great though,' said Ponytail. 'Sometimes they play music for twenty-two hours at a time, uninterrupted.'

'Is that fun?' said Penelope.

'Only if you like flutes, darling, and honestly, who does? In their heart of hearts,' said the blond man as he walked by. Then he was gone.

Penelope walked to her dorm in dejection. Her mother was simply confused.

'But I guess I just don't understand where it is. Do you know where it is? Why is it over a radio station? Who was that guy?' she kept asking Penelope.

'No. I don't know,' said Penelope as she trudged past the library. She wondered if these were the dorms where Ted Kaczynski, the Unabomber, had lived. She remembered from her experience reading conspiracy novels that when Ted Kaczynski was a freshman, he lived outside the Yard, which was apparently the place where the administration put the aberrations of the Harvard community. Penelope wondered what the admissions committee had thought about her. It was probably her essay on car seats that put them off.

When they finally arrived at the dorm, Penelope and her mother were pleasantly surprised. It was redbrick and had white trim. Even if Pilgrims hadn't actually lived in this building in particular, it still looked as if they could have. That was all that Penelope could have desired.

'This is nice,' said Penelope's mother. 'I'm gonna get the car.'

'OK,' said Penelope. 'I'll wait inside.'

Inside the dorm there was a large lobby and a spiral staircase. A boy wearing a butter-yellow polo shirt was moving a mini fridge up the stairs. Penelope thought about the man in the rumpled linen suit. It was possible he lived in her dorm – but she doubted it.

After Penelope's mother arrived, they lugged all of Penelope's possessions up to the third floor and opened the door. The room was composed of a large common room with a bedroom on either side (a single and a double). There was also a small white bathroom next to the single, which was good because Penelope's mother was petrified of coed bathrooms. Penelope assumed she was in the double, since the single seemed to be taken already.

Penelope examined her room, which was shared with a woman who had a predilection for aggressive neatness. Her bedspread was white. Above her bed, she had a poster of Madeleine Albright wagging her finger beneficently. Penelope didn't even know they made posters of Madeleine Albright. 'Bully for her,' Penelope intoned softly so her mother couldn't hear.

After contemplating things of a minute, while her mother put together a shelf in the common room, Penelope decided to make her bed. She put up her posters, which mainly consisted of one five-foot-wide panorama of Diego Luna doing a split on the set of *Dirty Dancing: Havana Nights* – Penelope had decided the poster would be an excellent conversation topic, because that is a movie everyone likes. She then put her desk lamp on the desk. She felt done.

'I really feel ready,' she announced to her mother, who was holding a screwdriver between her teeth.

'Good,' said her mother.

'I think we are all done.'

'Put your toiletries in the bathroom,' said her mother, pointing in that direction.

Penelope sighed. She went back to her room and got her pink shower caddy, which contained shampoo, two hair dryers, and four razors, all in various phases of oxidation. Her roommates had left barely any trace of themselves in the bathroom, each decorously displaying only one clean razor and no shower caddy, as if already demonstrating their superior hygiene and sophistication. Then she opened the medicine cabinet. It was filled with tiny bottles of pills, most of which were Valium.

Penelope closed the medicine cabinet and went back into the common room.

'Well,' said her mother, 'the shelf is done.'

'Awesome,' said Penelope. The shelf seemed to be missing one leg. Penelope put a book on it.

'Have you unpacked everything?'

'Yup,' said Penelope.

'Well, then I guess I better be getting back,' said Penelope's mother, bursting into tears.

'Oh, Mom ... Don't be sad.' Then Penelope started crying too.

'You are going to have the best time here. Finally you are going to have friends, and maybe even a boyfriend.'

'I don't want to yearn after impossibilities,' said Penelope, hiccoughing.

'OK,' said Penelope's mother.

'I am gonna miss you though.'

'We are gonna miss you so much too. Call me as soon as your roommates show up. I think you might really like that Lan girl.'

Penelope walked her mother downstairs and watched her get in the car and drive away. This was it. She was on her own.

Many people have said that you can learn from history, or that history repeats itself, but Penelope did not agree with either of those droll sentiments, at least in application to her social life. Because sometimes history has new eras of unprecedented behavior, and that is what Penelope was hoping to happen to her at college

It was now four o'clock. All she had to do was wait for her roommates to come back so they could all skip laughingly to dinner.

Penelope's roommates still weren't back yet. It was now nine p.m. She had been lying on the floor of the common room watching the only available channel on the TV for three hours. Luckily she found a rerun of the day's *Oprah* in which Oprah interrogated teen prostitutes. It was pretty hard-hitting.

'But why did you turn to sex to make money?' Oprah was

asking a sixteen-year-old blond girl who seemingly had no idea why she didn't become a bank teller.

Enough of this! thought Penelope. In her exceedingly detailed fantasies about college, this is not how she thought the first night was going to progress. She got up and decided to investigate.

The dorm looked menacing when empty, kind of like a manor house where a vicious housekeeper might convince you to throw yourself down the stairs. Penelope shivered and crept down the hall. As she neared the second floor, she heard voices coming from a small room directly below her own. The door was ajar. She knocked. Someone yelled, 'Who's there?'

'It's me, Penelope. I live upstairs?' She pushed open the door. Inside the room, which was much like her own, there were four boys, two sitting on a blue corduroy futon and two sitting on the floor. The two on the futon were looking at their laptops. The two on the floor were sharing a beer. They all stared at her in a pointed but uninterested way. Then they went back to their activities.

'Nikil,' said a boy sitting on the futon, who was wearing a pair of thin rectangular glasses, to the other boy on the futon who was not wearing glasses, 'do you know Sheila Bronstein?'

'That name sounds really familiar,' said the one that was presumably Nikil. 'Did she go to Stuy?'

'No, Science,' said Glasses.

'Those girls were all so busted,' said Nikil. 'But it's weird. I feel like I know her. It sounds so familiar.'

'Do you want to play checkers?' asked Glasses.

Nikil nodded. Apparently he and Glasses were the only ones talking/able to play checkers. Everyone else stayed motionless on the floor, while Glasses and Nikil went to find the checkerboard in a large Tupperware full of other board games.

'Hi, I'm Penelope,' said Penelope again to the other two. 'I'm from Connecticut.'

'Hi, I'm Jason,' said a remarkably egg-like person with red mottled skin and a mop of flaxen hair. The effort of salutation seemed to exhaust him. He lapsed into silence.

'Ted,' said the other one. Ted looked a little like Penelope would expect Mark Anthony to look, as he had small curling bangs.

'Do you live here?' asked Penelope.

'Indeed,' said Ted. 'Jason lives across the hall.'

'I wonder what across the hall is like,' said Penelope.

'What?' said Ted.

'Nothing,' said Penelope.

Nikil and Glasses came back from the Tupperware. They seemed surprised that Penelope was still there.

'Hi,' said Penelope. 'I'm Penelope. I'm from Connecticut.' Then she remembered her mother's admonition to be silent. It was too late now. Pretty soon she would be talking about the car seat.

'You guys are the only people who I have met in the dorm,' she continued.

'Yeah,' said Glasses. 'That's 'cause everyone else is at the panel.'

'The panel? What panel?' Penelope asked.

'Oh, the panel on medical school admissions,' said Nikil.

'But medical school is like six years away from now,' Penelope said.

'Yeah, I'm more interested in finance. But I'm waiting for the one on law school. That's on Thursday,' said Nikil.

'Me too, man,' said Glasses. They high-fived.

'I mean, it's not like this is some blow-off week,' said Nikil, addressing everyone and no one. 'This week's for us to take stock of our futures. We have to take placement exams, we have to meet with our proctors, we have to choose our classes. It's going to involve a lot of time. I'm planning on having a busy semester.'

'What are the placement exams?' asked Penelope.

'Did you read the freshman orientation materials at all?' asked Nikil, aghast. 'The placement exam is the test they give this week to place us into the correct required math and English courses.'

'Oh, those,' said Penelope. 'I thought those weren't a big deal and we couldn't study for them or anything. When are they?'

'In a couple of days,' said Glasses. 'That's why we're staying in tonight. We can relax a little later at the ice cream social. I am going to at least see if I can get into Math 55.'

They high-fived again. Penelope noticed for the first time that Glasses was wearing a mock turtleneck even though it was approximately 105 degrees outside.

'I didn't realize the placement exam was so soon. But I mean, there is nothing you can do to prepare for them. We don't have to stay in. This is our first night here, in college,' said Penelope.

No one replied to this, so Penelope started giggling.

'You know, when I was little . . .' she started.

'What are you gonna major in?' asked Ted, as if sensing disaster was ahead.

'It's "concentrate." As in, "What are you going to concentrate in?"' said Glasses. He slowly placed one red checker upon another red checker. This seemed to please him immensely.

'Um, I don't know. Maybe English,' said Penelope.

'I have never heard that before,' said Ted.

'English?' said Penelope.

'Well, that is what it is called,' said Glasses. 'It's not called a major. It's called a concentration. Personally, I think that terminology makes it much clearer.'

'I agree,' said Nikil.

'So I would say, "I am concentrating in English," when actually I am majoring in it?' said Penelope, feeling that awful giggle in the back of her throat.

Nikil's eyebrows arched downward, as if too exasperated to hold themselves in place.

'Yeah,' he said.

'Oh,' said Penelope. 'OK, well, I'm gonna go. It was really nice meeting all of you. I just live upstairs so, you know, you can come up there anytime. I don't have any checkers though, but ah, well, OK. Good-bye!' She left. Ted followed her.

'Do you live on the third floor?' asked Penelope.

'No,' said Ted. 'I live in that room. Like I told you before.'

'Oh,' said Penelope.

They walked up the stairs in silence.

'I think the panel is getting out soon,' said Ted.

'Oh, do you? That's good. I have yet to meet my roommates. Have you met them?'

'What are their names?'

'Lan and Emma.'

'Nope,' said Ted. 'There are some real winners here though.'

'That's good to know and, also, self-evident,' said Penelope. Fortunately they were practically at her room.

'Thanks for walking me back,' said Penelope.

'That's OK,' said Ted.

'OK, bye!' yelled Penelope as she darted into her suite and shut her door briskly behind her. It was the fifth-longest conversation she had ever had with a boy. She lay down on the futon with a pit in her stomach.

Emma came back first. She was prettier than Penelope had thought she would be, in a pointy kind of way. Even her forehead came to a point in the middle of her head.

'Hey, are you Penelope?' she asked Penelope, who was still lying prone on the futon. Penelope jumped up.

'Oh, hi!' said Penelope. 'Yes, that's me. Are you Emma?'

'Yes, hi.' She held out her hand and Penelope shook it. 'How long have you been here?'

'Oh, not long,' said Penelope. 'I talked to some kids downstairs for a while. They're a little weird.'

'Oh,' said Emma. She put her bag down on the double. She was the Madeleine Albright owner.

'How was the panel?'

'The panel was really informative, actually. The application statistics were horrible, of course, but, I mean, when are they not?' Emma exploded into a hooting laugh. Penelope watched her in awe. She continued. 'You know, I interned in a hospital for six summers, so I kind of get the whole culture of hospitals. It's a very very intense work environment, which I would be totally fine with because that really fits my personality, but I think I'm just too compassionate for it. I feel other people's pain a little too much, you know? I mean, I cry just thinking about hurting someone, and imagine if you had to cut someone open? I just can't imagine doing it. I don't really know how doctors go home every day and live with themselves, to be honest. So I don't think I want to go to medical school, but I thought it was pretty important to check it out, you know?'

'Yeah,' said Penelope.

'I just want to keep all my career options open at this point. In high school, I was involved in twelve extracurricular activities, all of which helped me explore my future. And it was this totally great experience. Fencing was really my first love –'

'When did you get here?' Penelope blurted out.

Emma blinked.

'We got here yesterday. I stayed with my parents in the hotel and we moved in early this morning. You have to make the reservations like a year in advance, so the minute I got the letter last year my parents made a reservation at the Charles Hotel. They just left.'

'Oh, cool,' said Penelope.

'My father is going out of the country on business next week.'

'Neat,' said Penelope.

'He speaks fluent Russian. It really helps when you travel the world. Russian is a world language now, which is pretty amazing.'

'That is amazing,' said Penelope. 'Does he walk around in a fur hat in Moscow?'

'No,' said Emma. 'He's not even going to Moscow. He just knows Russian because he is a very erudite man.'

'I have always wanted to wear one of those hats,' said Penelope.

'Oh,' said Emma. She went into her room, which was also Penelope's room. Penelope sat back down on the futon and kicked her foot against the floor a few times.

'You're from Connecticut, right?' said Emma from the bedroom. 'I think I read that on your contact information.'

'Uh, yeah.'

'Choate?'

'Excuse me?'

'I mean, like, did you go to Choate? As in Choate Rosemary Hall? I know some kids there.'

'Um, no,' said Penelope.

'Oh,' said Emma, who seemed disappointed.

There was a pause.

'Do you think you will miss your high school?' asked Penelope.

'In what way?' said Emma, popping her head out of the bedroom.

'Oh, I don't know. Like your friends or something.'

'I loved high school. It was really challenging. I mean literally, we had some of the brightest people in the country there. The math department taught college-level differential equations to sixth graders. We spent most of the day recreationally betting on the stock market.'

'That sounds fun,' said Penelope.

'So yes, I think I will miss it. But not as much as I will like it here.' Emma went back into their room and started to organize her part of the closet, which seemed to take up the entire closet.

'Oh, me too,' said Penelope. 'Have you met this Lan woman?'

'Lan? Yeah, we said hi.'

'What is she like?'

'She's nice,' said Emma. She closed the bedroom door. Penelope lay down on the futon again. She fell into an unsettling half sleep, while Emma jabbered on the phone in the next room. Penelope didn't usually sleep with the lights on, but apparently Harvard made her have narcolepsy. She kept lapsing into a dream where a giant car seat was coming to eat her and all she could do was plead with it for mercy in Latin. Which was really weird because she didn't even speak Latin.

Penelope woke up with a start. A person who must have been Lan was hovering five inches from her face.

By the time Penelope sat up, Lan already seemed bored with her discovery. Almost instantaneously, she seated herself on the windowsill and started to roll a cigarette.

'Hey,' said Lan in a completely inflectionless voice. Long bangs obscured the top half of her face. She was wearing a black T-shirt emblazoned with a decal of a snowman wearing sunglasses.

'Hi,' said Penelope. 'I'm Penelope.'

'I know,' said Lan. She started to lick the paper of her rapidly forming cigarette and then paused. 'Do you want one?' she said, gesturing to her creation.

'No,' said Penelope. 'I don't smoke, but a lot of my friends do, ha.' That was a lie. None of Penelope's friends did anything but occasionally miserably meet up at a local Chili's.

'OK. I wasn't really going to give you one,' said Lan. She lit her cigarette and blew smoke out the window.

'Did you go the panel?' asked Penelope.

'Yeah,' said Lan.

'Oh,' said Penelope. 'Did you like it?'

Lan was silent.

'What did you do afterward?'

'I watched a movie.'

'Oh, that's cool,' said Penelope.

'Not really,' said Lan.

'I guess not,' said Penelope. 'Who did you see it with? Have you met anyone cute? Boys, I mean?' Penelope winced.

Lan was silent again.

'Um, what are you going to concentrate in?' asked Penelope.

'Biomedical engineering,' said Lan.

'That's really cool. I can't do anything with numbers, or engineering. I'm more of a language person myself, or maybe history, but I kind of hate history, so I don't really know.'

'How can you hate history?' said Lan, throwing her cigarette out the window.

'I mean, I don't hate the fact that there is history in the world. That would be stupid. But sometimes I think it's kind of boring. I don't know.'

'OK, I'm going to bed,' said Lan, and stalked into her room.

Penelope was alone in the common room. She immediately fell asleep on the futon.

2.

An Ice Cream Social

The day of the placement exam, Penelope woke up with a stiff neck. At first she forgot she was at Harvard. Then she remembered.

Penelope had a full day ahead. She had a placement test, a proctor meeting, and an ice cream social. Even though these activities seemed to be conceived with an immature seventh grader in mind, she was glad of their existence. She had spent the last couple of days watching *Oprah* while everyone else studied for the placement exam, and it was getting very emotionally tiring.

Penelope padded over to the bathroom to take a shower. Emma was gone and her bed was immaculately made. Lan's room was dark and locked shut. Penelope thought she smelled pot emanating from under the door. She knocked.

'Hey, do you want to get breakfast?' she asked through the door. There was no answer. 'OK, you don't have to.'

Penelope showered. She put on her favorite jeans and a

blouse with a Peter Pan collar. She partially blow-dried her hair, braided it, and went to breakfast.

Annenberg Hall, where breakfast was served, was a gigantic Victorian gothic structure tempered only by the tenets of Christian Science from reaching true *Harry Potter* levels of grandiosity. The ceilings were cavernous. The stained-glass windows depicted Christopher Columbus and various Greeks. Marble busts of forgotten governors of Massachusetts decorated the walls. Breakfast didn't really deserve this building. The breakfast offered – a cold, cheerless affair involving fried chicken – definitely suffered for the comparison.

Penelope saw Emma right away. She was sitting at a long table in the corner, animatedly talking to four other girls. All the girls were wearing pastel iterations of the same jacket, which looked like it was originally made for fox hunting. Penelope scanned the room. There was Emma, and then there were miles and miles of sparsely populated tables. She decided to sit down with Emma and be friendly.

'Hey, can I sit here?' asked Penelope.

'Oh,' said Emma, 'we were just leaving.' The girls nodded in agreement. 'We have to study for the placement exam.'

'Isn't that exam just to test out what you know, so they can put you in the right class?'

'But don't you want to be in the highest class possible? I mean, I am at least going to try to get into Math 55.'

'What is Math 55?' asked Penelope.

'It's the hardest math class! It's actually the hardest math class in the world. It takes geniuses like eight hours to do the problem sets. You're so funny. Anyway, we have to go,' she said, and left. The gaggle of girls traipsed out behind her.

Penelope sat down at the deserted table. She toyed with her

fried chicken, which she now realized was stuffed with broccoli. She looked around the dining hall. Everyone had their old calculus books out to study for the math placement exam. Penelope started eating her chicken very quickly.

Then Ted sat down next to her.

'Oh, hi,' said Penelope.

'Oh, hi,' said Ted. 'Were those girls your roommates?'

'One was,' said Penelope. 'They had to go. Why aren't you sitting with your roommates?'

'Because they are studying for the math placement exam and leaving messages on random girls' Facebook walls.'

'Why aren't you doing that?'

'I don't know,' said Ted. He eyed the broccoli stuffing suspiciously. 'Can I ask you something?' he said.

'Shoot,' said Penelope, who winced again.

'I do not understand why everyone is going insane over the math placement exam. School hasn't even started yet. Math 55 sounds like hell on earth.'

'I know, seriously. It's weird,' said Penelope. She felt relieved all of a sudden.

'The ice cream social actually sounds fun in comparison.'

'That is when you know things are bad,' said Penelope.

'How is this fried chicken? It looks amazing,' said Ted.

'It is,' said Penelope. She picked up a glob of broccoli stuffing and zestfully shoved it in her mouth. Obviously, she had to go.

'Well, it has been fun, Ted,' she said.

'Where are you going? Not you too. Are you really going to study for the math placement exam right now?'

'Um, no. But I have to get ready and everything. I need to get a ruler.'

'What? Why?' said Ted.

'Oh, ha ha. Maybe not a ruler,' said Penelope, realizing that

she had never used a ruler during a math test. 'Well, anyway, I
have to go.'

'OK,' said Ted.

Penelope stood up and started to gather her tray. She felt bad
about how abrupt she was being, but she also felt that if she
prolonged the encounter unnecessarily, she would make some
horrible gaffe, like talking about Charles Dickens's penchant for
spiritualism, which was something she discussed in the longest
conversation she ever had with a boy. She wanted to be nice to
Ted because he was being nice to her. He was sort of good-
looking too, like a Roman senator who was sensitive and
unused to fighting in wars.

'So are you coming to the proctor meeting?' she asked, sitting
down again. Ted looked confused.

'Well, it is mandatory, so I guess so. I don't know why they
call them proctors. They are mostly just grad students who live
in the dorm.'

'Oh, me too,' said Penelope.

'What?' said Ted. 'Well, I'll see you at the meeting.'

'Definitely,' said Penelope. She picked up her tray and stood
up. As she walked out, she hit her leg on the side of the table
and stumbled, almost spilling broccoli and chicken bones everywhere.

'I'm fine,' she said.

The placement exam went relatively well. In the middle of it,
Penelope forgot calculus, but she figured she could always take
Counting People for her math credit if all else failed. She had
seen this class in the course book and thought it sounded interesting. Counting was something she was excellent at.

After the placement exam, Penelope began her long solitary
trudge toward Pennypacker. Other kids were leaving the exam

in globs of newly formed acquaintances, talking, perhaps even having a good time. Penelope had no idea when these friendships were formed. Was it while she was sleeping on the futon? Was it during the placement exam? She hated to think it was at the panel. The ironies of her ignorance were sometimes too hard to bear.

It was very hot still, and Penelope's blouse stuck to her back. The trees did not move, the sun was too yellow. The Yard looked stately if remote. No one was playing touch football on it, that was for sure. Maybe the man wearing the rumpled linen suit at registration had actually been a mirage. He looked like what she had thought Harvard men were going to look like before she went here, although now that she was here, none of the students looked remotely like that.

Penelope got to her dorm in about ten minutes. She decided to go up to her suite and see if she could walk to the proctor meeting with her roommates. Emma was in their room, violently brushing her hair.

'Hey, Penelope!' said Emma as soon as she heard the door slam.

'Yes?' said Penelope.

'What did you get for question three? Did x equal one-quarter or one-half?'

'I don't remember, uh, one-half?'

'I definitely got one-quarter. I think if you take the derivative of what's under the parabola, that's what you get.'

'Oh, maybe,' said Penelope. 'I don't know.'

'It's one-half, weirdo!' Lan bellowed from her room. 'Just accept it.'

'I didn't even know she was home,' said Penelope.

'Yeah,' said Emma, 'she was done with the exam in an hour.'

Penelope heard Lan slam a drawer shut in her room very loudly.

'Hmm. Well, do you guys want to go down to the meeting now? It starts in like five minutes,' said Penelope.

'No, you go ahead. I have to brush my hair.'

'Really? I can wait.'

'No. It's really all right.'

'OK,' said Penelope. 'Emma?'

'Yes?' said Emma.

'How do you know those girls from breakfast this morning? They seemed really nice.'

'Oh, from around. My parents are friends with their parents or something. You know how it is.'

'Oh, yes,' said Penelope.

'I'm hanging out with them tonight, actually. After the ice cream social, we are going to the Owl.'

'Oh, cool,' said Penelope. 'What is the Owl?'

'It's a finals club. Anyway, you should probably go.'

'Oh, you're right. I should. Lan?' she yelled at her door. 'Do you want to go to the meeting with me?'

'No,' said Lan.

'OK, I'm going,' Penelope said. Then she turned and paused. 'Do finals clubs have anything to do with the Masons?'

'What are you talking about?' asked Emma.

'I don't know,' said Penelope. 'Bye!' she said, and left.

The meeting was held in a small, green-carpeted room in the basement of Pennypacker. About five minutes after Penelope had seated herself on an uncomfortable chair next to a broken TV, Emma and one of the breakfast girls strolled into the room. Emma gave Penelope a tight smile but did not wave. Lan, of course, did not show up.

The room was sporadically populated. On the other side of the TV, Glasses and Nikil were vying for the attention of a girl who had a moderate to severe case of acne. Jason and Ted were splayed morosely on a plastic couch. There were other people whom she could not identify huddled near a pool table; most were wearing oversized Harvard paraphernalia. Some looked fourteen. Some looked twenty-nine. No one was wearing a linen suit or leather shoes, unless you counted sneakers. Penelope tucked her legs under her. Suddenly, a man entered the room.

'Hey, guys, sorry I'm late,' he said. 'I'm Jared.' Jared was short and wearing flat-front pants that did not have back pockets. Penelope wondered what this meant.

'I'm Jared, your proctor.'

Ted rolled his eyes at Penelope. Penelope kept her face expressionless.

'I guess you want to know a little bit about me.' Jared cleared his throat noisily. 'I, uh, am getting my PhD in economics at the grad school. I am interested in developing countries and the way that they interact with their water sources. For fun, um, I'm on the Ultimate Frisbee intramural team.' Penelope saw a neon-yellow plastic disk peeking out of Jared's leather messenger bag. She wondered if he had added it to his satchel for emphasis before the presentation.

'So I am your proctor. Well, what does that mean? It means that I am your resource. I live here, in Pennypacker, so anytime you guys have a problem I am here to help. And obviously, if you are having trouble with economics, I think I can handle it.' The crowd mustered a disappointed laugh.

'Obviously, there is no drinking or drugs allowed in this dorm. If I find that you guys have been drinking, I will have to report you to the dean. The whole process is detailed on this handout.' Jared passed out a bunch of pink papers. Penelope stuffed hers into her purse without looking at it. She figured she could use it for gum later.

'Now over the summer you guys were given a small book of essays. It came in your housing packet. I hope you guys have read through them because we are going to have a little discussion about them.'

Everyone took out a thin cream booklet. Penelope tried to recollect if she had received such an item in her housing packet. She vaguely remembered her mother looking through some kind of booklet, proclaiming it interesting, and then throwing it out. She often threw things out when Penelope least expected it.

'OK. Today we are gonna discuss "Self-Reliance" by Ralph Waldo Emerson. It's on page thirty-six. Now when you say your comment, just introduce yourself and hopefully we can learn everybody's name,' said Jared. Everyone obediently turned their pages. Penelope was relieved. She had read the essay in school before. As long as she was not asked to quote the thing at length, she should be fine.

'OK. Now that we are all on the same page.' Mild tittering emanated from the pool table. 'Why would something like this essay be specifically appropriate for the start of your first Harvard semester?'

Several hands were raised. Glasses was called upon.

'Well, I think Emerson is trying to stress the fundamental humanity of the individual. I mean, at the risk of being obvious, "Self-Reliance" is, at its core, about self-reliance. The transcendentalist message is really important for us now, at this time in history.'

Glasses looked smug. Jared looked pleased. It seemed that this was exactly the way he had envisioned the conversation going.

A guy wearing a backward baseball cap then raised his hand.

'I don't know. It kind of reminds me of Adorno. I'm Eric, by the way.' Eric shot a condescending glance at Glasses, who had the wherewithal to look abashed.

Jared was giddy. 'Elaborate,' he commanded, shoving his hands in the space where his back pockets would be.

As the conversation dragged on, each person essentially doing free association with German philosophers utterly unrelated to Emerson, Penelope got to thinking. *Is this supposed to be a bonding activity?* So far, no one had introduced themselves properly. No one had told an interesting fact about their past or their favorite color. They hadn't even fainted into each other's arms. Penelope was sorry for this. She had even prepared an interesting fact about herself, if it came to that. It was that she sat in a car seat until fourth grade. Very few people could say that for themselves.

If this was the only chance she was going to get to bond with her classmates, she figured she might as well make the most of it. So she raised her hand.

She never got called on. The free association had moved to France and a couple of guys from the pool table got into a debate about Foucault, which took up the rest of the bonding period. Jared looked simply fascinated. By the end of the meeting he was practically brimming with pride.

'Now this, ladies and gentlemen, reminds me why I loved undergrad so much. You will never have conversations like these again!' he said as they departed.

'I can't imagine what Jared was like as an undergrad,' said Ted to Penelope as they went upstairs.

'Probably very interested in water sources,' said Penelope.

After the discussion Penelope had very little time to go back up to her room and change before the ice cream social. It was her third outfit of the day. She decided to wear a sundress that was sort of low cut in the front. If she was ever going to seduce anyone, it might as well be now. Maybe the man in the rumpled suit would be around. Maybe they would meet and immediately hit it off. 'It was the ice cream social,' he would say at their engagement party in Naples, 'that started our love.' Penelope would laugh and her mother would laugh too, on a satellite feed, because she was desperately afraid of planes.

While Penelope was changing, Lan emerged from her room, which now smelled like paint thinner. Lan was wearing a black T-shirt with iron-on letters that spelled I HEART LIFE.

'Hi,' said Penelope. 'Why does your room smell like paint thinner?'

'I was painting in there,' said Lan.

'I don't think you're allowed to paint your room.'

'Shut up,' said Lan.

'What?' said Penelope. Lan had gone into the bathroom.

Emma came into their room while Penelope was trying to fix her bra straps under her sundress.

'That's an interesting dress,' said Emma, throwing her bag, a green leather satchel redolent with unnecessary chains, on her bed.

'Do you like it?' asked Penelope.

'What are you doing tonight?'

'The ice cream social, I think. I mean, what else is there?'

Emma did not answer. She walked over to her bureau and took out her makeup bag. She started applying very dark eyeliner to her bottom lids. 'Did you like the talk downstairs?'

'It was pretty awful.'

'Yeah,' said Emma.

'I kind of zoned out during it.'

'Me too. Does my eyeliner look OK?'

'Yeah, it looks great!' said Penelope.

'Good.' Emma pursed her lips and glanced at Madeleine Albright.

'Well, I'm off. I'm getting drinks at Noir with my friends

before this thing. I think I'll only go for like five minutes before
I go to the Owl.'

'You're getting drinks at a bar?' asked Penelope.

'Yeah.'

'How will you get in?'

'I have my friend's fake. It always works, at least in New York.
They probably won't even check here.' Emma laughed wildly,
this time a sort of braying sound.

'Well, have a good time,' said Penelope.

'Thanks,' said Emma. She picked up her bag, checked her cell
phone, snorted, texted someone, and strode out of the room.

Penelope floated into the common room and planted herself
on the futon. Lan was milling around in the bathroom, opening
and shutting the medicine cabinet really loudly. Penelope didn't
feel hungry but decided she should go to dinner. This time she
didn't even bother asking Lan to go with her.

After a long, lonely dinner, in which Penelope enjoyed a heap-
ing plate of canned corn with a side of what was supposed to be
chicken masala, she decided to make her way over to the ice
cream social. She walked very slowly. Penelope always felt
uncomfortable when she arrived at things on time. She usually
played Tetris on her cell phone until there was a good-sized
crowd somewhere, but her mother (in one of their many pre-
college pep talks) told her she was not allowed to play Tetris in
front of people anymore. Penelope's mother did not believe that
people played Tetris at social events, despite what Penelope told
her about the prom. Penelope told her mother that she was
being closed-minded and then Penelope's mother canceled
Penelope's subscription to Tetris. So now she didn't have it anymore.

She shouldn't have worried. The ice cream social was

mobbed with people who had all packed themselves into Harvard Yard for the event. There was no more ice cream, unless you liked strawberry – and Penelope didn't. Penelope walked around the perimeter of the gathering, wishing for Tetris and searching for people she knew. Emma and Lan were nowhere to be seen. She saw Adorno Eric playing with a hacky sack. She saw Glasses and Nikil trying to chat up a girl who was carrying a Razor scooter over her shoulder. Then she saw Ted and Jason glumly eating ice cream near a tree.

'Hi,' said Penelope, and sat down beside them.

'Oh, hello,' said Ted. 'How has your evening been?' Jason continued to shovel ice cream into his mouth at a rapid rate.

'Oh, fine. I hate strawberry,' said Penelope.

'Terrible!' said Ted.

'You are a freak!' said Jason. It was at this point when Penelope realized both of them were very drunk. Jason was almost completely crimson and sweating profusely. Ted was drinking whiskey out of a flask.

'Where did you get that flask?' asked Penelope.

'At 7-Eleven,' said Ted. 'Are you having a good time here?' He took a gigantic swig of whiskey and coughed slightly.

'Oh, not too bad. The strawberry situation is pretty depressing and my roommates aren't here, so . . .'

'Do you want to go? It's pretty awful,' said Ted. Jason had put his ice cream cup on his head and was lying against the tree, eyes closed.

'Where are you guys going? I just got here, so I don't know. Are you going to the Owl?'

'What is the Owl?' said Ted.

'I don't know,' said Penelope truthfully.

'No, we are not going there. We are going back to my room to drink more whiskey out of this flask. It is much funner in my room. We have been drinking there for about four hours. All of them were blissful. Just look at Jason.' Penelope did look at Jason, who was snoring.

'OK, I guess I can leave,' said Penelope.

'Up, Jason,' said Ted. Jason got up groggily and gagged. His entire face was red except for a thin strip of skin above his upper lip, which was greenish. Penelope took him by one arm and Ted took him by the other.

As they staggered away from the Yard, Penelope passed Glasses and Nikil. The Razor scooter girl had abandoned them. Now they were talking to another girl with dirty pigtails, drooping eyes, and the body of a quail.

'So where did you go to high school?' asked Nikil.

'Milton,' said the girl.

'Oh, cool. Bronx Science,' said Nikil.

'Stuy,' said Glasses.

'Did you know Sharon Dwoskin?' asked Nikil. 'I think I met her at an Academic Decathlon thing in Alaska.'

'That sounds familiar, but I don't know. Westinghouse took up all my time,' said the girl.

'Cool,' said Glasses.

'OK, we have to get out of here,' said Ted. He hoisted Jason up and started walking. Penelope trotted after him.

Jason vomited three times on his way to Pennypacker: once behind a suspiciously phallic monument covered in tarp and twice in front of a Chinese restaurant. He was a joyless drunk. He repeatedly referred to Penelope as 'the Whore of Babylon' and refused to drink any water. Penelope had never seen anyone this wasted in her whole life. At her high school, people smuggled vodka in water bottles to class in the mornings, but they were always very businesslike about it.

Finally, they arrived at the door to Pennypacker. Jason's face was covered in vomit and dirt. His hair looked oddly like a toupee.

'You look like you swallowed a fucking lemon,' said Jason to Penelope.

'Oh God. Penelope, can you open the door please?' said Ted, and hoisted Jason over his shoulder and carried him up to his room. Penelope flitted in the vicinity, occasionally patting Jason's shoulder.

Ted threw Jason onto his futon. Jason found this very funny. Then he fell asleep.

'I want to put him in his room, but I don't know where his key is, and I also don't want him to choke on his own vomit. Maybe he should stay on this futon for a while. What do you think?' asked Ted, his hand on his hip.

'Uh, sure,' said Penelope. 'But I don't want to wake him up.'

'We can go in my room,' said Ted.

'Oh,' said Penelope. 'OK.'

In all the novels that Penelope had read, puberty progressed in a certain, similar way. One got one's period at twelve. One dabbled abortively in popularity at thirteen. One French-kissed at fourteen. None of this was so for Penelope. She did not get her period until she was fifteen, and even then it was a bit of a struggle. She was never really given the opportunity to abandon her true friends for more popular drug users and learn from the experience. And she had never, really, properly made out with someone before.

She wasn't completely inexperienced. She had kissed people briefly. When she was a junior in high school she had a boyfriend named Greg for a week and a half. Greg had a lisp that only she could hear. Penelope's mother wouldn't let her have boys in her room, so she and Greg used to hang out in her living room and play Ping-Pong. Greg would talk about *Dune*. Penelope would pretend to play the piano, and eventually the entire experience began to resemble an absurdist play. Only chaste kissing occurred, like monks through some kind of grate.

Thus when Ted said to Penelope, 'Why don't we go into my room?' Penelope was mostly gripped with a cold fear. Yet she steeled herself to adversity and decided to follow him in there anyway. She had to grow up sometime.

Penelope entered Ted's room and stood in the doorway pretending to examine her phone, which, once again, did not have Tetris on it. Ted's room was entirely spartan except for a copy of *The Fountainhead* posed prominently on a plywood bookcase. Ted sat on his bed and took out his laptop.

'Do you want to listen to some music?' asked Ted.

'Sure!' said Penelope, still standing in the doorway. She scratched her head.

Ted stared at his computer screen for a moment, lost in concentration. Then he seemed to find something he liked, which was 'Crash into Me' by Dave Matthews Band.

'Come, sit here,' said Ted, and patted a space on the bed next to him. Penelope moved over to his bed and sat there, taking off her shoes and crossing her ankles. Dave Matthews started singing really softly. Penelope thought of pretending to throw up and then thought the better of it, because she could never really throw up on command like some people and she had not had anything to drink, so she would have to say the vomit was the result of a stomach virus, which is far less excusable.

'I love this song,' said Ted.

'Hmm,' said Penelope.

'What kind of bands are you into?' asked Ted.

'Oh, all kinds of bands,' said Penelope.

'Like what?' Ted's leg was really close to Penelope's leg. He was wearing shorts, which was embarrassing.

'Ah, gee, I don't know,' said Penelope, racking her brain on how to get this strand of conversation to stop. 'Whitney Houston, maybe.'

'Totally,' said Ted, not listening. Ted was bobbing his head to the music and Penelope wondered if Ted was secretly terrible, yet able to hide it effectively in the waking hours. She didn't really know him. And a sense of humor can sometimes be a disarmingly superficial thing. Still, she had come into his room. She was contractually obligated to make out with him. College students make out. It is just what they do. Ted was probably expecting her to lunge at him at any moment.

'This song really reminds me of my senior year,' said Ted.

'Really? I think it came out when we were nine.'

'My girlfriend was really into it.'

'Was she? That's cool,' Penelope said. This was a curveball.

'When I left for college, she made me a mix with this on it.'

'Wow,' said Penelope. 'That is awesome. It is hard to make mix tapes. I always have trouble, you know, because what do you really put after Ace of Base?'

'I just miss her,' said Ted, as if he did not hear. 'We broke up right before I came here. She's out in California, you know? That's far away.'

'I know,' said Penelope.

'And like, I don't know what she's doing. What did we do tonight? Go to an ice cream social?'

'Um . . . yes,' said Penelope.

'She is probably at a frat party or something. Do they even have those here?'

'I don't know. I don't think so.'

'Yeah, I didn't think they would.' Ted stared at *The Fountain-head* glumly.

They sat in silence for a moment. Penelope twiddled her thumbs.

'You are really great to talk to,' said Ted.

'Thanks,' said Penelope.

'You are like the only normal person here,' Ted said, inching closer to Penelope on the bed, brushing his ridiculous shorts on the side of her arm.

'I have never ever been told that before,' said Penelope.

'This school is pretty weird, don't you think?'

'I am not sure we can make that determination yet.'

'What does that mean?' said Ted.

'I mean, we have only been here for like a second. We don't really know if it is or not,' said Penelope.

'Yeah, I guess. Wow, I bet Sarah is fucking some guy at a frat party,' said Ted, who then kind of started to cry.

There was probably no person in the world worse equipped by nature and cumulative experience to handle drunk crying than Penelope. Her discomfort with all forms of maudlin emotion combined with her inability to distinguish drunken crying from real crying made her especially terrible in a situation such as this.

She ineffectually patted him on the arm.

'It's OK. I mean, I'm sure she is not doing that.'

'But what's stopping her? Oh God, I want to kill myself,'

'Don't do that,' said Penelope. 'It is stupid to kill yourself over empty conjecture.'

'Yeah, I guess you're right,' said Ted. He lay on his bed, his knees curled up in a C shape. Penelope sat up awkwardly.

'Here, lie down next to me,' said Ted. He pulled her down next to him. The bottom part of his neck was rife with pimples and infected stubble. He was not very good at shaving, it seemed. The man in the rumpled linen suit would probably be great at shaving. But beggars could not be choosers.

'Penelope,' said Ted.

'Yes,' said Penelope.

'I really feel a connection with you,' said Ted, staring into Penelope's eyes without blinking.

'Thanks,' said Penelope.

Ted touched her face. 'You don't have to be Helen of Troy, you know. You can just be you.'

Penelope sat up like a shot.

'It's late,' she said. 'I should go.'

'OK,' said Ted. He did not seem particularly displeased.

'See you around though,' said Penelope, putting on her shoes.

'Yeah, definitely,' said Ted, still lying down.

Four days later, Penelope's mother called her. Penelope was outside reading a book.

'Hi, Mom,' said Penelope.

'Penelope!' screamed her mother.

'Hello!' said Penelope.

'So. How is it? Do you love it?'

'It's interesting,' said Penelope.

'What does that mean?' said her mother.

'I don't know. I mean, how does anyone quantify experience?'

'Oh God, Penelope. Are your roommates assholes or something?'

'Yeah. I don't know. I think one of them huffs paint.'

'What about the other one?' asked Penelope's mother.

'Oh, I never see her. She knew all these people before she got here. She color coordinated the closet.'

'So then what have you been doing?'

What had Penelope been doing? One night she took a bus, which she thought went to another part of campus (Radcliffe) but instead went to Brandeis University. She walked around Brandeis for a while. It was deserted. She talked to some graduate students recovering from the aftermath of a Wilco concert. She went home.

Another night she stood on her stoop for a couple of hours. A homeless man carrying a grease-stained paper bag approached the stoop and started playing the harmonica. Several people came out on the stoop when they heard the harmonica and started playing their own instruments, including Adorno Eric, who brought out a cello. The homeless man started singing about fisting a woman and everyone went inside.

'Oh, nothing really,' said Penelope. 'There was a panel on medical school admissions a couple of days ago.'

'But you don't want to go to medical school,' said Penelope's mother.

'I know,' said Penelope.

'When do classes start?'

'Tomorrow.'

'When do extracurricular activities start?'

'I don't know.'

'You should join an extracurricular activity. What about the chorus?' said Penelope's mother.

'But I've never sung before,' said Penelope.

'That is what chorus is for,' said Penelope's mother.

'No, it isn't.'

'It is for learning how to sing. I bet there are a lot of cute guys in the chorus.'

'I bet there aren't,' said Penelope.

'Well, fine, Penelope. You don't have to take my advice.'

'I just don't think cute guys flock to the chorus, that's all.'

'Are there any cute guys in your dorm?' asked her mother.

'Not really. Though maybe they are hiding. People are kind of staying in their rooms to prepare for classes,' said Penelope.

'Why would they be preparing for classes? Classes have not started yet,' said Penelope's mother. 'Maybe you aren't going to the right places.'

'I don't know where else to go. I mean, if people aren't around, they aren't around. I'm not going to chase after them begging them to be my friend.'

'Penelope. Having friends requires a certain amount of effort. You need to get out there.'

'Fine. Fine,' said Penelope. Her mother was wrong. She did put in effort. She just didn't know where anything was or where anyone was going. Sometimes she would stay in the common room with the door propped open, hoping that someone would see her inside and ask her if she wanted to come out with them. This strategy had not worked yet.

'Well, that is all I am saying.'

'OK.'

'Are you reading?'

'No,' said Penelope, who hid her book near a vine.

'Good. Because you can't just read all the time. You have to be proactive. I love you. I have to walk with Liz now.'

'OK. Have fun walking.'

'Bye! Make an effort!' said Penelope's mother.

Penelope decided to go back to her room. Classes were going to start tomorrow. She had to lay out her outfit, apply a face mask, and whiten her teeth with whitening strips to prepare.

When she got back to the dorm, Emma was in the common room looking at the course book.

'Hey,' said Penelope. She put her book back on the broken shelf.

'Hi. Do you know what classes you're going to shop tomorrow? I've made a schedule for myself.' Emma pointed to a laminated, color-coordinated sheet of paper dangling off the futon. 'But I am still really stressed out. I don't know if I should take EC 10 or not. My dad says I should. He thinks every educated person should know the fundamental principles of economics. I mean, I think I agree with that to an extent. And I decided to opt out of Math 55 so I could have more bandwidth for other things. But I just don't know. What if I go into environmental law? I don't want people to think I am just motivated by money. I have a lot of principles that really do motivate me and I really want that to come across on my CV.'

'I don't think courses end up on your résumé,' said Penelope.

'Of course not, Penelope,' said Emma. 'God.'

Emma busied herself with the course book for a while. Penelope stood there awkwardly, staring at Lan's door, which she had decorated with a large KEEP OUT sign.

'What are you doing for required courses?' Emma said abruptly.

'I don't know. Maybe a music class,' said Penelope.

Emma sputtered. 'I would really get my sciences out of the way.'

'Yeah, I should probably do that,' said Penelope.

'I e-mailed the professor for EC 10 but he hasn't e-mailed me back. Can you believe it? God, what the hell else are they doing? I think I need to call my dad,' said Emma, who then made a shooing motion with her hands. Penelope did as she was told and went into their bedroom closing the door behind her. She got into bed with her shoes still on.

The one thing that Penelope found quite surprising about college was how often she was alone. At home she was constantly being pestered by her mother or eating at McDonald's with her depressing friends. Here she did everything by herself and she couldn't seem to stop. At dinner tonight, for example, she sat next to a kid who had recently bought a genetically engineered apple at a food festival. It was orange. Penelope liked him, but when she asked him to hang out later that night, he said he would be busy looking at the apple's skin under a microscope. Now she had forgotten his name so she could never look him up, even if she wanted to.

Maybe she would think about joining the chorus. She always did feel a spiritual kinship with Whitney Houston.

3.

A Death on the Nile

Penelope found shopping for classes to be an oddly pleasant experience. She was alone in that. Emma woke up simultaneously crying and screaming at her father (who was apparently in Russia) on a technologically advanced international cell phone that she used only in emergencies. Lan didn't shop for classes. As she told Penelope when she walked in on her in the bathroom that morning, each class sounded sort of interesting until you actually went to it. Then you would realize that you would rather be watching a light show.

For the first time in a week, Penelope was in the company of other people for a sustained period of time. This was invigorating, even if she didn't talk to any of them. She got to see all the other students, striding with purpose from class to class, the good-looking ones wearing pants with embroidered lobsters on them, the bad-looking ones wearing rollerblades. All of them, it seemed, had printed out a laminated schedule of the classes they were set to attend. Many of them were taking copious notes on their laptops, even though the subject of the class was usually something like 'Welcome to Class' and Penelope felt she could remember that pretty well without writing it down.

In every class she visited, including the English class where the professor discussed at length whether Shakespeare was handsome or not and the class about Bach's extremely boring yet mobile life, she saw Ted. She even saw him in Counting People, and she thought he was good at math. This was strange to Penelope for many reasons, but mostly because Ted had studiously avoided her since the ice cream social. She had seen him around sometimes with Jason, usually in the mornings eating breakfast; but he had completely stopped saying hi to her and one time pretended he did not see her when she was going up the stairs and he was going down them. So unless Ted really had the exact same scholastic interests as her, which she highly doubted considering the whole *Fountainhead* debacle, he was following her around. Penelope could not tell whether she was pleased about this or not.

Slightly later in the day, after Penelope had gone to several classes, she headed over to the Memorial Church basement to try out for chorus. The basement was filled with people milling around, humming, and sitting on folding chairs. Penelope wrote her name down on the sign-up sheet and sat down in a folding chair and pretended to hum to herself. Next to her, a man with a head of wet-looking red curls was discussing his week very loudly with two round-faced girls.

'Finally, I just had it. I said to her, "If you want to do the Tchaikovsky, do the Tchaikovsky, but don't come crying to me if everyone tells you it's just trussed-up folk music."' Both girls nodded.

'Honestly, I can't deal with Vivien's emotional breakdowns and handle my course load this semester,' said Wet Curls. 'I mean, it's amazing how much work I have this week already.

How are you?' he asked the round-faced girl on his left, who had her braids pinned around her head like a milkmaid's.

'I mean, same as you. I'm swamped with work,' she said, sighing. Penelope wondered how this could be true. It was the first day of classes. There were no official assignments and no homework for another week. 'I was supposed to go out to dinner with my roommate for her birthday last night, but I had too much to do.'

'I know how you feel,' said the other girl. Just then, Ted walked in. After agonizing slightly, he came and sat next to Penelope.

'Ted,' said Penelope, 'I didn't know you sang.'

'Oh, this is a chorus?' said Ted.

'Yes,' said Penelope.

'Well, actually I do sing. I am great at it.'

'Cool,' said Penelope. 'I am not.'

'Then why are you here?' asked Ted.

'I just felt like it,' said Penelope.

'OK,' said Ted.

'Attention!' said Wet Curls, who was apparently the leader of this operation. He had moved up to the front of the room and was brandishing the sign-up sheet. 'I know you guys wanna catch up – it's been a long summer.' Penelope heard giggling behind her. *They show a lot of mercy here when you make a bad joke,* Penelope thought. *Or not even jokes, really. Statements.* 'But we have to get down to business with auditions. We do not want to have a repeat of last year's disaster!' Knowing glances plus more laughing. Wet Curls was obviously well loved. 'I'm Ron, for those of you who don't know. I'm the president. And this is Cindy, our music director,' said Ron, pointing to the milkmaid, who was now mutely standing next to him.

'Hi,' said Cindy.

'For all you auditionees, Cindy is going to become your best friend. She is the one you can come to with all your problems, complaints, everything. I'm a little too busy wrangling alumni to deal with all that stuff, but we are both going to be sitting here every week watching you guys audition until we have our new group members. Anything you want to add, Cindy?'

'No,' said Cindy.

'All right, so I guess we better get to it. You guys know what the audition process is, I'm sure.'

'No,' Penelope whispered to Ted.

'Auditions last for a week or so and there are three major cuts. Eventually we will teach you guys some of our old standards, but today, you are just singing the solo piece you prepared. Cindy and I will be right here in the front row, watching you. Who wants to go first?'

'We have to sing a solo piece?' Ted asked Penelope.

'I didn't know that either,' said Penelope.

'We should leave, maybe,' said Ted.

'I disagree,' said Penelope. 'This might be our last opportunity to make a difference with the power of song.'

'Penelope O'Shaunessy?' said Ron, looking at the sign-up sheet. 'Are you here?'

'Just one second,' said Penelope. 'I have to decide what song I am singing.'

'Oh, ha ha,' said Ron, looking uncomfortable. The other people in the room, fellow auditionees, no doubt, swiveled around and looked at her. Penelope noticed that many of them had laminated sheet music.

'Well, do you want to go later?' asked Ron.

'No, no,' said Penelope. 'I'm ready now.'

'OK,' said Ron. 'Come up to the front, please.'

'Cool,' said Penelope.

*

After the audition, Ted and Penelope walked back to the dorm together. It was a while before they spoke.

'Do you want to know what my favorite part of that audition was?' said Ted.

'What?' asked Penelope.

'When Ron called your rendition of "Try Again" by Aaliyah "spirited."'

'Well, it is a spirited song. It was in *Romeo Must Die.*'

'It really doesn't have much of a tune when there is no background playing,' said Ted.

'No, I suppose not,' said Penelope. 'Personally, I thought you were going to discuss that girl who sang 'Memory' from *Cats*. It was rather ingenious when she started scratching the pole like that. Just like a real cat.'

Ted looked at Penelope.

'I really liked what you sang too,' Penelope blithely continued. 'I didn't know "I've Been Working on the Railroad" went so high. What a moving song, I suppose. Excellent job.'

'Thanks,' said Ted.

'Do you think we will make it to the next round?' asked Penelope.

'No,' said Ted.

'Too bad,' said Penelope. 'I bet the *Cats* girl will make it.'

'I think she really wants to be in it.'

'Probably,' said Penelope.

They walked along in silence.

'Do you know what classes you're taking?' asked Penelope.

'Not yet,' said Ted. 'Maybe that one, Images of Shakespeare? Are you gonna take that?'

'Oh, definitely,' said Penelope. 'I think I may also take that one about Bach.'

'I might also take that. It gets lit and arts B out of the way, at least,' said Ted.

'Yeah,' said Penelope.

'What about the others?' said Ted.

'I haven't quite decided yet. Maybe Counting People?'

'Sounds like a good plan,' said Ted. They were at the stoop. Ted and Penelope stared at each other for a brief yet awful moment. During this moment, Ted ran his fingers through his hair, causing his bangs to stick out perpendicularly from his forehead like a visor. Penelope moved to go inside.

'Listen, Penelope,' said Ted. 'I just want to apologize for the other night at the ice cream social.'

'Oh, Ted,' said Penelope, 'what ice cream social?'

'I guess I don't really remember what I did. I was really drunk, and I have this feeling I acted like an asshole. You probably had to take care of me or something. I'm sorry.'

'Ted, you were fine.'

'I was just so drunk. I don't remember anything. Did I do anything really embarrassing?'

'No,' said Penelope. 'Gosh, no.'

'Good,' said Ted.

'Well, I'm going inside,' said Penelope.

'Penelope . . .'

'What?' said Penelope, her hand on the door.

'Nothing,' said Ted. 'It's just I hope you aren't mad, that's all.'

'Oh, I'm definitely not,' said Penelope. 'Thanks for saying that though.'

'Sure,' said Ted.

Two days later, Ted and Penelope were in Shakespeare class. They sat next to each other now. As long as Ted didn't mention the Helen of Troy business, Penelope felt this was within the realm of propriety. He was taking all her classes, after all. They might as well be friends. She also didn't have to go to dinner alone anymore if they were friends. So there were many advantages to the relationship.

'Was Shakespeare fat? Well, according to this late seventeenth-century woodcut, he most definitely was,' said the professor.

'He doesn't look that fat. I think she's being a little harsh,' whispered Penelope to Ted.

'Hey, Penelope. I just got an e-mail. We can look and see if we got called back to chorus tryouts.'

'You check,' said Penelope.

Ted checked.

'We're both called back! Auditions are on Sunday! Are you excited?'

'Did the *Cats* girl get called back?' asked Penelope.

'I think so, uh, yup.'

'Well, then I don't even have a chance. But yes, I suppose I'm excited.'

'We have to learn some "old standards" of the group. What do you think that means?'

'I don't know,' said Penelope. 'Maybe barbershop quartets. Since you have such a high voice, that might be really good for you.'

'Thanks, I guess,' said Ted.

'I can't believe it's on a Sunday,' said Penelope.

'Yeah. That sucks. Ron wrote a note at the bottom of the audition sheet saying, "There is no rest for the weary."'

'Is that a joke?' asked Penelope.

After class was over, Ted and Penelope walked across the Yard to Annenberg Hall for lunch. Jason was already sitting in their usual spot, which was a corner table next to a frightening bust of Governor John Winthrop. Jason seemed to tailor all his mealtimes to Ted and Penelope's, even though he refused to talk to either of them while he was eating. He did seem to like

Harvard food a lot. Today he was making short work of chicken cheesesteak with a side of beets.

'You know,' said Ted after he and Penelope sat down, 'I am glad I am doing something musical now. I always liked music. I was in a band in high school, you know.'

'What was it called?' asked Penelope.

'Ted Only Knows. We practiced at my house, so that was why it was called that,' said Ted.

'Cool,' said Penelope.

'So, Penelope,' said Ted, 'what are you doing this weekend?'

'I don't know.'

'There is a party at the Ten-Man in Currier tonight.'

'Ooh, a party. I have not gone to one of those yet,' said Penelope.

'It should be fun. Ten guys live there this year and they always have parties. Nikil knows one of them for some reason,' said Ted. 'Well, do you want to go?'

'Sure,' said Penelope. Jason sighed.

'Oh, shut up, Jason,' said Ted. 'It's tonight. I'll call you after class.'

Penelope beamed at Ted. It was humid out and Ted's bangs were hovering over his forehead in cloudy curls, almost as if they didn't exist. *If only they didn't,* Penelope thought.

Later that day, after another interminable lecture about Bach's childhood predilection to crawl in and out of organs, Penelope returned to her room. Lan was in the common room reading. This was unusual. Penelope had seen Lan only four times since she started school, and three of those times had been in the bathroom.

'Hey, Lan,' said Penelope, closing the door behind her. She felt the irrepressible urge to sneeze.

Lan said nothing.

Penelope sat down at her desk and took out her laptop. On the second day of classes, in a state of manic tidiness that involved several calls to Russia, Emma had said there was not enough space in their room for two desks and moved Penelope's desk into the common room. As a result, Penelope was currently sitting about four feet away from Lan's cigarette.

Penelope tried again. 'So,' she said, 'what are you reading?'

'A mystery,' said Lan.

'What's it called?' asked Penelope.

'I forget.'

'Oh,' said Penelope. 'That's cool. I love mysteries. I used to have a crush on Hercule Poirot. From ages eleven to thirteen.'

'That's weird,' said Lan.

'Yeah,' said Penelope. 'Wow. I need to do some homework!' They sat in silence. Lan read. Penelope sneezed ten times in a row. Maybe she was getting a cold. It would be a fitting punishment for constantly saying idiotic things.

'Hey, Penelope, guess what?'

'What?' said Penelope.

'I got a cat today. His name is Raymond.'

'Really? That's cool. For your home? In California?'

'No! For here. For the dorm. He lives in my room. I think I can train him to go to the bathroom in the toilet.'

Penelope's eyes started to water. Another thing her mother had told her not to mention in mixed company was her debilitating allergies. Penelope's mother said there were many negative stereotypes associated with allergies but declined to mention specifically what they were. She was, often, infuriating.

'Oh, Lan,' said Penelope. 'That *is* awesome. It's just that I am really allergic to cats, like really allergic.'

'Oh,' said Lan.

'Yeah, my eyes swell up and everything, from the cat hair and stuff.'

'It's a hairless cat,' said Lan, not looking up from her book.

'Oh, really? Wow. Well, I guess that's fine then,' said Penelope. 'How does it look?'

'Cute,' said Lan. 'Well, I have to go to my room.'

'What are you doing tonight?' asked Penelope as Lan put out her cigarette on the floor.

'Watching my iTunes visualizer,' said Lan. 'What are you doing?'

'Well,' said Penelope, 'I am going to a party at the Ten-Man in Currier. I haven't been to a party yet here, so it should be pretty fun.'

'Oh, Jesus,' said Lan. 'I wouldn't be caught dead at one of those.'

'Why?' said Penelope.

'Because it is always terrible when nerds pretend to be cool,' said Lan. 'I bet they even have an ice luge to drink beer out of or something.'

Just then, the cat came out of Lan's room. Part of its ear was missing. It was also covered in gray fur.

Lan and Penelope stared at each other.

'Bye,' said Lan, and ran into her room. The cat followed.

Penelope sneezed. Then she wondered how you could train a cat to pee in a toilet.

One of Penelope's more unfortunate qualities was her tendency to view social occasions, such as parties, as cataclysmic events that would shape her destiny. She was often disappointed. Disappointment, however, did not lead to greater insight. Penelope still applied her eyeliner with a certain fatalism even before the most banal of activities, such as grocery shopping.

After Lan disappeared into her room, presumably to play with the 'hairless' cat, Penelope could barely concentrate. She tried to read an article about Bach's father's organ and gave up. The prospect of the night's activities was too exciting. What if she met someone really handsome? What if this person had chin-length blond hair? What if she charmed this person not just with wit but also good looks? What types of things would she say during that process?

Penelope alternately tried on clothes and thought increasingly fantastic thoughts for the next three hours. She missed dinner, dithering. By the time Ted finally knocked on her door, she had already changed her nail polish twice.

'Hey, Penelope,' said Ted, hanging awkwardly near the doorway. 'Wow.'

'What do you mean, wow?' said Penelope.

'I was just wondering if you wanted to go downstairs and pregame in Nikil's room.' Nikil had been having 'pregames' since the beginning of school, but Penelope had never been invited. Sometimes she thought she might just go, uninvited, as people were wont to do in movies about college, but she never did.

'Aren't we going to the party?' asked Penelope.

'Well, we are, but that doesn't start for a while. There are a couple of things going on tonight actually, but they all start later.'

'OK,' said Penelope. 'Let's go. This is exciting.'

Penelope and Ted walked down the stairs.

'I don't think this pregame will be exciting,' said Ted.

'Why not?' asked Penelope.

'First, I have been to pregames at Nikil's before, and I know what they are like. And second, this is always Jason's favorite part of the evening. He only likes pregaming. He always falls asleep at actual parties,' said Ted, and opened up Nikil's door.

Nikil and Glasses were sitting on their futon, typing on laptops. Jason, very red in the face, was sitting on the floor nursing a beer. Aside from a rather truculently displayed vodka bottle on the coffee table and two girls texting furiously next to it, it was exactly the same scene as the first night of school.

'I thought pregames were different from this,' said Penelope in an undertone to Ted, who was making a beeline for the vodka bottle. 'I thought there was going to be beer pong.'

'You thought wrong. Drink this,' said Ted.

'What is it?'

'Straight vodka,' said Ted.

'Ted, I can't drink straight vodka,' said Penelope.

'Penelope. You must. Down in one.'

'Maybe I will sip mine. I think that is what they do in Russia.'

'Hey, Ted,' said Glasses, finally looking up from his computer screen. Nikil was still typing. 'What's up?'

'Nothing,' said Penelope, who took a dainty sip of her vodka while holding her nose.

No one said anything after that. Eventually, one of the girls got up and sat on Glasses's lap. Glasses looked enormously pleased. The girl had the largest breasts Penelope had ever seen. She was also very bug-eyed. Penelope wondered whether she had some kind of gland issue.

'Hi! I'm Catherine, nice to meet you,' said the girl. She held out her hand and Penelope shook it. 'Do you live here?'

'Oh, yes,' said Penelope.

'Awesome,' said the girl. 'I live in Grays, but I hang out here all the time. It's basically like I live here.' Then she oriented her body completely in the direction of Ted.

'Are you going to the thing in Currier tonight?' she asked him. Ted took another gulp of his vodka and grimaced.

'I think so,' said Ted.

'Everyone has been saying it sucks and that we should go to Eliot.' Eliot was another dorm for upperclassmen. Penelope had heard it was one of the nicer ones.

'Why does everyone say it sucks?' asked Ted.

'Just like nobody is there. And they haven't set up the luge thing yet. I dunno. I think we should go to Eliot.'

'I mean, whatever you guys want to do. I think we should go to the Ten-Man, but I am flexible,' said Ted.

Catherine then turned toward Glasses. She kissed him on the forehead.

'What do you want to do?' she asked Glasses, smoothing his hair with the flat of her palm.

'I don't know,' said Glasses. He looked stunned.

'Well, fine, let's go to Currier. But it's gonna suck,' said Catherine. Glasses's awkwardness in the face of such hair-styling did not seem to faze her. Penelope was mentally congratulating Catherine on the inner resilience it must take to pursue such an utterly unromantic individual when it occurred to her that Glasses was not her real object. Catherine was staring at Ted with an intensely bug-like expression.

'Well, if we are going to go to Currier, we might as well take a shot before we go,' said Catherine to Ted. 'Emmeline, come here!' said Catherine to her friend. Emmeline – the picture of plump, plain docility – waddled over.

Catherine set up several paper cups and poured vodka into them. Nikil stopped typing on his computer, and the whole of the party assembled somberly around the coffee table.

'OK, guys, bottoms up,' said Catherine. 'One, two, three ...'

'You know? I already have vodka, in my cup here, that I am sipping, so I think I am fine,' said Penelope.

'Oh, come on, Penelope,' said Ted.

'Yeah, come on, Penelope,' said Catherine. 'Take a shot.'

'Well, OK,' said Penelope.

'We'll all do it together,' said Catherine. 'One, two, three . . .'

Penelope had her first shot ever.

'So what classes are you taking?' yelled the guy whom Penelope was dancing with. Penelope forgot his name. He was sweating profusely. Dancing was a very aerobic activity for him, as it involved many aggressive leg kicks.

'Oh, you know,' said Penelope. 'What classes are you taking?'

'EC 10, Justice, Math 21, and Expos. And I am auditing a physics class. I don't know. I'm taking it kind of easy this semester.'

'But what a finely balanced course load you have! It says to me that you have a finely balanced mind. Like Hercule Poirot's,' said Penelope, tapping her head significantly.

'That's so weird! That's exactly what my guidance counselor said about me when I graduated high school. That I was well rounded,' said her dance partner.

'Wow,' said Penelope. 'That is cool. Maybe I should be a guidance counselor.'

Penelope had been at the party in Currier for approximately fifteen minutes. She was the drunkest she had ever been, which is why she was dancing. No one else was, because almost no one was there. However, there was much effort to make the gathering seem festive. The lights were off. Beer bottles were strewn everywhere. An elaborate ice luge was set up in the middle of the room. Glasses was drinking beer out of it while Nikil pumped his fist in the air and cheered him on. Penelope felt an intense sense of embarrassment whenever she looked at that ice luge. Catherine, Emmeline, and Ted were standing in a cluster next to a makeshift bar. Catherine was wearing an incredibly small spaghetti-strap tank top. Every time

Ted said anything at all, she hugged him. Ted's back was to Penelope, so she couldn't see his reaction to all the affection. Jason was sleeping in a heap on the floor. Emmeline was texting.

'Are you having a good time?' asked Penelope's dance partner.

'Hmm . . . Where is everyone?' asked Penelope.

'Well, our tutor came in like right before you guys came, because it was sort of loud in here, and we didn't register the party.'

'You have to register the party?'

'Yeah, you have to tell the administration the Thursday before you have a party. And this was kind of spur of the moment, so we didn't register it. Our tutor broke it up. Also, we didn't get the beer luge to work until after everybody left.'

'I can see now that it is working,' said Penelope, staring at Glasses, who was now trying to shove Nikil's face into the luge.

'Woo! Yeah, man! College!' said Penelope's dance partner at a blistering volume, presumably at Glasses and Nikil, who wooted back.

'Wouldn't more people have to be here for this to be collegiate? Or maybe the luge would have to be less elaborate? Or more elaborate. Something would have to be different I think. The luge would probably play a big part in it,' said Penelope. Her dance partner kicked quite high in response.

'Wow. You almost hit your own face with your leg!' said Penelope. 'That's quite impressive.' Just then, Ted walked over to her.

'Penelope, do you want to go to Eliot with us?'

'That would be good I think,' said Penelope.

'OK, well you should say good-bye to your friend here,' said Ted.

'I am sorry, my friend, I have to go,' Penelope said, patting him on the arm.

'OK,' said her dance partner, 'see you around.' He did not seem too regretful to see her go. *Such accomplished dancing is best done alone,* thought Penelope.

Currier was in the Radcliffe quad about a half mile away from Harvard Yard. All the dorms were coed now, but the inconvenient distance between the old girls' campus and the main campus remained the same. To get back to the regular campus, where Eliot was, Ted, Penelope, and their friends had to take a shuttle bus.

The bus was extremely crowded. There were no seats. Someone had vomited earlier in the night and it was rolling around on the floor. Catherine, Emmeline, Jason, Glasses, and Nikil were stuck in the front of the bus. Ted and Penelope were pushed very close together in the back of the bus. All the handrails were taken, so Penelope had to hang on to Ted's coat.

'Oh, hi,' she said.

'Hi!' said Ted. 'Did you have fun?'

'No,' said Penelope.

'But you kept dancing with that guy. Was that fun?'

'I couldn't really keep up with him. He was too good at dancing,' said Penelope.

'You're a decent dancer though,' said Ted. 'I saw. I thought you did a pretty good job.'

'What a lie,' said Penelope. 'Did you have fun?'

'No,' said Ted.

'That is because you weren't dancing. At the next party, I want you to do the worm on the floor.'

'Are you serious?' asked Ted.

'I am just looking out for your welfare. If you want to have fun, that is what you must do,' said Penelope.

'Thanks, Penelope,' said Ted. He scratched his scalp, temporarily moving his bangs off his forehead. Then they flopped back down again like a leaden weight.

Ted took out his flask and drank out of it.

'Want some?' he asked Penelope. Penelope shrugged her shoulders.

'Sometimes I wonder if you are an alcoholic. Like William Faulkner,' said Penelope. She took a sip. It was warm vodka.

'Eww,' said Penelope. 'My mouth is numb.'

'Are you OK?' asked Ted.

'Is the pope in Rome?' asked Penelope. She laughed. This was one of her mother's favorite expressions.

Just then, Catherine, narrowly avoiding stepping in vomit, made her way toward the back of the bus.

'This is where you guys were! I was so worried!' said Catherine.

'Why?' said Ted.

'Oh, I don't know. I was worried you weren't going to see us when you got off. We have to get off like right now. Come on, Ted.' Catherine grabbed his arm and Penelope followed behind them.

The Eliot party was stuffed with people, which was good, but the lights were on, which was hard. Some people were dancing like crazed, uncoordinated animals. The rest were collecting in small terrible groups around the room.

Penelope was standing in a group with Ted, Catherine, Glasses, and a sophomore named Phoebe who was regaling them all with a story of her summer internship.

'I worked like fifteen-hour days. And sure, it was hard. But, in the end, it is an architectural dig in Malta. It's going to be hard. But it's also going to be interesting. I wish I could have planned my sophomore essay more, but hey? Trade-offs.'

'Is that Mariah Carey I hear?' said Penelope.

'I think so,' said Ted.

'Didn't you just love Malta? I always think it's so impressive,' said Catherine. She put her arm in the crook of Ted's arm.

'Cool,' said Penelope. 'I am going to go dance. Come on, you.' She pointed at Glasses and then took him by the elbow and led him away to the dance floor.

'Penelope,' said Glasses, once they were dancing, 'how do you know so many words to Mariah Carey songs?'

'I don't really know,' said Penelope. She was watching Catherine shimmy up and down Ted like a pole.

'You are a good dancer,' said Glasses.

'Thanks,' said Penelope.

'Do you want another drink?' said Glasses.

'Not really. I keep seeing two of you, and that's not correct,' said Penelope.

Almost immediately after Penelope uttered this sentence, Glasses grabbed each side of her face and kissed her, mostly with his incisors, on the mouth. Eventually Penelope wrangled loose, but it took her a good thirty seconds. She saw Ted out of the corner of her eyes as she struggled for freedom. He looked shocked. She also heard Catherine laughing. Her laugh was very annoying, probably due to her gland problem.

'Hey,' said Penelope when she finally extricated herself. 'Why did you do that? I didn't think you even liked me very much.'

'I don't,' said Glasses. Then he vomited on Penelope's shoes.

'Oh,' said Penelope. 'Well, I think that's that.' She went to go find her pocketbook.

When Penelope arrived at the entrance of Pennypacker, it was 2:30 a.m.

She still had vomit all over her shoes. She tried rubbing her shoes in the grass, but that seemed to make it worse. She walked home by herself, as everyone else was going to get burritos at a late-night Mexican place. Ted had stayed behind with Catherine to help her decide what burrito she wanted.

As Penelope walked home, she saw hundreds of people walking around, all dressed up for some kind of festive gathering. Where were they going? She hadn't seen any of these people actually inside any parties. Did they dress up to mill around the campus with a sense of purpose? Were they just going to go home? Were they all going to go to a Mexican restaurant?

Penelope wearily climbed the stairs to her suite and opened its door. Emma was not back yet, but she very rarely slept in their room now, or maybe slept at all. Lan was not home either, as her door was open. Penelope sat down on the futon. She took off her vomit-soaked shoes and threw them in the bathroom, hoping they wouldn't splatter. She picked up a copy of *Beowulf* that happened to be lying on the floor and started reading it. Someone was eating someone else, but Penelope could not tell why or if either was Beowulf, when Raymond the cat ran out of Lan's room and jumped up on the futon to hiss at Penelope.

After a couple of minutes of uninterrupted hissing, which Penelope did not reward with any attention, because she had read about this very situation in her mother's book *Dr Spock's Baby and Child Care*, Raymond stopped abruptly. He put his head on Penelope's knee, which is exactly what Dr Spock said would happen. Penelope patted him. She fell asleep on the futon, sneezing.

Penelope awoke the next day to a searing headache. At first she thought it was because Raymond was sleeping on her head. Yet even after she removed him, and put Neosporin on the places where he clawed at her scalp and drew blood in revenge, she felt no relief. The pain of Raymond's not inconsiderable talons was nothing to the pain and attendant light sensitivity that was now pulverizing Penelope's brain. Every time she sneezed she felt she was about to vomit. Penelope decided that the best medicine for this sort of affliction was sleep and proceeded to lie back down on the futon.

Just then, she heard a violent knocking at the door.

'Penelope!' yelled Ted. 'Open up! We're late!'

'Late for what?' yelled Penelope, prostrate on the futon. Raymond had resumed his position on her head and was, in a friendly way, digging his claws into the tops of her ears.

'The auditions! Remember? Open up.'

'Oh, right,' said Penelope. She sat up. When Raymond saw that Penelope was going to head toward the door, he jumped down from her head, forced himself into her arms, and demanded, by a series of hisses, to be carried over to the door as well. Penelope opened the door with her free hand. Ted was standing there wearing a red polo shirt.

'Penelope! We have to go! Are you still wearing your clothes from last night? Also, you are holding a cat.'

'Yes, his name is Raymond.'

'Is he yours?'

'No, he is Lan's,' said Penelope.

'He looks feral,' said Ted.

'I definitely think he is,' said Penelope.

'Get changed!' said Ted.

Penelope went into her room. She took off her dress from last night and threw it, haphazardly, in her bureau. She found an inoffensive outfit lying crumpled next to her bed and put it on. She went to the bathroom and splashed her face with bracing water until the bags under her eyes looked more pronounced. She brushed her hair and put it in a ponytail. She looked in the medicine cabinet to find some aspirin and found several unpronounceable drugs that were not aspirin.

'OK, let's just go,' said Penelope to Ted as she grabbed her coat and slid out the door. 'And try not to talk very loud.'

'OK,' said Ted.

They were about a block away from Pennypacker when Ted said, 'Did you make it home OK last night?'

'I mean, I am alive,' said Penelope. 'But I am going to strenuously emphasize to Glasses there that he should never drink again.'

'Glasses? You mean Mike?'

'Perhaps. The one who vomited on my shoes.'

'Yeah, Mike. The guy who kissed you.'

'Hmm,' said Penelope.

'Are you OK?' said Ted. 'You look green, kind of.'

'Oh, sure. I'm fine,' said Penelope.

'It seemed like a really toothy kiss,' continued Ted, indefatigable in the cause of truth, because of objectivism. 'Was it?'

'It was on the toothy side,' said Penelope. 'I think. That point in the night is rather hazy to me. I think I blocked it out.'

'I wish I had blocked it out,' said Ted. 'It was pretty disturbing. Especially when he hurled on you.'

'I know,' said Penelope. 'I wonder if my shoes will ever be the same. Did you have fun?'

'Not really,' said Ted.

'Oh, why not? Didn't you have fun with Catherine?' Even as she said it, it sounded hollow to her ears.

'Catherine? Yeah, I guess she's OK. She's kind of annoying. Like she kept going on about that burrito, and when we got there, she made me pick the meat, and I picked steak, and then she said she didn't eat red meat, which is understandable, but then why did she make me pick it, you know? She was fine after that, I guess. I didn't think the parties were very fun, that's all. I mean, I never think the parties are very fun here.'

'Yeah, I don't know,' said Penelope. Suddenly, her headache

overwhelmed her. 'Wow, I feel so ill. I don't think I can audition for this chorus. I think I'm going to faint.'

'You must,' said Ted. 'I already got you up. It would be a waste of all the effort that you spent in getting here.'

'True,' said Penelope. They were at the door to the church basement.

'OK,' said Ted. 'Let's go inside.' Ted opened the door and Penelope followed him. They walked down a long, carpeted hallway toward the music practice room. The whole basement smelled faintly of mildew. Penelope wondered why the interiors of all religious buildings she had ever been in smelled of mildew. This church was nondenominational too, which seemed somehow worse.

The basement was eerily silent considering there was a choral practice going on. However, this soon made sense when they got to the practice room and a choral practice was not going on. The room was empty.

'What the hell?' said Ted. He started reading a piece of paper that was plastered to the door.

'Why is this room empty? Did we miss it?' said Penelope in a strangled tone. She hoped they had missed it. She was trying to think of things that would make her forget the crushing pain in her head. So far she had come up with the face of Millard Fillmore, who many people have maintained was the best-looking US president.

'Oh, the practice isn't until tomorrow,' said Ted. 'I thought it said today.'

'Oh,' said Penelope. She closed her eyes.

'Well, I guess we can go to brunch now,' said Ted.

When Penelope and Ted arrived in Annenberg Hall for brunch, they saw Glasses, Nikil, and Jason eating at a table near the marble bust of James Russell Lowell. James Russell Lowell had been a Victorian professor and his bust had the distinction of being the only one in Annenberg that declined the use of a shirt. All the other busts wore shirts, and some had ties.

'It is often hard to tell the difference between narcissism and bravery,' said Penelope gravely to Ted. Her headache was finally going away.

Nikil, Glasses, and Jason were huddled as closely together as people with lunch trays could possibly be huddled, and they seemed to be having a rousing conversation. This was out of character. They usually ate in silence, or while group reading, or while doing a puzzle. As Penelope walked closer to them, she could hear Nikil's winded, nasal, and frighteningly high laugh. Previously, Penelope had heard Nikil laugh only in response to very violent Internet cartoons, so she was immediately put on her guard.

When the boys saw Penelope and Ted coming toward them, their demeanor changed. The conversation stopped. Nikil gave everyone a significant glance. Jason started whispering very animatedly to Glasses.

'Hi, everyone,' said Ted, and sat down at the table. The whispering ceased abruptly.

'What are you guys doing here?' said Nikil. 'I thought you had chorus practice or something.'

'We messed up the time,' said Ted.

Jason giggled.

'Oh, man,' said Jason.

'You should have texted us,' said Nikil.

'Why?' asked Ted.

'Catherine is with us,' said Nikil. He cleared his throat. 'She's getting a waffle.'

'That's fine,' said Ted in a clipped tone.

'That's fine?' said Nikil.

'That's awkward!' yelled Jason. This made Glasses start laughing.

'It's fine,' said Ted. 'I'm going to get food.'

'Me too,' said Penelope.

Penelope ran after Ted.

'Let's not get waffles,' said Ted. 'They take too long.'

'OK,' said Penelope. They entered the servery as far away as possible from the waffle line.

Penelope helped herself to two large servings of corned beef hash. Then she said, 'Those guys are acting kind of funny, huh?'

'I guess,' said Ted.

'OK, maybe they aren't,' said Penelope.

They went back to the table. Catherine had just arrived from getting her waffle. She was wearing see-through striped pajama pants, pink furry slippers, a zip-up Harvard sweatshirt, and a lime-green spaghetti-strap tank top without a bra.

'Hey,' said Catherine in a soft, tremulous way. Ted started eating his cereal quickly.

A painful awkwardness overawed the table.

'Hey!' said Penelope, who had been looking at Catherine's waffle. 'I didn't know the waffle irons here had the Harvard coat of arms on them.' Catherine's waffle was much like a normal Belgian waffle, except there was a large divot in the middle where syrup and butter were collecting. Embossed in the divot was the Harvard motto, 'Veritas,' emblazoned in a shield.

'Oh, yeah,' said Catherine. 'All the waffles have the Harvard coat of arms on them. I think it's so cute!'

'But does it ruin the waffle-eating experience?' asked Penelope.

No one said anything to this. Ted ate his Marshmallow Mateys with a stricken look. Jason and Glasses started whispering to each other again. Penelope looked up at the face of James Russell Lowell and resolved to read his biography, if he had one.

'I'm gonna go,' said Ted. He got up from the table. Penelope had never seen anyone eat cereal that quickly. She hadn't even started on her second lump of corned beef hash. By the time she finished this thought, Ted had already bused his tray.

'Me too,' said Nikil, who also stood up. 'I have so much work to do it's ridiculous. I'll probably be working for the rest of my life.'

'What do you have to do?' asked Penelope.

'I have a paper I need to get a head start on. It's due in four weeks,' said Nikil. 'And I have to prepare for class. You can't go to class unprepared.'

'Well, you can,' said Penelope.

'No, you can't,' snapped Nikil. He turned on his heel and walked away.

Glasses and Jason stood up hazily, as if unsure of what to do.

'Well,' said Glasses, 'I guess we better be going too.' Glasses glanced absentmindedly at Penelope. She wondered if he remembered that yesterday he had kissed her and vomited on her shoes. It seemed like he didn't.

'Yeah,' said Jason.

'OK,' said Penelope.

And with that he and Glasses walked away. This left Penelope and Catherine sitting across from each other. Penelope ate more corned beef hash.

'Those boys are so cute, aren't they?' said Catherine.

'Hmm?' said Penelope.

'I love all those guys,' said Catherine. 'They are hilarious.'

'Ha ha ha,' said Penelope.

'Still,' continued Catherine, drumming her fingers on the table impatiently, her eyes flitting around the room like moths, 'it's nice to have girl time. I need to hang out with girls more. I never hang out with girls.'

'They are dumb,' said Penelope.

'I know, right?' said Catherine. 'Last night was so fun. Did you have fun?'

'Maybe,' said Penelope. 'I left sort of early.'

'Oh, really?' asked Catherine.

'Well, that guy vomited on my shoes,' said Penelope.

'Oh, right! That was hilarious!' said Catherine.

'Yeah,' said Penelope.

'Mike was just like, "Who was that girl?" afterward. It was so funny.'

'That's weird because I think he definitely knows who I am. Since I live so near him. And we made out yesterday,' said Penelope.

'Can I tell you something?' said Catherine. She lowered her voice and pivoted her entire torso onto the table, narrowly missing her waffle. 'Do you promise not to tell anyone?'

'Sure,' said Penelope. Inwardly, she was filled with dread. She usually made people mad when they confided in her.

'You really have to not tell anyone about this, OK?' said Catherine.

'OK,' said Penelope.

'So,' said Catherine, 'last night we were just hanging out, and Ted was being really cute with me. You know, helping me order at the Mexican restaurant and just like flirting with me a lot, and I was a little like, "What is going on here?" I never really thought of him that way.'

'Really?' said Penelope.

'Yeah. So after we went and got Mexican food, Mike and Nikil were like really tired and went to bed, but I just wasn't tired. Do you know how that is? And Ted wasn't either. So he and I were just hanging in his common room, doing shots or whatever, and then I kind of went to sleep on his lap, and the next thing I knew we were making out on the couch. And then we went to his room and I slept over.'

'Wow,' said Penelope. Penelope had never heard of anyone who, in the process of doing shots, fell asleep on someone's lap. *Catherine must also have narcolepsy,* she thought.

'We didn't have sex,' said Catherine quickly. 'I'm not that kind of girl.'

'That is so cool,' said Penelope.

'This morning he had to leave really early because of chorus practice. I kept saying I thought it was tomorrow, but he kept insisting it was today. And it was tomorrow! I was right. Why do you think he thought it was today?'

'Well, maybe he can't tell time,' said Penelope. Her head was starting to ache again. She rubbed her forehead with her index finger.

'When I woke up, I came out into the common room, and Mike and Nikil couldn't believe I was still there. They were so funny about the whole thing, really protective. I think they view me as a little sister.'

'That is nice,' said Penelope. Jason and Glasses's conduct this morning suddenly made far more sense, although 'protective' was not what Penelope would have termed it.

'We should probably bus our trays,' said Catherine.

'Sure,' said Penelope. She followed Catherine, who was walking toward the conveyor belt on which everyone laid their dirty lunch trays.

As Penelope approached the food conveyor belt and laid her tray upon it, she thought more about how everyone had acted at breakfast. The giggling, the yelling of 'awkward' after interactions that were just that very thing, all the abrupt departures. The flagrant nerdiness of the proceedings was shocking, she decided.

Of course, Penelope was not unused to nerdiness. She had hung around with nerds her whole life, or tried to, for nerds can be very exclusionary. However, the nerds in her high school would shamble quietly down the hall, or invent a Sim family after school. They were small, damp spirits who did not like it when Penelope showed up at their birthday parties because she was hopeless with a glue gun. These Harvard people were different types altogether. They were so aggressive in all their utterances, almost as if they really thought they were being very cool. *But how could that be?* thought Penelope. It was a puzzle.

Catherine and Penelope left the dining hall. They both started walking in the direction of Pennypacker, which was, in addition to being above a radio station, the farthest dorm away from Annenberg.

'So how was chorus practice?' asked Catherine as they walked by Canaday, the riot-proof dorm the administration built in the 1970s after a student squirted a water gun at the Harvard president.

'Well, I didn't actually go to it,' said Penelope.

'Oh, right,' said Catherine. 'Was it weird getting up so early in the morning for no reason?'

'It was, actually,' said Penelope. 'Especially since I think I was really hungover. Do you know anything to cure that? I was thinking of buying an egg and a bottle of Tabasco sauce and mixing them together. Except I don't have a cup.'

'That sounds gross,' said Catherine. 'Did Ted mention anything to you about what happened last night?'

'What?' said Penelope.

'Did he say anything about me this morning?' asked Catherine.

'I don't know,' said Penelope. That seemed to be the most decorous answer. Penelope had often heard that it was bad form for men to talk about their sexual conquests outside very specialized circumstances, like a cigar salon.

'Really?' said Catherine. 'He said nothing?' She looked crestfallen.

'Well, maybe he did,' said Penelope hurriedly.

'Really?' said Catherine, perking up. 'What did he say?'

'Well,' said Penelope, 'he said you guys went to a Mexican restaurant and that he helped you order.'

'He said that? That was so funny.' Catherine laughed, a tinkling laugh, at the memory.

'Yeah,' said Penelope. 'It sounded it.'

Luckily they were almost at the door to Pennypacker.

'Well, I guess I am going up to my room,' said Penelope. She yawned.

'Oh, me too,' said Catherine.

'Really?' said Penelope. 'OK. You could come and watch a DVD with me if you want to.'

'Do you have work to do?'

'No,' said Penelope.

'I have so much work,' said Catherine. She sighed. 'But I can't anyway. I just came here to see Mike and Nikil for a sec.'

'Oh, OK,' said Penelope.

'It was so fun to hang out with you. I feel like I know so much more about you now! We really need to hang out more,' said Catherine.

'Yeah, definitely,' said Penelope.

'OK, bye!' said Catherine, who sprinted up to Ted's suite, where Glasses and Nikil also lived.

'Lan, do you know the guy who lives downstairs, the one with the glasses?' asked Penelope. She was sitting on the futon watching the movie version of *Death on the Nile* a couple of hours later. Hercule Poirot was striding around the deck of a ship wearing a white Panama hat. He was questioning a woman wearing a fur stole. Lan was in the bathroom with the door ajar, holding Raymond over the toilet.

'Why would I?' said Lan.

'I don't know,' said Penelope.

'Pee. Goddamn you!' said Lan to Raymond.

'Well, anyway, the guy downstairs, he kissed me,' said Penelope.

'Gross,' said Lan.

'I know,' said Penelope. 'It really was.'

Lan slammed the bathroom door shut, and Penelope went back to watching her movie.

After a couple of minutes, Penelope heard a knock on the propped-open door to her suite. From where she was sitting, she couldn't see who was knocking, so she decided to investigate the situation, as *Death on the Nile* had made her wary of surprise entrances. When she finally approached the door, she saw two forlorn creatures cowering in the space between the recycling bin propping the door open and the doorjamb. One was a boy with a tiny head and noticeably large feet. The other was a girl with a shin-length braid. They both looked like they had recently been crying.

'Is Lan here?' said the girl in a quavering voice.

'No, I am not here!' yelled Lan from the bathroom.

'She's not here,' said Penelope apologetically.

'I just heard her,' said the boy.

'Does she have the problem set?' said the girl, looking as if she was about to cry again. 'It's taken us twelve hours to do the first problem. And there are ten problems, and it's due in five hours.'

'Close the door and I'll slip it under the door!' yelled Lan from the bathroom.

'Should I close the door?' asked Penelope.

'You better do as she says,' said the boy, who took the recycling bin out of the doorway and quickly shut it. When Lan heard the door shut, she came out of the bathroom and strode into her bedroom. Eventually, she emerged brandishing a piece of paper, which she slipped under the door. Penelope heard some muffled thank-yous from the exterior and then the sound of feet pattering down the hallway. Once she was sure the creatures had left, she opened the door and put the recycling bin back where it had been. Lan was standing with her back against the bathroom door, smoking a cigarette and looking very annoyed. Raymond was sitting beside her, also looking annoyed.

'Hey, Lan,' said Penelope. 'So I guess you are in a math class.' Lan looked at her with a stone face.

'What math class are you in?' asked Penelope.

'Math 55,' said Lan.

'That's the hardest math class!' exclaimed Penelope.

'Everyone here is retarded,' said Lan.

'Oh?' said Penelope.

'I am going to drop out,' said Lan. She went into her room. Penelope sat back down, opened up her laptop, and started watching *Death on the Nile* again.

A couple of minutes later, Penelope heard another knock on her propped-open door. It was Ted, and he strode in the room without waiting. It was a night of popularity apparently.

'Hi,' said Ted. He sighed ponderously.

'Hi,' said Penelope.

'Can I come in?' asked Ted.

'Sure,' said Penelope. Suddenly, she was filled with an overwhelming desire for him to go away. Ted flopped onto the futon next to her.

'What are you watching?' asked Ted.

'*Death on the Nile*,' said Penelope. 'It's really good.'

'What's it about?' asked Ted.

'A death on the Nile,' said Penelope.

'Oh,' said Ted. 'I wanted to talk to you.'

'Well, the thing is,' said Penelope, desperate to avoid this, 'is that I was watching this movie and I have no idea who the murderer is!'

'Oh, OK,' said Ted. 'Can I watch it with you?'

'Sure,' said Penelope. They watched the movie together. Penelope felt very uncomfortable. The entire time Hercule was striding up and down the deck of the ship, which always used to be her favorite part, she thought about what Ted wanted to talk to her about. She figured that he would try to explain why he hooked up with Catherine and neglected to mention it. The idea of such explanations filled Penelope with a profound sense of embarrassment. Why did anyone ever have to explain anything? If Penelope ran the world, it would be filled with benign misunderstandings, but no one would ever talk for more than five minutes at a time. She kept moving slightly away from Ted on the futon, which in turn made him crane his neck closer to her computer screen, blocking her view.

'I don't understand what is happening,' said Ted.

'Well, they haven't solved the crime yet, but they are about to,' said Penelope. 'That is why he is trying to get all of those people into one room.'

'I don't get this movie at all. Can we just talk?' said Ted

'Sure,' said Penelope. She snapped her laptop shut with unnecessary vehemence, hoping that Ted would get the hint, which he did not.

'So,' said Ted.

'What have you been doing all day?' asked Penelope.

'Oh, I dunno. I've just been in my room,' said Ted.

'Cool,' said Penelope.

'Yeah,' said Ted. He stared at the futon. 'Anyway, Penelope . . .'

'What is your favorite movie?' asked Penelope.

'What is my favorite movie?' Ted looked at her uncomprehendingly.

'Yes,' said Penelope. 'What is it?'

'I don't know. Maybe *Reservoir Dogs*?'

'Oh, weird,' said Penelope. 'I would have thought *Ben-Hur*.'
They both fell silent.

'I'm sorry brunch was so weird,' said Ted. 'I was going to tell
you about Catherine.'

'Oh, it's OK,' said Penelope. 'You didn't have to, ever.'

'There just didn't seem to be an opportunity, you know? I
wanted to tell you walking over to chorus, but it just really didn't
seem like the right time. And then, brunch. I don't know. Those
guys were so weird about it. It wasn't like I planned on hooking
up with her. I even wanted to hang out with you but you had to
go home.'

'I had to go home because someone vomited on my shoes,'
said Penelope.

'Yeah, that guy you made out with. I can't believe you made
out with him.'

'Well,' said Penelope, 'it was the result of an inevitable chain
of events.'

'It just sort of happened,' Ted continued. 'We got back to the
room and one thing led to another. I was so drunk. She tried to
have sex with me on the couch in the common room!'

'Wow,' said Penelope.

'Then we went into my room. It was so weird this morning,'
said Ted.

'Hmm,' said Penelope.

'I just got out of there as fast as possible,' said Ted. 'I sort of
knew we didn't have practice today but I wasn't sure. She kept
grabbing hold of my legs with her legs all night.'

It was at this moment Penelope realized that these con-
fessions were not only embarrassing her, but they were making
her rather piqued. She couldn't really say why. Maybe it was
because she had forgiven but not forgotten the Helen of Troy

incident. Maybe it was because she thought they were in bad taste.

Ted stared at the floor for some minutes. Then he said, 'Well, I should probably be going.'

'Really?' said Penelope. She hoped she sounded sufficiently regretful.

'Yeah,' said Ted. 'I have huge amounts of work to do. I will probably never get it all done in time.'

'OK,' said Penelope.

'So I'll see you at chorus tryouts tomorrow?' asked Ted.

'Oh, uh, OK,' said Penelope. That sounded like a catalog of horrors. Penelope decided she would fake a sickness to get out of it. Perhaps an ear infection.

'Good,' said Ted. 'Well. Bye.'

'Bye!' said Penelope

Ted walked out the door. Penelope opened up her laptop and returned to her movie.

4.

In Which Penelope Reaches the Zenith of Her Literary Ambitions

'Hey, guys. I'm Jared. I'll be your Counting People TF this semester. Welcome.' Jared started clapping, and shortly, everyone else followed suit, including Penelope, even though Raymond had bit her hand that morning and it still ached. Lan said she thought he had rabies. Penelope hoped that wasn't true.

It was the first week of discussion sections and official home-work. Harvard had a lot of lecture classes, and in order to compensate for the lack of individual attention associated with that format, each lecture class also had a once-a-week manda-tory discussion section taught by TFs, or teaching fellows. These were usually graduate students who had specialization in the class's material.

TFs determined a student's final grade, so who one's TF was was very important. Students competed for the easiest TF with a sort of death aggression. They called their professors at home.

They made up fake prior commitments so they would be free only during their favorite's time slot. Emma had changed all her TFs in two days. Ted had switched into two of Penelope's sections. Penelope did not know how to do any of this and therefore accepted Jared as part of her inalienable destiny. The one nice thing about Jared was that she knew him already since he was the proctor of her dorm. Although it remained to be seen if he even remembered her from the 'Self-Reliance' conversation.

'I figured we'd talk about the readings in the packet today, but first I just want everyone to go around the room and say their names, introduce themselves, and say why they were interested in this class. I think I know some names from the list here, but I just want to make sure,' said Jared. Penelope smiled at him. She always felt bad for men in necklaces. While she was wondering about why that was exactly, a tall blond man burst through the door carrying several leather-bound notebooks of varying sizes. To Penelope's surprise, she realized that this was the man in the rumpled linen suit. He was actually a student.

'Oh, damn, sorry I'm late,' said the man in an accent that was an odd mixture of British and something that sounded like German. 'I must remember to add punctuality to my list of accomplishments.'

The class giggled nervously. A guy in a Harvard sweatshirt started whispering to the guy next to him, who was also wearing a Harvard sweatshirt. Penelope resented them.

'You have to be on time next time,' said Jared in a low, stern voice. 'What is your name?'

'Gustav,' said the man. He ran his hand through his hair, which was abundant.

'Hesse-Cassel?' asked Jared,

'The very one,' said Gustav. He sat down and took off his

trench coat, only to reveal another jacket underneath, a tweed sports coat that had red driving gloves stuffed prominently in its pockets

'Well, Gustav, you might as well go first. Where are you from? Why do you want to take this course?'

'Well, origin is rather difficult to determine. I'm German, really, but then my grandfather was rather great friends with Juan Perón. Buenos Aires, for purposes of simplicity.'

'Oh,' said Jared. 'I love Argentina.'

'Really? Why how terribly charming!' said Gustav. He let out a loud laugh. This utterance was so exaggeratedly British it almost toppled headlong into German.

'Why do you want to take this course?' asked Jared in a high, panicked voice.

'Oh, I dunno, I suppose I've always liked counting really.'

'This is a demography class,' said Jared.

'Yes, I know,' said Gustav. 'Counting is integral to that field of science, I believe.'

'Next? Who wants to say their name next?' yelled Jared.

In all of Penelope's years as a human living on earth, she had never in her life seen anyone nearly as handsome as Gustav. She knew this from far away, but she especially knew this now that he was up close and personal. He was unlike anyone she had ever encountered. His hair was longish, he had a dimple in his chin, all his clothing was rumpled. The men of Connecticut, even at their best, had a certain healthy straightforwardness to them that Penelope found singularly trying. Gustav looked like a jewel thief. A man like that would never just walk into a McDonald's.

'Oh, I will go next,' said Penelope. 'My name is Penelope.'

'Awesome,' said Jared. 'And you're a freshman? I recognize you from Pennypacker, I think. Are you are one of my proctees?'

'Yes,' said Penelope, unaccountably embarrassed.

'Well, welcome, Penelope. Glad to see you again. So tell us, why do you want to take this course? Just quickly.'

'Um, why? Well . . . you have to do a report on a country. So that's pretty fun.'

'It is fun,' said Jared. 'It's the most fun I have all year. Those papers are always so interesting.'

'Yeah, so that,' said Penelope.

During class, Gustav took notes in his leather-bound notebook with a tiny ballpoint pen of military precision. He didn't speak again. When it was over, Gustav slowly gathered up his belongings. He took a white linen handkerchief out of his front pocket and used it to dust off the outside cover of his notebook. *For fingerprints probably,* Penelope thought. She was in love.

The next day, Penelope tried to look Gustav up on Facebook. Penelope did not use Facebook or the Internet very often. When Penelope was little, her mother discouraged her from using the Internet because she was afraid that Penelope would be the victim of online bullying. Even now, Penelope was a hesitant joiner of websites.

Luckily, it was easy to find Gustav on Facebook. Unluckily, all she could see was a picture of him in jodhpurs in the middle of the desert, his face obscured by a giant Panama hat. Penelope decided against friending him. Everyone says it is usually better to play hard to get, she thought.

While Penelope was trying to figure out which desert Gustav was in by Google-imaging deserts, her mother called her.

'Hi, Mom,' said Penelope.

'Penelope! You finally called!'

'I thought you called me.'

'I can't really talk now. I'm going into the grocery store. But how are you? Good? Did you get into the chorus?'

'No,' said Penelope. 'I didn't want to go to the final audition. It just didn't seem very fun. I didn't feel very well.' Ted had not seemed to buy the ear infection story, especially since Penelope called him and told him about it in a very hoarse voice, only realizing later that an ear infection probably would not affect that part of your body. Penelope had successfully avoided talking about it with him since.

'Oh, OK,' said Penelope's mother. 'How are you feeling about it?'

'Oh, fine.'

'You know, I know you didn't want to go on that day, but maybe you could go up to that guy Ron and ask him if you can still be involved in some of the chorus stuff. Like maybe they need a stage manager or something, you know? Then you sit in at some of the practices at least, and that might be really fun, to sit in. You could go on all the bus trips and stuff.'

'No,' said Penelope.

'Because I was talking to Liz the other day, and she said she knew someone who did that.'

'I don't want to do that,' said Penelope.

'Well, fine, Penelope. But that is what people do.'

'It's not,' said Penelope.

'Well, you're wrong, Penelope, totally wrong. I'm not going to get into it, but you are. How else will you make friends unless you do something?'

'You can wordlessly make friends by challenging them to a game of Tetris. Which is why I need Tetris back,' said Penelope.

Penelope's mother sighed. 'How are your roommates?'

'Oh, they're fine. Lan got a cat.'

'Penelope! A cat? But what about your allergies?'

'They are bad.'

'You need to tell her that. Aren't cats illegal in the dorms?'

'I don't know. Lan told me they were legal as long as you told no one about them,' explained Penelope.

'Oh God, Penelope. Well, what about Emma? How is she?'

'She's OK,' said Penelope.

'What does she do for fun? Maybe you should ask her to dinner or something. Maybe you guys could go to the movies.'

'I don't know. I don't think she would want to do that. She is pretty busy rearranging the furniture in our room. And I don't think she likes me very much, to be honest. More and more of my stuff has ended up in the common room.'

Penelope's mother sighed again.

'That's too bad. How is school going?'

'Oh, fine,' said Penelope.

'That's good. Hey, I have an idea. What about joining the literary magazine? Remember when you were in high school and you were on the literary magazine?'

'No, I don't remember that because I wasn't on the literary magazine.'

'Yes, you were! Remember? I can't believe you don't remember. There was that girl on it who had that scrunchie collection, and you used to always talk about it.'

'Mom, that was the president of the debate team, and I was never on the literary magazine and neither was she.'

'Well, why do I remember dropping you off at school for a meeting of the literary magazine then? I remember that, Penelope. You were definitely on the literary magazine.'

'I really was not on it.'

'Fine. Anyway, I was thinking about this the other day and I think you should try out for the literary magazine. They have one of those, right? If they do, I think you would really like it. You like reading. And you could meet all different people from the ones in your dorm.'

'Do you think German-Argentineans would work on a literary magazine?' said Penelope.

'I don't know, probably,' said her mother. 'A German-Argentinean? Where are you meeting those? Isn't that kind of like *Marathon Man* or something?' She started laughing her silent laugh.

Penelope waited until she finished. Then she said, 'But I just don't like literary magazines. In books I always hate it when people talk about their own poetry.'

'There is no time like the present to try things out. If you hate it, you can quit, but I bet it's better than being left alone in your room with a disgusting cat. I'm in the checkout line of the supermarket now so I have to go. Call me tomorrow! Oh, also, am I still forbidden from coming to Parents Weekend?'

'Yes,' said Penelope.

'You really aren't going to change your mind?'

'No,' said Penelope. 'Trust me, you would hate it. All you do is sit in on classes.'

'OK. I would hate that,' said Penelope's mother. 'Bye, Penelope. Let me know how everything goes.' And then she hung up.

'Hey, Catherine, I have to ask you a question,' Penelope asked, she thought, very casually.

'Hmm?' said Catherine.

'Have you ever heard of a guy named Gustav?' asked Penelope. She was sitting on the futon. Catherine was lying on her stomach on Penelope's floor. She was wearing her slippers, tiny navy-blue athletic shorts, and an uncomfortably long tank top that was at once too short to be a dress and too long to be a shirt. She was heavily made up.

'Is he a freshman?' asked Catherine. 'Because I know a guy

named Goose who's a freshman. He's really funny. He lives in Grays with me and he's on the water polo team. Everyone on the water polo team is like hilarious.'

'I don't think he's a freshman. I think he's like a sophomore or a junior or something,' said Penelope. 'He's from Europe kind of.'

Even after Facebook stalking and another discussion section, Penelope still had no more real information about Gustav. Once she overheard a cell phone conversation he had right before he went into section in which he referred to demography as 'too too sick-making.' Penelope could not agree more.

'How do you know him?' asked Catherine.

'He is in my Counting People section.'

'I have never heard of him, I think,' said Catherine, who was looking out the door into the hallway. Someone was coming up the stairs. It was Penelope's upstairs neighbor Harold, already the president of the model train club. Catherine went back to her reading.

This was the third time this week that Catherine had burst into Penelope's suite and asked to study with her. Penelope was starting to wonder if this was going to be a nightly occurrence. Already, it had started to fall into some kind of routine. Catherine would lie on her stomach, limbs splayed everywhere, on the cold, wooden floor. Penelope would offer her a seat, which she would refuse. Then Penelope would go back to studying and Catherine would get distracted by every single person who came up the stairs.

'I was thinking I might try out for the literary magazine,' said Penelope.

'What?' said Catherine. She was highlighting her textbook.

'The literary magazine?' said Penelope. 'Maybe I won't.'

'Oh, the *Advocate*,' said Catherine.

'Yeah,' said Penelope.

'You want to comp the *Advocate*?'

'Excuse me?' said Penelope.

'That's what you call trying out clubs here. "Comping." I am comping like six things right now. Nikil told me that I was almost comping more things than him, which is ridiculous because he is comping like ten things.'

'Oh,' said Penelope.

Catherine sighed and repositioned herself on the floor so that she was looking at Penelope, but her torso was still pointing toward the door. 'Penelope,' she said, 'I need to ask your advice.'

'Why?' said Penelope, frightened.

'I don't know what to do about Ted. At all,' said Catherine.

'What were you thinking of doing?' asked Penelope.

'Well, I told you how we hooked up and everything, right?'

'Oh, yeah,' said Penelope. Penelope knew everything about this fleeting hookup that one could possibly know.

'Well, now I don't know what to do. I mean, I think he really likes me, but I can't help feeling like, what if he wants to be in a relationship? Do you know what I am saying? I am not sure I want that.'

'Well,' said Penelope, 'the good thing is that you aren't in a relationship with him.'

'True,' said Catherine. She did not seem as satisfied by this as Penelope thought she would be. 'What are you doing right now?'

'Well, there is that paper for Images of Shakespeare due tomorrow, so I am writing that.'

'Oh, right. That is the class you are in with Ted. What is yours on?'

'"Fat but Fit? The Mad Scottish King and Shakespeare: A Comparative Study."'

'That's interesting,' said Catherine in a bored voice. They

were silent for a while. Penelope wrote two paragraphs about King James's distant ancestor James the Fat.

'Do you think he wants to be in a relationship with me?' asked Catherine suddenly.

'James the Fat?' asked Penelope.

'Ted,' said Catherine.

'Oh, sure,' said Penelope.

'You do? Really? Why do you think that?' asked Catherine. 'Hold on, what is that singing? It's so high.' Someone was singing 'I've Been Working on the Railroad' in a really high voice, and it sounded as if that person was coming up the stairs.

'That's Ted,' said Penelope.

'No, it isn't. That sounds like a girl,' said Catherine.

Suddenly Penelope saw Ted's face in her doorway.

'Hola, Penelope,' he said. He kicked her recycling bin out of the way and stepped through the door. 'Where is that cat of yours?'

'In the bathroom,' said Penelope.

'You should tell Lan to get rid of the cat,' said Ted rather loudly. Penelope was glad that Lan had soundproofed her door.

'Maybe' said Penelope. 'She almost got it to pee in the toilet the other day. It's a very smart cat, especially considering its feral antecedents.'

'Or the fact that it is feral now,' said Ted.

'Hey, Ted,' said Catherine, batting her legs together like a 1950s teenager.

'Oh, hi,' said Ted. He sat down on the futon next to Penelope. Penelope could smell alcohol on him from where she was sitting, two feet away.

'Are you drunk?' asked Penelope.

'I was drinking with the chorus people. How is your ear infection?' asked Ted.

'It's really good,' said Penelope.

Ted gave her a wondering look.

'Did you do the EC 10 problem set?' asked Catherine. She moved onto the futon and sat between Ted and Penelope.

'Not yet,' said Ted.

'It's pretty easy,' said Catherine.

'I'm not too worried,' said Ted. 'Penelope, why did you have to get an ear infection right before the chorus tryouts? That *Cats* girl got in instead of you.'

'You can never tell when sickness will strike,' said Penelope.

'She said she was going to comp the *Advocate* instead,' said Catherine.

'Not instead,' said Penelope. That was the thing about Catherine. Every time Penelope thought she wasn't listening, she was in fact actually listening.

Catherine turned to Penelope and placed her hand on Penelope's arm. 'I wasn't going to say anything before but, Penelope, that's pretty ambitious. They don't let anyone get on when they are a freshman. I don't think it's the best idea.'

'Oh, really?' said Penelope.

'When did you decide to do that?' asked Ted.

'Yesterday,' said Penelope. Ted looked hurt, but Penelope didn't care very much. Ted was wearing unseasonable shorts again. Penelope realized that not everyone could wear a rumpled suit, but at the same time, you could at least try to wear a rumpled coat.

'Well,' said Ted. 'I am super-tired.'

'Me too,' said Catherine happily.

'OK,' said Penelope.

'I should probably go to bed,' said Ted, who stood up. He threw his hands over his head and yawned, causing his T-shirt to ride up and expose a small, quaggy expanse of skin. Penelope averted her eyes.

'Before I go to bed, I also should probably tell Nikil

something about the EC 10 problem set,' said Catherine, looking at Ted.

'Bye, Penelope,' said Ted. He walked out of her room.

'Bye!' said Catherine. 'I should probably go do that! Ted, wait for me!' In a flash she was gone, a soldier for romance.

The *Advocate* had its own building – a small white one that looked as if it used to be a barn. There was an unobtrusive bas-relief of a winged figure near the roof that implied that this was indeed the font of soaring literary ambitions; but if Penelope hadn't been previously informed that this was where the *Advocate* was situated (by Lan, who knew where everything was situated, even though she never went outside), she would never have seen it. *The disinclination on the part of the Puritans for florid showiness, though admirable and moral, did make things needlessly confusing,* Penelope thought.

Penelope climbed up the stairs to the second floor (the first seemed to be an elongated corridor of small, unoccupied rooms – the stables, Penelope figured). When she got to the top of the stairs, she walked into a crowded alcove where someone was making a speech. Penelope was late. She sat down Indian style in the back.

The room was sparsely furnished. Two shabby couches were pushed up against facing walls and one disarmingly long table was shoved next to a window, but that was about it. The floor was littered with cigarette butts. Affixed to the walls were countless wooden tiles with gold writing on them. Penelope looked at them closely. Written on the tiles were the names of all the past officers of the *Advocate* in each year. Penelope did not see the name of anyone famous.

'OK,' said whoever was talking. 'You guys know, I think, the basic premise of what this place is. Let's sit in a circle.'

Everyone assembled in a circle. Penelope noticed that there seemed to be two leaders of the meeting. One was an impossibly small brunet male in a commodious navy-blue cardigan, flannel shirt, and matching driving cap. The other was an emaciated blond female wearing a dirty slip, huge glasses, and Victorian boots. They were both holding decanters of red wine.

'So this is the fiction board. Hey, guys,' said the small guy.

'Hey,' said the girl.

'Let's try to make this less scary, I guess, and start with going around the room and saying your names or something. Or what about' – he looked at the girl – 'playing an icebreaking game? What do you think? I mean, that's what they always did in elementary school anyway.' Penelope had often wondered why a defining attribute of her generation was a nostalgia for things that happened in elementary school. What was so great about elementary school? Penelope always wanted to know. She had had a terrible time.

'OK,' said the girl. 'What should we ask.' Although this seemed to be a question, it was not said like one.

'I don't know. Hmm. What should we ask them? Maybe everyone should go around and say what their favorite bad French action movie is. Like if you're a *Nikita* fan or not. If you're not a *Nikita* fan, just get out right now, OK?' said the small guy.

'I think it should have something to do with fiction,' said the girl.

'OK, OK, I got it then,' said the guy. 'Let's go around and say what fictional character you would fuck if you could. That's awesome. OK, say your name, concentration, where you live, what kind of literature you like, and, uh, who you want to fuck.'

Everyone else in the group tittered nervously.

'OK, I'll go first,' said the guy. 'My name is Scott. I'm a VES concentrator. Live in Adams House. I would definitely most want to fuck Margherita Erdman from *Gravity's Rainbow*. Because she was so hot in that.'

'I'll go next,' said the girl. 'I'm Gwen. I'm a lit concentrator. I live in the co-op. It's a pretty great place. Uh, I specialize in postwar French poetry and literature, but I like anything that plays with structure in any language. I guess I would want to fuck Borges, the character.'

'That's a good one,' said Scott. 'Wow, that's such a good one. OK, who wants to go next, guys? And then we will go in a circle.'

'Uh, I'll go next,' said a girl with very short, dark bangs and tiny wire-rimmed glasses like a World War I staff sergeant's.

'OK, Lisa,' said Scott.

'My name is Lisa. I'm a junior. I'm VES with Scott. I live off campus, on Story Street, so not too far away.'

'God, I remember when Gary Sherman lived there,' said Scott. 'That place was just, insane.'

'Gary Sherman was insane,' said Lisa.

'Remember when Gary came to *Advo* initiations dressed as a panda-opticon? So funny. You remember that, don't you, Gwen?'

'That was hilarious,' said Gwen.

'That guy was so fucking smart. He was kind of a dick, but so fucking smart,' said Scott.

'Yeah, totally,' said Lisa.

There was a brief silence.

'And, um, I guess I'd have to say Humbert Humbert from *Lolita* is who I would want to fuck,' said Lisa.

'Cool,' said Scott. 'Very cool. Who's next? You?' said Scott, pointing at Penelope.

'Me? Oh, OK,' said Penelope. 'Hi, um, my name is Penelope. I don't have a concentration yet, since I am only a freshman.'

'Just so you know, and really, just so everybody knows, it's not

very likely that anyone will get on the *Advocate* as a freshman
unless you are just totally phenomenal. We usually don't take
any. You really just don't know how to think quite yet when
you're a freshman. Usually you need a couple of semesters
under your belt to think on the level that we're thinking at, you
know? I mean, it does happen. I got on as a freshman. But still,
I wouldn't get my hopes up,' said Scott.

'Oh, OK,' said Penelope. 'Do you want me to leave?'

'Oh God, no, I just wanted to let everybody know. Just so
they don't take it personally. Where are you?'

'I live in Pennypacker.'

'And who would you want to fuck? Any character from literature at all,' said Scott.

'Oh, gee, I don't know.' Penelope had not expected to go this
early. For some reason she thought they were going to go the
other way around Lisa, and busied herself with looking at more
tiles while she was talking.

'Come on,' said Scott. 'We are not going to judge you. This is
supposed to be fun.'

'Moby-Dick,' said Penelope. Penelope knew her mother
would be very disappointed if she brought up Hercule at this
juncture.

'The whale?' said Scott.

'Sure,' said Penelope.

'Hmm,' said Scott. 'OK.'

Scott went around the circle. After Penelope, there were two
girls who wanted to sleep with Mr Rochester and Mr Darcy,
respectively. One sophomore boy said he wanted to sleep with
Sappho. Penelope thought it was a little unfair to bring up
authors, but nobody said anything.

After the icebreaker was over, Scott gave another speech, this
time about how Norman Mailer and T. S. Eliot were members
of the *Advocate* and that it means something to be on the board.

He read a little from *The Waste Land*. Then he gave out two short stories that people had submitted to the *Advocate* in the past. Everybody read the pieces in silence. The first piece had no periods at the ends of any of the sentences. The main action seemed to involve drinking orange juice and killing a homeless man. It mostly consisted of a very detailed description of the orange juice. The other story was about someone from the South stealing a jar from a store.

After about ten minutes of reading, Scott and Gwen asked everyone to discuss the pieces. Lisa and the sophomore boy dominated the discussion. Everybody liked the orange juice one.

'I just think it's very visceral,' said Lisa, 'the way the orange juice and the killing of the homeless man are on the same level of meaning.'

'I totally agree,' said the sophomore. 'It reminds me a lot of those kind of short, more structurally playful submissions to the *New Yorker*.'

The Southern one was met with mixed reviews.

'I like the almost muscular simplicity of the prose?' said Scott doubtfully.

After a while, the discussion petered out and Scott stood up and resumed his position in the front of the room.

'OK, that was awesome,' said Scott.

'Yeah, really great, everyone. Great discussion,' said Gwen.

'As you guys must know, there is a party coming up. Obviously it is themed. Obviously, if you are a comper, you have to dress in the theme, no ifs, ands, or buts. And, uh, we will let you know what the theme is in your e-mail update. Also, for next time, you guys need to come up with your own submissions. It can't be of your own work. It just has to be something you find. And we'd like you to write a couple of short essays about what you think these pieces really mean, why you think they'd be a good fit for us, what their strengths and weaknesses are and everything. We're not trying to be intellectually intimidating here; we're just trying to see what you guys can do in this setting. Um, thanks so much for coming and good luck on midterms. I know I will be in here with a glass of wine all week, studying my ass off.'

Penelope came away from the *Advocate* meeting mulling over what she thought were the two main takeaway points. The first was that Gustav did not appear to be a member of the *Advocate*. That was disappointing. Somehow, also, the longer she had sat at that meeting, the less likely it had seemed that Gustav would burst through the door. Fortunately, there was another fact she gleaned from the meeting; the *Advocate* was having a party.

Penelope had not gone to a party since her fateful evening at the Currier Ten-Man suite. This was for two reasons. The first reason was that there were no parties to go to. There didn't even seem to be people milling around anymore, trying to go to parties. On a typical Friday night, the majority of the students in Pennypacker stayed in their rooms or went to the library. Penelope found this astounding. Even though the last party she went to had involved vomit on her shoes, she still wanted to give socialization another chance. A party, Penelope's mother once said, is a really good way to get to know people.

The second reason was a general weirdness. Penelope was still laid up from her ear infection during the last pregame, but she had heard such a full report from Catherine that it almost seemed as if she attended it. From nine p.m. to eleven p.m., Glasses and Nikil played video games while everyone else watched them. From eleven p.m. to two a.m., music was played and Glasses, Nikil, and Jason danced homoerotically with one another while Ted ignored Catherine and texted on his phone.

Precisely at two a.m., Glasses and Nikil went to bed, Jason retired to his room, and Catherine and Ted were left alone in the common room. From two a.m. to four a.m., Ted and Catherine hooked up for the second time ('It was very sweet,' said Catherine). So the pregames had lost a lot of their charm, it seemed to Penelope.

Although Penelope briefly flirted with the idea of dropping out of the *Advocate* process after the first meeting, she decided to stay on for one more week and go to the party. Deep in her heart, she held out Gustav-related hopes. Even though Gustav hadn't been at the meeting, it didn't necessarily preclude him from making an appearance at a party. He was a fun-loving, adventurous individual and he could just happen to show up.

The next day, Penelope was in her English Survey section with Ted. Penelope's TF, a frightened-looking woman who always wore a scarf that looked like a long, boring Oriental rug, was talking about their first paper. Apparently, she had been inundated with phone calls and e-mails about it.

'Do you see the difference here? I don't want a paper about the meaning of class in *Beowulf*. But maybe I do want a paper about the meaning of upstairs and downstairs in *Beowulf*. Does that make sense?'

'Did they even have stairs during Beowulf's time? I thought they lived in those very long huts,' whispered Penelope to Ted.

'That's what makes it all the more interesting as a paper,' said Ted.

Penelope nodded.

'So just push your analysis a little more. OK, you can go,' said the TF. Everyone filed out.

'How did the meeting at the literary magazine go?' asked Ted as he and Penelope were walking down the stairs.

'It was cool, sort of. Did you know that T. S. Eliot was a member of the *Advocate*?'

'Yes,' said Ted.

'Well, I did not,' said Penelope.

'What are you doing now?' asked Ted. 'Do you want to get lunch?'

'Oh, I would, actually, but I can't because I have to meet with Jared the proctor. He is also my TF for Counting People, and he wants to talk to everyone individually about their midterms.'

'That's kind of nice of him,' said Ted.

'Yeah, well, he wears a necklace,' said Penelope.

'I don't see what that has to do with anything. Well, I guess I'll just peel off here then,' said Ted.

'OK, bye,' said Penelope. She ran toward the Science Center.

The Science Center was given to Harvard by the Polaroid Camera company and was rumored to look like a Polaroid camera from the sky, which Harvard denied. Inside, it was decorated in jarring primary colors and had many different useless staircases. Penelope came to this building very rarely. It was where all the science classes met. It was also where Jared the TF's office was.

Penelope took the elevator to the third floor and knocked on the door to Jared's office.

'Just a minute,' yelled Jared through the door. 'I'm with a student.'

'Oh, OK,' said Penelope. She sat outside in the hall. She took her Images of Shakespeare paper out of her bag and looked at it. 'Fat but Fit?' had gotten a pretty good grade, but it was covered in comments. At one point the TF had scrawled, 'You have no idea what a semicolon is, do you?' in the margin but then crossed it out.

After a couple of minutes, Jared opened the door a crack.

'Well, that's a very interesting story,' Penelope could overhear Jared say, 'but I have another student waiting in the hall, so I think I better cut this discussion short. I didn't really know they had yurts in that area of the world.'

'You could have knocked me over with a feather, old chap, when I saw those yurts, there of all places. The Jeep almost destroyed one, actually. Luckily, Goldsmith has a tremendous ability to maneuver when under pressure,' said a voice that sounded suspiciously British and German.

'Well, that's good,' said Jared.

Penelope saw Gustav get out of his chair and turn toward the door. He was going to walk right by her.

'You can come in now,' said Jared to Penelope.

'Oh, OK,' said Penelope. Gustav was walking toward her. He was wearing a navy-blue silk jacket, a light blue button-down, and cream twill pants. It was not seasonal, but that was because, thought Penelope, it was winter in the Argentine.

'So sorry to keep you waiting,' said Gustav to Penelope. He winked. Penelope quickly slunk into a chair inside Jared's office so she wouldn't fall on the floor.

'Bye, all,' said Gustav, and he was gone.

'Hey, uh, Penelope, welcome. Can you close the door?' said Jared.

'Sure,' said Penelope, who pushed it closed from her seated position.

'Are you feeling OK?' asked Jared.

'Oh, yeah,' said Penelope.

'Great, well, then, let's get down to business. So, Penelope. You are a freshman. So first I just want to ask you, you know, how everything is going. How is your first semester at school? Are you adjusting OK?'

'Oh, fine,' said Penelope. 'It's been good.'

'How's Pennypacker been treating you?'

'Fine,' said Penelope.

'Have you been to the radio station?' asked Jared.

'Yeah,' said Penelope. She had never been to the radio station, but she had to feign understanding of it so often it almost seemed as if she had. It always made her nervous when people brought it up.

'I proctor in Pennypacker now, but when I went here I lived in Straus as a freshman, so I was lucky. It was near Annenberg too, and I was a breakfast eater!' Jared laughed.

'You went here for undergrad?' asked Penelope.

'Yeah, it was, uh, six years ago now, that I was a freshman.'

'Cool,' said Penelope.

'I still have friends from Straus. We get together for unofficial Straus reunions in Boston sometimes. I loved it there. Later on, I lived in Lowell House, and I got very into my house life, through intramural rowing, which I suggest you do when you move into a house because it is a great place to meet people.'

'Rowing! That seems so difficult,' said Penelope.

'It is!' said Jared. 'Mostly, I just met the best people here. There were just so many great conversations. Probably the best conversations you'll ever have.'

'Yeah,' said Penelope.

'I just remember staying up late and not wanting to go to bed, because everyone was so interesting, but then having to tear myself away, because I had to go to bed! That was the best part, really. Do you like your classes?'

'Yeah, I like them OK,' said Penelope.

'Um, do you have any questions for me? What do you have to say about this class? Do you like it? Do you have any constructive criticism?'

'The class is really fun. I never knew anything about demography, really, before this, so I'm glad that this class has allowed me to, you know, literally think about what counting people actually is.'

'That's so great,' said Jared. 'That is just what we want.' He smiled at Penelope. Penelope smiled back. 'I was worried that you thought the class was boring.'

'No!' said Penelope. 'What made you think that?'

'Because, you know, you seem sort of distracted during class sometimes. It's part of the reason I set up this meeting with you. I just wanted to talk with you and see what's going on with you, you know?' said Jared.

'But I thought you were setting up these meetings with everyone,' said Penelope.

'I am,' said Jared. 'But I was going to have a talk with you anyway about how distracted you get.'

'Oh, I'm sorry,' said Penelope. 'What do I do that makes you feel I'm distracted?'

'Yeah, well, you never really comment very much. You never take any notes. Sometimes you just stare into space. Participation in the class is important, you know? It's something I take very seriously. I like to have people really engaged in this material.'

'Oh, I'm sorry,' said Penelope. She felt a little like throwing up.

'And then there was this whole part in your first test – oh, here's your test,' Jared took out Penelope's test and passed it to her. She got an 84. 'You didn't do too badly on it, really, but you lost so many points on this question, and actually, to a lesser extent, on a lot of questions, for a similar thing.' Penelope looked at her midterm and saw it was covered in purple hysterical-seeming marks. Jared was not a red-ink traditionalist. 'Like, do you see? This essay question was about population density in the New World. You wrote a paragraph on the population densities in the New World before the plague, which, though fascinating, is not what the question asked, because the whole point of the question was how population in the New World was affected after the plague.'

Which makes sense, because a plague kills people. And I mean, how do you even know about population densities before the plague?'

'I don't know,' said Penelope.

'I just feel like, and I know this seems harsh, but that you're not trying very hard to do well in this class. You never come and see me during office hours. If you are not free to come to my office hours, I can always spare some time to talk – just call me and make an appointment. We could even discuss it over dinner if you have no other time to meet. You can even come up to my room in Pennypacker. We live in the same dorm. I want you to take this class seriously. Do you take it seriously?'

'Yes, I do,' said Penelope. 'I take it very seriously. I think I just didn't read the question right.'

'But if you were careful and if you cared, you would have read the question right and understood what I was asking you. Do you think you need to go to the Bureau of Study Counsel and get some study strategies?'

'I don't know,' said Penelope.

'Well,' said Jared, 'I just want you to get the most out of this class that you possibly can. I want to help you. Demography is important.'

'I know it is,' said Penelope.

'Good,' said Jared in a satisfied way.

'OK,' said Penelope. She got up from her chair.

'Oh,' said Jared, 'thanks for waiting before.'

'No problem,' said Penelope.

After two more classes and a quick dinner by herself, Penelope went back to her room to do her homework. She checked her e-mail and found two missives of interest. The first was from the *Advocate*:

Advo-cats –
'If you shut your eyes and are a lucky one, you may see at
times a shapeless pool of lovely pale colours suspended in
the darkness; then if you squeeze your eyes tighter, the pool
begins to take shape, and the colours become so vivid that
with another squeeze they must go on fire.'
peter pan party
friday 10
   find your inner child and molest it

It seemed that the 'theme' of the party was *Peter Pan*.
Penelope hated costumes. She hated Halloween. When she
was little, it was always too cold to wear her costume without
a leotard under it, and the whole thing had seemed pregnant
with negative associations ever since. It was depressing to
think she had to dress up as a fairy, especially being of average
height.

The second e-mail was from Jared.

Hey, Penelope,
I really enjoyed talking to you today. I just wanted to check in
with you and let you know that I am free anytime you want
to discuss any problems or questions you have about the
homework, the class in general, or getting through freshman
year. You can e-mail me day or night. I am usually by a
computer, even at three in the morning. Or just come by my
room! The life of a grad student can be pretty miserable
sometimes. :(
   I know the transition from high school to college can be
really tough. It demands a lot from you, and I know that you
probably have a lot on your plate right now and feel
stressed. We all do!
   Attached is the link to the Bureau of Study Counsel.

Perhaps you can call and schedule an appointment for a
tutor? Also, would you like to go to dinner in the dining hall
on Wednesday and go over the problem set?

Best,
Jared

Penelope threw that e-mail in her trash.

Lan came out of her room. She was wearing a T-shirt with a
cat on the back of it. The cat looked a little like Raymond, but
it had different-colored eyes.

'Lan?' asked Penelope. 'I have a problem. My TF wants to
meet with me. Again. And he already met with me today.'

'Eww,' said Lan.

'I know. And he wants to meet in a dining hall,' said
Penelope. 'He's the proctor in Pennypacker too. What should I
do?'

'I would never meet with him ever again,' said Lan.

'Really?' said Penelope. 'Isn't that a little disrespectful?'

'No,' said Lan.

'Would you write him an e-mail, maybe, explaining why you
can't meet with him?'

Lan gave Penelope a withering glance.

'OK,' said Penelope. 'How was your day?'

'Fine,' said Lan. 'I painted my room again, so don't go
inside.'

'I won't,' said Penelope.

Lan snorted and shut her bedroom door.

The day of the *Advocate* party, Penelope decided that she was
not going to dress the theme or wear a costume of any kind. If
anyone asked her what she was dressed as, she would say a Lost
Boy, and wore a brown dress to back up that claim.

Penelope waited in her room until about midnight before she went over to the party. She was nervous. She hated going to things alone. She couldn't get ahold of Catherine, which meant Catherine was probably with Ted. Even if Catherine was around, Penelope wasn't sure that she could bring her. Scott had warned all the compers in a follow-up e-mail that the parties were very exclusive, and it was doubtful they themselves would get in, much less a guest.

Eventually, Penelope walked over to the *Advocate*. When she got to the door there was a man standing outside it. He was wearing a gigantic alligator mask and a green spandex jumpsuit. He was one of the smallest men Penelope had ever seen. His kneecaps were the size of Sacagawea coins.

'Hi,' said Penelope. 'I'm here for the *Advocate* party?'

'What's your name?' said the man, muffled by the alligator mask. He was holding a clipboard with a list on it. He looked at it now.

'Penelope.'

'I don't see you on this list,' said the Alligator. 'Are you a comper?'

'Maybe,' said Penelope.

'I don't see you. I'm sorry.'

'Oh, that's OK,' said Penelope. 'I can go home.'

Just as Penelope was turning to leave, someone came up to the Alligator and started talking to him. It was Scott. He was wearing a tricorn hat, a black curly wig, and an entirely red spandex jumpsuit, which exposed his unexpectedly lush chest hair. Penelope realized he must be Captain Hook. She was surprised at the choice of a body suit over the more versatile pantaloons.

'Hey, hey, hey, hey, man,' he said, grabbing the Alligator by the waist. 'That is my comper.'

'Oh. I didn't know who she was,' said the Alligator.

'Yo, buddy,' said Scott. He was touching the Alligator's face. 'It's OK.'

'OK, you can go inside,' said the Alligator to Penelope. Scott and he were embracing each other.

The *Advocate* was completely pitch-black on the bottom floor. Penelope thought she saw outlines of wings and tutus shifting around in the blackness, but it was hard to tell what they were doing or where exactly they were positioned, symbolically, in the *Peter Pan* saga. She saw blaring lights on the second floor and climbed the stairs.

One thing that Penelope could attest to, afterward to Ted when he asked, was that this party was much more spirited than the one she had been to in Currier. For one, everyone had really embraced the theme and, in addition, spandex seemed to be a unifying force in their interpretations. To Penelope, the use of spandex in a costume always implied, at the very least, a willingness to show the outline of your hip bone in the spirit of fair play.

In the middle of the room, there was an old-timey projector that was playing *Peter Pan*, the Disney version, on the ceiling. It was right at the part where Peter sings 'What Makes the Red Man Red?' while blowing into a pipe. Even as a child, Penelope never understood that part of the movie. The sound was off and nobody seemed to be paying attention to the film anyway. Instead, everyone was dancing to a very slow, very obscure song that until now Penelope had never thought anyone could ever dance to.

Penelope felt very overwhelmed. She knew no one, Gustav apparently had not made it to this party either, and seeing *Peter Pan* projected on the ceiling was actually kind of scary. Everyone was dancing in a way that involved a lot of jumping on the part of the males and a lot of adorable hand motions and shaking of the head on the part of the females. If Penelope's mother had been there, she would have worried that someone was going to drop their cigarette on the floor, cause a fire, and condemn everyone to die in a burning barn.

After watching *Peter Pan* for a while, Penelope decided to get a drink. She didn't even want to drink alcohol, necessarily, but she needed something to occupy herself. There were boxes of wine on the long table in the front of the room that a couple of people were dancing on. When Penelope reached the table, all the wine boxes were empty, and there were no more cups. She scanned the room and spotted a bar in the corner and decided to make her way there.

To her surprise, while walking to the bar, she finally spotted people she knew. Behind the counter, she recognized Lisa from the fiction comp, who was wearing a bathing suit covered in feathers (Was there a bird in *Peter Pan*? Penelope could not remember this) and talking to the sophomore who wanted to sleep with Sappho. The sophomore was wearing an eye patch on his eye and a tattoo of a mermaid on his biceps. Penelope saw a bottle of Jack Daniel's on the counter and got an idea. She would make herself a drink and then slowly insinuate herself into their conversation. She just had to think up an icebreaker.

Penelope made herself a concoction of whiskey, orange juice, and milk. She took a very long time doing it, hoping that Lisa and the sophomore would see her and say hi. They did not. After putting eight slices of lemon into her drink in an effort to buy time, she decided she had to break into their conversation by forced means.

'Hey, guys,' said Penelope. 'Do you know where the bathroom is?'

They both looked at her blankly.

'Uh, no, sorry,' said the sophomore.

'Oh, OK,' said Penelope. She almost wandered away, but she steeled her resolve.

'Aren't you guys in my group?' she asked.

'Are you comping the fiction board?' asked Lisa.

'Yeah,' said Penelope.

'Oh, yeah,' said the sophomore. 'I'm John.'

'Lisa,' said Lisa. Penelope nodded slightly at both.

'This party is so nuts,' said John.

'It's always like this. Everybody here is insane. But it's so awesome,' said Lisa.

Penelope nodded again. What could she say? She touched a pierced ear to see if the hole was still there.

'Do you want a drink?' John asked Penelope. 'There is some Jack Daniel's here. I think we drank all the wine, which is too bad.'

'Oh, that's OK,' said Penelope. 'I already have one.'

'Nice,' said John.

'Where are you from?' asked Penelope.

'Pittsburgh.'

'Great.'

'It's so boring now,' said John in an authoritative voice. 'I mean it's fine. It's like a fine place to grow up and everything, but it just used to be this really cool place in the seventies. It had this underground art culture that was really compelling. Everyone was strung out on heroin and could lead these very interesting lives because unemployment was so high. Now, at least where I live, there are just Starbucks everywhere. It's just totally corporate and weird.'

'Oh,' said Penelope.

'John, what were you saying before?' asked Lisa.

'About what?' said John.

'I forget what we were talking about,' said Lisa.

'I thought we were talking about when Professor Parker went to that party at Story Street or something,' said John. He laughed. 'I don't really know though.'

'That was before,' said Lisa.

'Oh, yeah, I think I was saying something about how long I have been spending in that fucking editing room,' said John. 'But how now, I finally decided what my objective is for my movie.'

'What is your movie about?' asked Penelope.

'Well, it's more about an effect right now. Plot-wise, it's kind of hard to explain.'

Suddenly, Lisa started pointing. 'John, guess who's here? You'll never guess. It's Gary Sherman. I wasn't sure he'd show up.'

'The panda-opticon guy? Oh my God. Awesome.'

Lisa pointed to a guy drinking a Pabst Blue Ribbon across the room. He had curly hair that was forcibly parted to the side and a handlebar mustache, and was wearing a vertically striped tunic and tiny bloomers.

'Is that mustache part of his costume?' asked Penelope. 'It really matches his hair though.'

'You have to come over and meet him,' said Lisa to John. 'Excuse me, Penelope.' She took John by the arm and ran in the direction of Gary Sherman. Penelope watched them. Lisa tapped Gary Sherman on the shoulder to alert him of her presence. Gary Sherman looked rather bemused at the liberty.

Penelope wandered over to a couch piled with coats and sat down on it. She watched the people dancing on the table. There were more of them. Scott, no longer wearing his Captain Hook wig, was leading a conga line on it. The table was gently swaying back and forth.

She had been sitting on the couch for a while when suddenly the man who was Gary Sherman sat down next to her. Lisa and John were nowhere to be seen. Gary Sherman twiddled his handlebar mustache. Then he spoke.

'Yo,' he said. 'That table is going to break.'

'What?' said Penelope.

'Do you see that long table with all those people dancing on it, in the front of the room?'

'Yes, I do,' said Penelope.

'Well, it's going to break,' said Gary Sherman.

Penelope looked at the table. It did seem to be swaying more violently now.

'Are you sure?' said Penelope.

'I'm positive,' said Gary Sherman, scratching his arm. 'Are you a comper?'

'Yes,' said Penelope. But her reply was muffled by the sound of the table breaking and all the dancers falling to the ground. A man in a headband seemed to take a particularly nasty spill. Penelope saw him rubbing his elbow while the others tried to clear the table debris off the dance floor.

'Come,' said Gary Sherman. He grabbed Penelope's hand and pulled her up off the couch.

'Let's go downstairs,' said Gary Sherman.

'OK,' said Penelope. She followed him.

'How old are you?' asked Penelope as they walked down the stairs.

'Twenty-seven,' said Gary Sherman.

'That is pretty old,' said Penelope. 'Why are you here?'

'I was in town. I always try to check in on what my fellow Advo-cats are doing.'

They were downstairs. It was still pitch-black. Gary Sherman opened a door into a small room. Inside this room, the lights were on, and there were three boys smoking marijuana on a couch. They did not acknowledge Gary Sherman or Penelope.

'Come back here,' said Gary Sherman to Penelope, gesturing to a table in the back of the room.

'OK,' said Penelope.

Gary Sherman picked up Penelope and sat her on the table. Penelope jumped off the table and stood next to it.

'So,' said Penelope, 'what are you dressed up as from *Peter Pan*? A pirate?'

'I am not dressed up,' said Gary Sherman, who was shimmying, dreadfully, to the rhythm of the muffled bass coming from upstairs. The music had resumed after the accident. 'This is what I wore to work.'

'Cool,' said Penelope. 'That's so cool. Where do you work?'

'I work at the Grolier Bookstore,' said Gary Sherman, 'down the street.'

'Neat,' said Penelope. 'So you live right near here.'

'Yeah,' said Gary Sherman. 'I write on the side.'

'That's fun,' said Penelope.

'These parties keep getting lamer though. It was at its best five years ago,' said Gary Sherman.

Gary Sherman took a packet of white powder out from his pocket and dumped the contents on the table. He took a card out of his pocket and organized it into a line. Then he sniffed it off the table.

'Do you want any of this?' asked Gary Sherman.

'No, that's OK,' said Penelope. 'I am worried I will get allergies.'

'Fair enough,' said Gary Sherman. He patted his nose protectively.

'Were you on the *Advocate* when you were a student here?' asked Penelope.

'These are the only cool people at Harvard!' said Gary Sherman. He took Penelope's hands and moved them in a waving motion to the beat of the music. Penelope kept her hands limp but Gary Sherman was really not taking the hint.

'Really,' said Penelope.

'Yeah,' said Gary Sherman. 'Everyone else is just a banker. Or a lawyer or something.'

'Oh, wow,' said Penelope.

'You realize later that those people are such a waste of space. They don't have interests. They don't listen to cool music. They are robots.' Then Gary Sherman took Penelope's hands and made them 'vogue' around her face. This was the last straw.

'Hmm,' said Penelope. 'You know what? I think I'd better go.'

'Why?' said Gary Sherman. 'The table broke. This party could become awesome.'

'It's sort of late,' said Penelope, 'and I have so many things to do. My roommates are at home. I am sure they want to know what I am doing . . .'

'Suit yourself,' said Gary Sherman. He quickly exited. After standing near the table for about thirty seconds, staring blankly at the door, Penelope also left the room and the party. Because the thing was, Penelope hated whimsy as she hated hell. It was the last time she ever set foot in the *Advocate*.

'Penelope. Are you whistling?' said Ted, or the voice of Ted. Penelope couldn't really see where he was. She was almost back to Pennypacker but it was very dark out, and she couldn't see very much in front of her. That was why she was whistling, to inform predators that she was alive and unafraid.

Ted stepped under the streetlight in front of Pennypacker, so Penelope finally spotted him. He had his phone in his hand. He was wearing cargo shorts, a white T-shirt, and a flannel shirt over the T-shirt, like a minor figure in Pearl Jam.

'You are like the best whistler I have ever heard,' said Ted.

'Thanks!' said Penelope. This was not the first time she had heard this compliment. She was an excellent whistler. Still, it was pleasing every time it was said. She smiled at Ted.

'What were you doing tonight?' asked Ted. He shifted his weight to his other leg.

'Oh, I was at that *Advocate* party,' said Penelope. She drifted toward the front door of the dorm and opened it. Ted followed her inside.

'Was it fun?' asked Ted. He followed her up the stairs too.

'Was it fun,' said Penelope. She thought about this. It was probably more fun than other things she had done in her life, but not by much.

'Why are you home so early?' asked Ted. They were almost at Penelope's door.

'I don't know,' said Penelope, fiddling with the lock and opening the door. Ted was going to come inside her suite, it turned out. He followed her into the common room and sat on the futon. Penelope gingerly removed her shoes and sat next to him on the futon, to be polite.

'Everyone says those parties are fun,' said Ted, crossing one leg over the other. 'Maybe you just didn't hang out with the right people.'

'Maybe,' said Penelope. 'What did you do tonight?'

'Me?' said Ted. 'Well, there is still a pregame going on downstairs. I was there.'

'Oh,' said Penelope. 'How was that?'

'Fine,' said Ted. 'Sort of boring. Nikil is going insane because he is comping the business board of the Crimson and also doing something at the Institute of Politics. He spent like five hours talking about it. I think he wants to be president or something.'

'Do you think he would be a good president?' asked Penelope.

'No,' said Ted.

'I think he would be. It's too bad he has already lost most of his hair. But maybe he can be secretary of state,' said Penelope.

'I just wanted to get out of there after a while,' said Ted. 'It's much better when you go. I wished you were there.'

'Really?' asked Penelope.

'I am so drunk,' said Ted suddenly.

'You are?' asked Penelope.

'I have been drinking like the whole day!' said Ted.

'I hope you don't vomit,' said Penelope.

'I won't.' Ted lay back on the futon and closed his eyes.

'Good,' said Penelope.

'Were there any guys at this *Advocate* party?' asked Ted in a too-loud voice, eyes still closed. He was acting very drunk now, like a drunk person in a movie.

'Well,' said Penelope. 'It was coed, yes.'

'Did you make out with anyone?' asked Ted.

'I don't think so,' said Penelope.

'Oh, Penelope. I am sorry.' He hiccoughed theatrically.

'For what?' asked Penelope nervously.

'That you had a bad time,' said Ted. He pulled at the back of Penelope's dress so that she had to lie on the futon right next to him.

'Yeah,' said Penelope. 'It's OK.'

At this, Ted laid his head on Penelope's shoulder. Ted's head was rather heavy for being comparatively small, Penelope thought. He was like a velociraptor. Penelope was more like a T. rex.

'Oh, man, Penelope,' said Ted. 'I am so tired.'

'You should go to sleep I guess,' said Penelope, sitting up. 'Maybe I should go too. Because I am semi-tired.'

'No,' said Ted. 'Don't go!' He pulled her back down on the futon.

'OK,' said Penelope.

They sat next to each other in silence for a minute or so, while Penelope tried desperately to think of something to say. During this silence, Ted went to sleep on Penelope's shoulder. It was amazing how many people Penelope knew who could go to sleep in a matter of seconds. Ted put his face in such a position that his lips were slightly grazing her upper arm. If she moved her shoulder, Ted would kiss her entire arm. She decided to stay in one place, frozen like a mannequin, to avoid this.

'Penelope,' said Ted into her shoulder.

'Yes,' said Penelope.

'Hi,' said Ted. Now he was kissing her shoulder. Penelope stared straight ahead. Then Ted started kissing her neck. All this was alarming. Penelope was not sure whether she was friends with Catherine in the classic sense, but she had a feeling that if Catherine burst in at this moment, as she was wont to do, she would think this was a breach of propriety on Penelope's part.

'Hey, Ted,' said Penelope, trying to laugh.

'What?' said Ted. He was moving up to her face. Penelope felt his lips on the corner of her mouth.

'Ted,' said Penelope, 'what are you doing?'

'Nothing,' said Ted. His mouth had migrated dangerously close to hers.

'What are you doing?' asked Penelope stupidly again.

'Nothing,' said Ted. He kissed her firmly on the lips. Penelope opened her mouth slightly in shock and Ted stuck his tongue rather aggressively through her teeth, where it flapped around like a dying fish.

Despite the fact that this style of kissing betrayed a history of sexual ineptitude on the part of Ted, it was not an entirely unpleasant sensation, and Penelope let it go on for some minutes. Eventually, however, Penelope felt like she had to get certain things straight to maintain moral consistency. So, in the midst of some awkward repositioning on the futon, she said:

'I have a question.'

'What is it?' said Ted.

'Are you dating Catherine?' asked Penelope.

'No,' said Ted. He repositioned Penelope so that her pelvis was uncomfortably jutting into his hip bone.

'But didn't you just hook up with her?' asked Penelope.

'Only twice. Plus, it's not like that,' said Ted. He kissed Penelope again on the cheek. 'She knows that.'

'Really?' said Penelope.

'Yeah,' said Ted.

'Well, OK,' said Penelope. 'I also have another question.'

'OK,' said Ted.

'Why did you say that thing to me about Helen of Troy?'

'What are you talking about?' said Ted, exasperated.

'That time you were drunk, and you said I wasn't like Helen of Troy or something. Do you remember that?'

'Oh, that,' said Ted. 'That was a joke!'

'Oh,' said Penelope.

Ted kissed her on the mouth again.

'But,' he said, laughing. 'You don't actually think you look like Helen of Troy, do you? That would be a little inflated.'

'It's not that I think I look like Helen of Troy,' said Penelope. 'But –'

'Someone is an egomaniac!' interrupted Ted.

'Ha ha,' said Penelope. It occurred to her that this was an odd binary for discussion, this Helen of Troy gamut. No one knew what Helen of Troy looked like. It also occurred to her that Ted wore shorts all the time even when it was objectively cold out, kissed like a dying fish, and was probably involved in some sort of secret engagement with Catherine that would inevitably conclude in a Gretna Green elopement.

'I am so tired,' said Penelope. 'I need to go to bed.'

'What?' said Ted. He looked stunned. Penelope was off the futon at this point, putting her hair back into its ponytail.

'I'm sorry,' said Penelope, putting on her shoes, even though she was only going to walk two steps into her bedroom. 'I am exhausted.'

'What's going on?' said Ted.

'I am just exhausted. I might have mono,' said Penelope.

'But you just had an ear infection!' said Ted, now putting on his shoes.

'I think it was a symptom,' said Penelope.

'Are you OK?' asked Ted.

'Yeah,' said Penelope. She was standing in front of the door with her arms crossed and her shoes completely on.

'Can I see you another time?'

'I am worried I am a permanent invalid,' said Penelope.

'What?' said Ted. He put on his shoes angrily. 'Well, bye, I guess.' He left then, muttering things under his breath.

5.

Caligula

'Penelope, you will never guess what happened!' said Catherine after she barged into Penelope's suite, knocking the recycling bin out of the doorway with her foot.

'What?' said Penelope. She was nervous that Catherine had found out about her activities with Ted the night before and was trying to lure her into a confession with a congenial, unsuspicious manner. If so, Penelope had to respect that. It was very Poirot.

'Ted and I are officially going out!' said Catherine. She flopped down on the futon next to Penelope.

Penelope swiftly put down her copy of the biography of James Russell Lowell. She felt shock but also a sense of expectation fulfilled. 'When did this happen?'

'Last night! Can you believe it?'

'How did this happen?' asked Penelope.

'We were hooking up last night and he just asked me. I didn't see him until really late. It was weird. He like left the pregame for three hours, and I was like, where did he go? But yeah, we are like *going out* going out,' said Catherine.

'That is really awesome,' said Penelope.

'I knew you would be happy for me,' said Catherine. 'I am also really happy for myself. He is totally obsessed with me.' Catherine lounged back against the futon seat. She was wearing a pink cropped angora sweater that was obscenely tight and shedding all over the futon. 'I didn't even really want to date him.'

Penelope did not want to say anything that would make Catherine suspicious about where Ted had been during those missing three hours before he asked the eternal question (although if Catherine were as good a detective as Poirot, it would be the nonverbal clues that would eventually betray the truth), so she decided to stay silent and think of something innocuous to say. Catherine yammered on about love, marriage, and commitments that stretched deep into the foreseeable future without seeming to mind.

When it became absolutely necessary for Penelope to speak, she was saved by Emma running through the door.

'Penelope. Thank God you're here!' she said. 'I need you to do me a huge favor!'

'What?' said Penelope. Emma was wearing a cable-knit sweater in a hideous shade of pale yet also fluorescent green. Penelope had never been so glad to see her.

'I need you to come down to the theater with me like right now.'

'OK,' said Penelope. Penelope did not know that Emma was involved in a theatrical extracurricular, but it didn't really surprise her. Emma was involved with every known extracurricular, including a hospitality service that provided refrigerators in dorms.

'Wait, why do you need to go to the theater?' asked Catherine.

'Oh, hi,' said Emma to Catherine. 'You can come too, who-ever you are.'

'We actually have met before,' said Catherine. 'The other day. I introduced myself on the stairs.'

'Oh, maybe,' said Emma. 'I am terrible with names. Penelope, I really need as many people as possible to help me out, OK? We really need people to play guards in this produc-tion of *Caligula*. You don't even have to talk! I am desperate. Even Lan is helping.'

'Wait, we have to play something?' whispered Catherine to Penelope. 'That is a huge commitment! I don't think I can do this.'

'Lan is helping?' said Penelope.

'Yeah,' said Emma.

'You asked her?'

'Yeah,' said Emma, looking uncomfortable. 'Why is that such a big deal?'

'I am coming,' said Penelope.

'I don't know, should I come?' said Catherine. 'I have so much work. I have my essay for Expos due, I have a problem set, I have an essay to write for a couple of comps I am doing. I am just totally swamped.'

'You don't have to come if you don't want to,' said Penelope.

'OK, I am coming,' said Catherine. 'I did a lot of theater in high school. I was the lead in almost every play, but it wasn't like the plays were for losers or anything. The cool kids did it too.'

'OK,' said Emma, as if she expected such an answer. 'Now let's go.' She whipped out her international cell phone and bran-dished it at the door. Everyone followed her to the theater.

The theater was housed in a large 1960s cement edifice of nonsensical geometry. Like many buildings of its time and era, it had a lot of windows but very little natural light to show for it. Penelope followed Emma inside the drama complex, past the larger main proscenium, to a tiny, filthy experimental theater in the back of the building. Inside this theater, a lot of people were talking worriedly in the middle of the stage.

'I finally found two people to play guards!' yelled Emma as soon as she entered the room. This pronouncement caused quite a stir. Everyone clapped, and a middle-aged man stood on a chair.

'Everyone sit down, please,' said the man standing on the chair.

'That's the director,' whispered Emma to Catherine and Penelope. 'Go sit down.'

Penelope and Catherine walked to the middle of the stage and sat down where everyone else was sitting. The director was still standing on a chair. He was a rangy kind of man with feathery hair that was more gesture than reality. He was wearing a black turtleneck, a black beret, and gaping jeans. He started to speak.

'Well, first off, I think I should introduce myself to the new members of our little cast of characters. I'm Henry Wills-Mather and I am the director of this year's production, *Caligula*.' Everyone gave Henry Wills-Mather a rousing round of applause. He continued:

'At one time, I was a student at this very college. Now I know what you are thinking. It was in what you would now call the prehistoric times. We didn't have cell phones, we didn't have the Internet. It was that wilderness called the seventies.' Everyone laughed.

'After I graduated from this fair institution, I worked in New York City for a long time, writing plays, directing plays, that sort of thing. Lee Strasberg, in the twilight of his years, once said to me, "Henry, you've really got something here." I was experiencing quite a bit of success, but I felt my life was missing something. And I realized what that was: working with kids and making them better writers, directors, teachers, and actors. I decided to come back here, a place I have so much fondness for, and share with you all as the artist in residence of off-campus housing. The administration was very pleased, if I do say so myself.

'And now on to business. Thank you, late arrivals! We had some dropouts to the cast late in the game, which was unfortunate. Luckily, Emma, our producer, found us some actors. I trust her to not lead us astray. She did find a somewhat accomplished lighting designer.' Everyone laughed at this and Penelope reflected once again on how she really had to adapt her jokes to reflect the vaudevillian changes in taste that were happening around this country.

'In all seriousness, we are so lucky to have someone who designed planetariums for so many years working for this very small, but I hope in a little way significant, endeavor.' Henry Wills-Mather gracefully gestured toward a corner of the room. 'Take a bow, Lan Wu,' said Henry.

'No,' said Lan.

To Penelope's utter shock, Lan was the lighting designer in question. Penelope had never seen Lan looking so out of sorts. She was wearing a shirt that said IT'S NOT RIGHT BUT IT'S OK: THE WHITNEY HOUSTON CONCERT TOUR. Penelope knew Lan hated Whitney Houston, because she asked her about that very early on. It was clearly a sign that something was amuck.

'Lan legitimately is the best lighting designer in California,' Emma whispered to Penelope. 'I was looking up lighting designers and I couldn't believe it. She has designed like five planetariums. She did the lights for the Rolling Stones reunion tour.'

'What?' said Penelope. 'Why?'

'I don't know. But I knew if I got her to do this, it would be a huge deal.'

'How did you get her to do it?' asked Penelope.

'I just asked,' said Emma brusquely. 'Lan was really nice about it.'

'Hmm,' said Penelope. She was watching Lan, who was in the process of tattooing herself with the nib of a pen.

'For those of you who have not read *Caligula*, I suggest you start,' said Henry Wills-Mather. 'It is an exceedingly bleak, unremittingly existentialist play. Our production is going to revolutionize the text. We have a new translation from the French, as done by yours truly. (I am an amateur linguist in my spare time.) And we have a radical new way of conceptualizing Caligula herself or himself. Bitty, dear, I would like you to stand up.' An unseasonably tan girl stood up. She smiled at everyone.

'Bitty is one of our Caligulas. Chris I would like you to stand up.' An adenoidal boy with a tiny rattail stood up. 'This is one of our other Caligulas. If you have ever read Caligula, you know that Camus is examining the two sides of the tragic king's personality: his subhuman logical side and his romantic emotional side. Our casting, and we will go into this more later, I think really reflects this. You two can sit down.' Chris and Bitty both sat down. 'New arrivals,' said Henry Wills-Mather. 'Stand up. Introduce yourselves!' Catherine and Penelope stood up. Henry Wills-Mather gave them scripts in binders.

Catherine spoke first. 'Hi, I am Catherine. I'm a freshman. I live in Grays. I'm considering a double concentration in economics and government. I actually do have a lot of experience in theater, so it is so funny I am doing this!'

'Hi, I'm Penelope,' said Penelope.

'Very good,' said Henry Wills-Mather. 'Now, Guards (I am going to call you all by your character names from now on, so as to make you feel more in tune with the people you are playing), although you do not have speaking parts, your role here is very important, very important. I want you to come with

a history for your character by our next rehearsal. Their likes
and dislikes, that sort of thing. Write an essay about them. Note
their entrances and exits. Are they worried about Caligula?
Proud of him or her? In love with him or her? That is what you
must think about to make your character real. I think that's
about all for you guys today. I have to work with the two
Caligulas one-on-one for the rest of our rehearsal time. You all
can go. Rehearsal schedules are attached to the scripts; let me
know if you have any conflicts. *Bonne chance!*' Penelope
glanced at Lan's corner. She had already left.

Penelope walked home with Catherine, who despite today's
intervening events was still on the subject of Ted.

'It's so funny that he is like my boyfriend now,' said
Catherine. 'Do I say, "My boyfriend, Ted," when I talk about
him?'

'Sure,' said Penelope.

'That feels really weird to me,' said Catherine. Just then, she
got a text.

'Cute!' said Catherine.

'What?' said Penelope.

'Ted wants to have dinner with me,' said Catherine.

'Where?' asked Penelope.

'At this Chinese food place,' said Catherine.

'Oh, cool,' said Penelope.

'Well,' said Catherine. 'Have fun with your dinner!'

'What dinner?' asked Penelope.

'I got to run,' yelled Catherine. She turned off in the direction of the Square.

Penelope was glad Ted and Catherine were going on a date.
She didn't want to see Ted in Annenberg after what had
occurred yesterday. But if Catherine and Ted were occupied,
she had no one to eat dinner with (she never faced Ted's roommates on her own), so she went and got a slice of pizza, and

read her e-mails on a public computer in one of the libraries. She got a rather long-winded one from Jared, in which he asked about her trip to the Bureau of Study Counsel and also why she did not respond to his last e-mail. Penelope wrote him quickly that her e-mail was broken and suggested that they communicate by letter.

When Penelope returned to her suite, she saw Emma lying on the futon.

Penelope assumed she was sleeping, so she tried to hang up her coat very quietly. As she tiptoed into the common room, she realized that Emma was not sleeping but sobbing, and rather loudly.

'Emma,' said Penelope. 'Are you all right? What's the matter?'

'Oh, Penelope,' said Emma. 'I didn't see you there.' Emma sat up. She looked theatrically miserable. All her makeup was running down her face in black streams. Her hair was matted in zoological clumps. She was wearing a sweatshirt that said NIGHTINGALE-BAMFORD on it. 'It's nothing. I'm just really stressed out.'

'About what?' asked Penelope. 'The play?'

'Not just the play, although that's really stressful too.' Emma's voice caught and she started to cry more.

'What is it?' said Penelope.

'I can't really talk about it,' said Emma.

'OK,' said Penelope. 'Do you want me to leave you alone?'

'Well, OK, I'll tell you,' said Emma. 'But you have to keep this really secret. You can't tell anyone. I mean, I don't really know who you even know where it would actually matter, but still, it's the principle of the thing.'

'Yeah, sure,' said Penelope.

'Well, it's just Pudding stuff.'

'Oh, OK,' said Penelope. She had no idea what Emma was talking about.

'It's like this finals club for freshmen,' said Emma in the breezy way she had of explaining things but not really explaining them. 'I'm punching it now. I really want to get into it, mostly because it makes it so much easier to get into the real finals clubs later, but also because I just think it will be fun and a great way to meet cool people who you will know forever.'

'OK,' said Penelope. 'Is that like an extracurricular?'

'No!' Emma said. She shook her head in disbelief. 'Kind of, I guess. You can't put it on your résumé, but like a ton of powerful people have been members of finals clubs and they can get you incredible jobs later. But I mean, that is not the point of it. It's supposed to be like for making friends or something.'

'Oh, OK,' said Penelope. 'Is it like a sorority?'

'No,' said Emma. She looked disgusted, but her disgust at Penelope's ignorance seemed to pull her out of the worst of her misery. She removed the excess eye makeup from her face and hiccoughed. 'It is way more prestigious than any kind of frat at a state school. There is one club for guys that if you haven't made a million dollars by the time you are thirty, they give you a million dollars.'

'That's awesome,' said Penelope.

'I want to get into one of the girl ones. If you get into a girl one, you get into the guys' ones for parties. Those parties are so much fun. They never get broken up by the cops and you don't have to register them or anything.'

'Could Lan join one?' asked Penelope. 'She hates cops. She told me that on Friday.'

'Oh, no,' said Emma. She laughed. 'You have to get selected to even try out. There is a whole application process with cocktail parties and stuff. It's called a punch. It's not like some random person could do it. The Kennedys couldn't even be in the million-dollar one.'

'They were bootleggers,' said Penelope solemnly.

Then Emma was sad again.

'So I have been doing those events all fall, and I just feel like I'm the person who's the least likely to get in. Of all the punches.'

'Oh, I'm sure that's not true,' said Penelope.

'Thanks, Penelope. But I know I have to work double time. That is why I am doing this play, really. Bitty is the president of the Hasty Pudding, and probably going to be president of the Bee (which is like the best girls' finals club), and I wanted to get to know her, so I volunteered to produce this play. But we have been having so many problems with all these people dropping out because they need to study. People really need to start taking personal responsibility.' Emma's voice rose to almost hysterical levels.

'It will be fine,' said Penelope.

'I know that,' snapped Emma. 'It's just hard. Sometimes I feel like I'm so different from everyone else who is punching the Pudding. Like everyone else's parents went to Harvard too. Everyone else's parents were in finals clubs too. I don't have that kind of legacy. My parents only went to Cornell.'

'I don't even know where my mother went to college. I should ask her,' said Penelope.

'All these other girls I went to school with, I don't even think they are worried about getting in. But I am super-worried.' Emma started to cry again.

'I am sure you will get in,' said Penelope. She patted Emma's head. 'You are just freaking out because it is almost over. How could you not get in? You did everything right.'

'Thanks, Penelope,' said Emma. While Emma tried to recover, Penelope got up and got a box of Kleenex from her desk.

'Here,' said Penelope. She gave Emma the box.

'Thanks,' said Emma. She took out a tissue and blew her nose loudly. 'Just telling someone made me feel so much better.'

'Oh, no problem,' said Penelope.

'Thanks for doing the play too. It's funny. I thought you were so weird when I first met you. Like one of the weirdest people I have ever met. Like just a freak.'

'Oh, really?' said Penelope.

'Yeah. And you know, while I was doing this, this Pudding stuff, I had to really think about my social position. You can't be walking next to someone who owns half of New York City and say hi to someone like you. This is a very delicate thing.'

'I could see that,' said Penelope.

'But today, I was just so desperate, I was like, "Whatever, I will ask her to do the play. I don't know anyone else who wants to do it." And now I think you are really fine. Like totally normal.'

'Thanks,' said Penelope.

Emma sighed.

'I really love it when people are honest with me. I am going to go to my room,' she said, and left.

Penelope went into the bathroom to brush her teeth. While she was flossing, Lan stormed into the bathroom and slammed the door behind her.

'Lan,' said Penelope. 'Hi!'

'Hi,' said Lan.

'I didn't know you were a lighting designer,' said Penelope.

'Emma said she would report Raymond to the proctor if I didn't lighting design this terrible play,' said Lan. 'I hope she dies in a ditch.'

'She did?' said Penelope.

'Yeah,' said Lan. 'Why would I ever want to do the lighting design for this stupid play? It doesn't even make sense at all! She just wants to brownie up to that bimbo who plays Caligula because she's the president of one of these finals clubs that Emma wants to get into. What a loser. I am going to paint her room black.'

'But that's my room too,' said Penelope.

This was greeted with silence.

'Do you really like Raymond that much?' asked Penelope.

'I like him OK,' said Lan.

'Can he pee in the toilet now?' asked Penelope.

'No. He is the stupidest cat I have ever met,' said Lan. 'His IQ is zero.'

'Oh,' said Penelope.

6.

Penelope Attends a Disturbing Party

A couple of days later, on the way to play practice, Penelope called her mother.

'Hi, Mom!' said Penelope.

'Penelope,' said her mother, 'I was starting to worry you were dead. I was two seconds away from calling a hospital. You haven't called me for a week. What have you been doing?'

'Oh,' said Penelope. 'Well, I am alive, and guess where I am going!'

'Did you get my calls? I called you twice.'

'I did. And now I am calling you back! Guess where I am now!'

'Well, I don't even want to know. Because I was very worried. You should have called me back much earlier.'

'I'm sorry,' said Penelope.

'Well, where are you?' asked Penelope's mother, mollified.

'I am on my way to play practice,' said Penelope.

'You are in a play? Oh, Penelope, that is great news! What's the play called?'

'*Caligula.*'

'What is that?' asked Penelope's mother.

'It's a play about this guy who kills his entire kingdom and has sex with his sister. I don't know, I haven't read it in a while.'

'Well, aren't you in it? Shouldn't you read it to refresh your memory?'

'Maybe,' said Penelope. 'I don't have any lines.'

'Still, Penelope,' said her mother, 'I think you should read it. What if the lead breaks her leg and you have to go on as the lead?'

'Well, there are two Caligulas, so I don't think that will happen.'

'There are two Caligulas. Why is that?'

'I don't know. OK, Mom, I am almost at the theater,' said Penelope.

'OK,' said her mother. 'How are your friends?'

'Bye!'

'What? Oh well, bye, Penelope,' said her mother.

Unfortunately, Penelope arrived at the theater at the same time as Ted and Catherine. They were just across the street from Penelope; Ted in his shorts, Catherine in a tiny pink tennis skirt and sweatshirt with a giant V cut in the front. Penelope hoped she could escape without saying hi to them.

Until this moment, Penelope had successfully avoided speaking or hanging out with Ted. This was a major feat considering the broad parameters of their former intimacy, but she had felt herself both too duty bound and embarrassed to see him once he had pledged himself to Catherine's stead. Penelope imagined Ted felt the same way. He had certainly stopped randomly dropping in on her since the dead fish incident, which was what Penelope had taken to calling it in her mind.

'Penelope!' yelled Catherine when she spotted her.

Penelope reluctantly turned around.

'Oh, hi,' said Penelope.

'Wait up,' said Catherine. When within arm's length, Catherine grabbed Penelope's elbow. Ted hung back, met Penelope's eyes briefly, and smiled. She did not smile back.

'Did you hear about Nikil?' asked Catherine, encasing Penelope's arm in a viselike grip.

'Um, no?' said Penelope.

'He didn't get on the Crimson Business Board. He got cut.'

'Oh, that's too bad,' said Penelope.

'He's really upset,' said Catherine with relish. 'I feel awful for him.'

'It's too bad that even things that seem so un-fun are also so competitive,' said Penelope. 'This was why I have always been against the Olympics, as a rule.'

'I think the business board sounds fun. You know what is not fun? I was up until four a.m. last night doing work,' said Catherine. 'How late were you up?'

'Eleven?' said Penelope.

'I'm worried I will fall asleep during this rehearsal.'

'Well,' said Penelope, 'good thing we are guards. They always go to sleep at inopportune times.'

'Are you going to Harvard-Yale, Penelope?' asked Catherine. 'We're not. Too much work.'

'I don't know,' said Penelope. 'What is it?'

'It's a football game, duh,' said Catherine. 'Oh my God, you are so out of it.'

'I have to head out,' said Ted. 'I have a class.'

'OK, baby!' said Catherine, brought to attention. She hugged Ted and then ruffled his hair. 'What are you doing later?'

'I don't know,' said Ted. 'What are you doing later?'

'I was thinking about watching a movie or something,' said Catherine.

'That sounds great,' said Ted. 'Penelope, do you still have that TV?'

'Yes,' said Penelope. Was he inviting her? She would make it clear that she was not attending. 'You can use it. I think there is a parade in Boston that I wanted to go to.'

Ted started laughing.

'Penelope, don't be ridiculous. If we are watching TV in your room, then you have to come! I don't think there is a parade happening anywhere.'

Penelope was struck dumb. She had flattered herself that their avoidance was mutual. Was he trying to be friends again? Did he want them all to be friends? Why had she said that about a parade? What parade happens at night? A night parade, she should have said.

'Cool,' said Ted. 'Let's all get dinner and watch a movie together. That will be fun.' He sauntered off, pleased. Catherine and Penelope entered the rehearsal room together.

'Ted insisted on walking me here today, isn't that sweet?' whispered Catherine as they opened the door.

'Yes,' said Penelope.

'Ahh, Guards,' shouted Henry Wills-Mather as soon as Penelope and Catherine entered the room. 'Just in time!'

Henry Wills-Mather was wearing the exact same outfit that he was wearing at the last play practice with the addition of a red scarf, which he had tucked into the neck of his black turtle-neck like a bib. The overall effect was curiously non-French.

'We are blocking the first act today and we have a lot of work to do, so let's hop to it!' The cast, many of whom were milling around the front of the stage, quickly gathered around Henry Wills-Mather.

'I want the Caligulas over there,' said Wills-Mather, flinging his arm toward a spot in the center of the stage. 'We are going to run the scene from your entrance. Octavius, Lucius, Cassius, Helicon, all to your places.' All the Roman senators gathered in groups of two or three around the stage. In nearly every group someone was kneeling and someone else was peering into the distance and pointing.

'It's supposed to seem like we interrupted you talking. So really act like you're talking!' said Henry Wills-Mather. The senators broke from their poses and started mouthing words and gesticulating wildly.

'OK. Guards, I want you to go to either side of Caligula.' Penelope and Catherine silently filed next to the two Caligulas.

'You are holding spears, so pretend to hold spears,' said Henry Wills-Mather. Penelope and Catherine both put their hands out in front of them, as if they were holding spears.

'OK. So I see you all have your places,' said Henry Wills-Mather. 'Let's take it from "But you know nothing."'

Boy Caligula came forward. He spoke in a high, nasal voice:

'But you know nothing!' he said, spitting tiny pustules of water into the air. 'Everything is important, the agrarian laws and finance. Everything is on the same footing: the grandeur of Rome and your arthritis attacks. Hear me, little steward.'

'We're listening,' said the Steward. Then Girl Caligula stepped forward.

'You are fair, is not it?' said Girl Caligula forcefully.

'No, no, no, no, no!' said Henry Wills-Mather. 'That is all wrong.'

'Phew. Do you think something is wrong with their scripts?' whispered Penelope to Catherine.

'No,' said Catherine shortly. Penelope wondered if she was a little peeved that she had to watch TV in Penelope's room this evening.

'I think he doesn't know French or something,' said Penelope.

'Penelope, he said he was a linguist. I don't think he would just lie about that,' hissed Catherine.

'Guards,' said Henry Wills-Mather. 'Do you know why I am stopping?'

Penelope and Catherine stopped whispering.

'Guards, your job in this play is very very important. Very important. Although you have no speaking roles, you add a very integral humanity to the theatrical landscape. That is why you are here. So when you stand there, woodenly looking at the action instead of psychologically participating in the action, well, it's very hard to watch.'

'I'm sorry,' mumbled Penelope.

'It's all right, Guard,' said Henry Wills-Mather. 'But just because you are not saying anything doesn't mean you can let your face go dead. What is going on in the mind of your character right now? You must always ask yourself that! You!' said Henry Wills-Mather, pointing at Catherine. 'What is going on with your character? What are you thinking about during this scene? A couple of days ago I asked you both to write essays about this.'

'Well,' said Catherine. 'Hold on, let me get my essay.' Catherine walked over to her bag and took a typewritten sheet of paper out of a binder. Penelope watched this with a heavy heart. This assignment had entirely slipped her mind.

'OK, so I was formerly a slave girl,' said Catherine, looking at her paper, 'sold into slavery against my will to pay off some parental debts. I fell in love with a slave boy but he was killed in a gladiator fight. In grief I worked my way up to being a guard in Caligula's army, where I hope to kill him.'

'Bravo,' said Henry Wills-Mather. 'That is exactly the type of thing I am talking about. Specificity. What I want now' – he paused – 'is for you to convey that to me.' He made a dramatic pinching motion with his hands. 'Make the audience your captors. Engage with what Caligula is saying. If you are feeling homicidal, I want to see it on the stage, OK?'

'OK,' said Catherine, beaming.

'You,' said Henry Wills-Mather, pointing at Penelope. He was on a roll now. 'How about you?'

'Me?' said Penelope.

'Who else would I be referring to, Guard?' said Henry Wills-Mather in an instructive way. 'What is your character's history? What brought you to this place, next to the Caligulas?'

'Um, well,' said Penelope. She had to think quickly. 'Hmm.'

'Do you need to get out your character essay?' asked Henry Wills-Mather.

'No, that's OK,' said Penelope. 'It's really just about, you know, being a guard.'

'OK,' said Henry Wills-Mather, smiling broadly at everyone. The cast giggled uncomfortably.

'On the Nile River,' said Penelope quickly. 'Where a horrible shooting accident happens and someone dies.'

'Hmm,' said Henry Wills-Mather.

'It radicalized me, as a guard,' said Penelope. 'A Belgian detective solves the mystery.'

'Bring that pain to your part,' said Henry Wills-Mather slowly and distinctly. He pinched the air with his hands again. They moved on.

Later that evening, Ted, Catherine, and Penelope were watching TV in Penelope's common room. In order to keep Catherine's antagonism toward her to a minimum, Penelope had hidden in her bathroom for most of the evening.

'Are you OK?' asked Ted, as Penelope was coming out of the bathroom after a particularly long stint inside.

'Oh, yes,' said Penelope. 'I was just cleaning.'

'Really?' said Ted.

'Yes,' said Penelope. Actually, she was putting the original French text of *Caligula* into Google Translate to prove some theories.

'This show is ridiculous. Don't you think so?' Catherine said to Ted. They were watching *Laguna Beach* at Catherine's suggestion.

'I mean, sort of,' said Ted, still looking at the TV. 'I can't believe she goes back out with that guy.'

'Well, I don't know,' said Penelope, sitting on the arm of the futon. 'He has the charm of a man with a square hairline.'

'Do I have a square hairline?' asked Ted.

'I think you have a widow's peak,' said Penelope

'I think you have a square hairline,' said Catherine. She sat on Ted's lap.

Just then, Emma came into the room. She was wearing leggings tucked into riding boots and a large monogrammed ring on her index finger. Once again, Penelope marveled at her ability to enter a room at just the right time. She laid her bag on the floor and sat down next to it.

'Hi, guys,' she said. 'What's up?'

'Nothing,' said Penelope.

'Hey, Emma!' said Catherine. 'Wanna watch TV with us?'

'I'm so sorry,' said Emma. 'I'm always forgetting everybody's names. Have we met? What's your name again?'

'I'm Catherine,' said Catherine. 'I'm in the play with you.'

'Oh, right,' said Emma. 'I'm so sorry. I just meet so many people. I can't keep anyone straight.' She did one of her hooting laughs, which succeeded in drowning out the sounds of *Laguna Beach* for a few seconds. 'What are you guys watching?'

'*Laguna Beach*,' said Ted.

'And your name is?' asked Emma, looking at Ted.

'Oh, this is Ted,' said Penelope.

'Oh, I remember this season,' said Emma. She resituated herself so she was sitting in front of the TV. 'I wish I could watch it. I'm going out pretty soon. Maybe I can stay for just one episode.'

'Where are you going?' asked Penelope.

'Oh, I am going to this party at the S—. I'm waiting for Bitty. She went to this drinks thing at the Pudding that I couldn't go to because I was working. Once she texts me, I'll head out.'

'OK,' said Penelope.

Emma settled on the floor and the group continued watching TV – Penelope sitting precariously on the arm of the futon, Catherine lying on Ted's lap.

'There are so many girls like that in California,' said Emma after one girl vomited from drinking too much.

'I know,' said Catherine, who nodded. 'They're so cheap. I get sick of looking at them. Those sandals are like what a whore would wear.'

'I've never been to California,' said Penelope.

'It's weird,' said Emma authoritatively. 'It's like a different culture. Like all the girls here from California have breast implants. It's like, can you imagine going to Harvard and getting breast implants?'

'Sure I could,' said Penelope.

'I'll leave in a second,' said Emma.

For the next two hours Emma, Ted, Catherine, and Penelope watched an entire season of *Laguna Beach*. Emma checked her phone approximately every five minutes to see if anyone texted her to go to the S— party. No one did. Once they had finished the final DVD, she seemed at a loss for what to do.

'I don't know why no one has texted me to go to the S— party yet,' said Emma as Penelope ejected the DVD and put it back in its case.

'That is weird,' said Penelope.

'I know,' said Emma. 'It's probably because it's hard to get service in the clubs. I bet that's it, actually.'

'I'm sure it's that,' said Catherine sympathetically.

'Maybe I should just head over. What do you think, should I head over?' asked Emma.

'I would,' said Ted.

'I hate to go to things alone though.'

'It does suck,' said Penelope. 'Do you have a game on your phone?'

'Oh God, I don't know what to do,' said Emma in a distressed tone.

'Penelope could go with you,' said Ted, lightly punching Penelope's arm. Penelope was not displeased with this sugges-tion. It was a much more sound excuse than a parade. She wished she had thought of it.

'Well, you couldn't go,' said Emma. 'They don't let random guys inside.'

'I know,' said Ted. 'That's why I said Penelope should go.'

'Or I could go,' said Catherine loudly.

'OK,' said Ted. He seemed even more pleased by this idea. 'Penelope and I will just stay here.'

'Actually,' said Catherine, 'maybe Penelope should go to the party. I should probably stay with you.' She got up, straddled Ted, and kissed him on the lips.

'Well, OK,' said Emma. 'Penelope, do you want to come with me?'

'Sure,' said Penelope.

'OK then,' said Emma, as if resigned to fate.

'I'll get my coat,' said Penelope.

Penelope went over to the coat rack near the door and put her coat on. She found lipstick in one of the pockets and applied it lavishly. Emma gathered her belongings and joined Penelope near the door.

'Well, bye, Ted. Bye, Catherine,' said Penelope.

'Tell me how it is when you get back. I'll probably be up,' said Ted.

'I will be too!' said Catherine.

'OK,' said Penelope.

'This won't be so bad,' said Emma.

'Maybe not,' said Penelope, thinking about lesser evils.

7.

Penelope Attends a Disturbing Party, Continued

Emma and Penelope walked over to the party in silence. Emma tried fruitlessly to call people. Penelope trudged beside her. It was cold out. Penelope was vaguely regretting this endeavor.

'We're almost here,' said Emma suddenly. They were on a wide street. It was lined with different kinds of brick buildings, some apartments, some Greek Revival-type houses. They stopped in front of an anonymous-looking edifice of the latter description, one side of which seemed to be a German bookstore.

'Just say you're my roommate.'

'I will,' said Penelope.

Outside the door of this establishment was a man sitting on a chair. He was about forty, tan, pockmarked, and wearing a leather jacket. He was holding a sheaf of papers.

'Hi,' said Emma. 'Emma Green.'

'Are you on the list?' asked the guy, looking at the papers.

'Yeah, I think so.'

'Hmm . . . There you are,' said the guy, checking her name off with a pen. 'Who's this though?'

'This is my roommate,' said Emma.

'Is she on the list?' asked the guy. 'What's her name?'

'She's not on the list, but can she still come in with me?'

'I don't think so,' said the guy, who Penelope realized was a bouncer, hired for the occasion. 'You're gonna have to check with one of the members. We're pretty full.'

'Oh, please!' said Emma.

'I'm sorry,' said the bouncer.

'I'll call the guy I know,' said Emma. She looked like she was about to cry.

'I can just go home,' said Penelope.

'Could you?' said Emma.

'Yeah, def,' said Penelope. 'I definitely could.'

'Oh, hey, Evan? Is that you?' said Emma into her phone. 'I have a friend here, and I need to get her inside. Will you come out here and tell the guy outside that it's OK? Oh, you will? Thank you so so much!' Emma hung up the phone, elated.

'Evan will be down in a minute,' said Emma to the bouncer. He shrugged.

'It's cold out,' said Penelope to the bouncer.

'Yes,' said the bouncer.

'Do you have gloves?' asked Penelope.

'I don't have circulation in my hands,' said the bouncer.

Evan opened the door. He was wearing pleated pants, a polo shirt, and a blazer. He was suffering from a terrible case of cystic acne.

'Thanks so much, Evan,' said Emma. She hugged him. 'Sorry I'm late.'

'Next time you should call me earlier if you are going to bring a guest,' said Evan. He beckoned both Penelope and Emma inside, and shut the door quickly behind them. They stood in a dark hallway. The music, an anonymous yet menacing techno, was quite loud.

Evan looked at the two girls. He stood on one foot. Then he switched to the other foot.

'How are you doing, Emma?' he said after a pause.

'Oh, great, well, not that great. I have a ton of work,' said Emma.

'Me too,' said Evan.

'Ha ha,' laughed Emma.

'Well, I guess we should really go inside. We don't want to just keep standing here,' said Evan. He walked down the corridor without waiting for an answer.

Emma grabbed Penelope's arm and started walking with her down the hallway. They followed Evan closely.

'Evan's father is the head of this bank in New York,' Emma whispered into Penelope's ear. 'His mother is Donald Trump's sister, I think.'

'Oh,' said Penelope.

They walked into the foyer of the club, which was forest green and adorned with a decorous smattering of dentil molding. To the left of the foyer was a billiards room, which had been converted into a dancing area with the help of a strobe light. It was stuffed with people bouncing up and down and, in the process, bumping roughly against the pool table in a way that looked like it hurt. On the right side of the foyer was a staircase. Every available wall was covered with either the head of a dead bear or a drawing of a live bear.

Evan started to go up the stairs. Emma grabbed his wrist.

'Can we go upstairs, Evan?' asked Emma. She held his hand in hers and looked at him pleadingly.

'Uh, sure. Yeah, definitely,' said Evan.

'Yay!' said Emma. She hugged him. She and Evan climbed the stairs, arm in arm. Penelope trotted behind them.

This was probably the nicest house that Penelope had ever been in in her life. It was rather shabby, of course, but only in the way that truly grand things are shabby. On every table, there was something old and mildly valuable, like a vase or a tiny statuette of a bear doing ballet. Penelope wondered how a group of eighteen-year-olds was expected to keep up something like this, but apparently they were quite good at it.

When they go to the top of the staircase, Evan and Emma led Penelope into a large room. Unlike the rest of the house, this room had all the lights on. Small groups of people were playing antique board games, like cribbage, at tables designed for such a purpose. One side of the room housed a grand piano and a couple of settees. The other side of the room featured a gigantic stuffed bear poised in the position of attack.

Emma and Evan went to the piano side of the room when Emma spotted Bitty, who Penelope remembered played one of the Caligulas.

'Bitty!' yelled Emma. She disentangled herself from Evan and ran toward her. Bitty was balanced on the corner of a Queen Anne end table sipping a glass of white wine. She was wearing an ivory-colored cashmere sweater and pearls. She had such an aggressive plainness about her, down to her unadorned hair and well-defined jaw, that it almost substituted for glamour.

'Emma!' said Bitty. She spoke in a gravelly voice, like she had just stopped shouting. They hugged. Evan ambled away and sat on a nearby settee.

'How was the Pudding?' said Emma.

'Fine,' said Bitty. 'I mean, boring as usual. We left early.'

'Where's Katrina?' asked Emma.

'Oh, she's playing backgammon with Roger,' said Bitty with a wave of her hand.

'Katrina is so hilarious,' said Emma.

'She really is,' said Bitty. 'Emma, have you met Leslie Danforth?' Bitty gestured to a man standing next to her with eyebrows so blond they were invisible.

'Nice to meet you,' said Emma.

'Does anyone want a drink?' asked Leslie Danforth.

'I think we all would,' said Bitty. 'Another one of these for me.' She tipped her glass toward Leslie Danforth, who gallantly took it.

'All right,' said Leslie Danforth, and walked away.

'He's a blast!' said Bitty.

'Doesn't his father own one of the British Virgin Islands?' asked Emma.

'His father is really involved with public radio,' said Bitty in a warning tone. 'They're great friends of ours.'

'Oh,' said Emma.

'We're going on vacation with them, actually, over Christmas break. To the Virgin Islands.'

'That will be amazing,' said Emma.

'It really will,' said Bitty. 'We're also going with Amelia Lucey. Do you known Amelia Lucey?'

'It sounds familiar,' said Emma.

'She's in the Pudding,' said Bitty 'Went to Exeter. She's hilarious. It's going to be a fantastic trip.'

'Oh, I know her now that you say it,' said Emma. 'She is hilarious.'

Leslie Danforth came back with the drinks.

'A white wine for you, a scotch for you, Emma, oh, and I'm sorry, I didn't see your friend back there. I didn't get you anything,' said Leslie.

'Oh, yes, Emma, who's your friend?' said Bitty.

'Oh, this is my roommate,' said Emma. 'Penelope.'

'Hi,' said Penelope. 'We're in the play together.'

'We are?' said Bitty.

'I play a guard,' said Penelope.

'Do you need me to run back and get you a drink?' asked Leslie Danforth.

'Oh, I can get it myself,' said Penelope. She walked toward where Leslie got the drinks from – a small mahogany-paneled study connected via pocket door to the antique board games room. In the study, there were three men in tuxedos smoking cigars.

'So what have you been up to?' said one of the men in tuxedos to another. Penelope could not see who was speaking, because she was busy making herself a mixture of rum, tonic water, and orange juice at the makeshift bar in the back of the room.

'I've been so busy with my new business. I'm working on a startup,' said one of the other tuxedo-clad fellows. 'It's an Internet-based company that's like Facebook but lets people with ecological businesses connect to one another.'

'That's a great idea,' said the first tuxedo.

'Yeah, we'll see,' said the second tuxedo. 'I think it really could be big.'

'I agree,' said the third tuxedo, a voice that could only be Gustav's. Penelope almost spilled her drink but still did not turn around. 'All those ecological fellows need to connect to one another. Really, I know at least four. They are crying out for a system.'

'Exactly,' said the first tuxedo.

Penelope turned away from the bar and slowly walked by Gustav and his friends on the way to the door. Gustav looked intensely handsome, so handsome that Penelope thought she couldn't realistically stay around much longer without mishap. Gustav did not seem to notice her. He was untying his bow tie when she left.

When Penelope returned to the antique board games room, Emma and Bitty were gone, and Leslie Danforth was playing a Chopin nocturne on the piano. Penelope briefly considered looking for her lost compatriots but decided against it. Neither of them seemed to like her very much, and Penelope's mother had recently given her a lecture about not hanging around with people who seemed like they were annoyed with her, as that would make them more annoyed. So instead she sat on the settee directly under the outstretched claws of the stuffed bear. She took a book out of her bag and set it down next to her. She sipped her drink. It tasted mostly of tonic water.

About fifteen minutes after Penelope settled herself in her seat, Gustav entered the room, cigar still in hand. He sat on an ottoman quite near Penelope's settee. He texted someone for a long time. Penelope kept her eyes bolted on Leslie Danforth, who was given to very elaborate hand gestures and closed eyes while playing piano.

Suddenly Gustav spoke.

'Are you reading?' he said to someone. Penelope kept looking at Leslie Danforth.

'You, in that sort of frilly neck thing, are you reading?'

Penelope whipped her head around. Apparently, Gustav was addressing her. He had turned his body completely in her direction and was staring at her.

'No,' said Penelope.

'Then why is there a book lying next to you on the couch?'

'Well, eventually, I was preparing to read,' said Penelope. 'I think.'

'Harrumph,' said Gustav. 'That seems rather antisocial.'

'I was thinking of reading aloud,' said Penelope. 'To everyone.'

'But how would anyone hear you over the din of the piano?' asked Gustav.

'I would shout,' said Penelope.

Gustav shook his head. Then he turned away to watch Leslie Danforth, who could, apparently, play only one Chopin nocturne. Periodically, people clapped for Leslie Danforth, but he did not let accolades distract him from his task. He would bow and start again, like a player piano. Penelope assumed her conversation with Gustav was over. He had started to look at his phone again. She gave herself permission to exhale, and was inwardly rebuking herself for the reading aloud comment, when Gustav spoke again.

'My God,' Gustav said suddenly. 'Are you twiddling your thumbs?'

'No,' said Penelope.

'I just saw you,' said Gustav.

'Well,' said Penelope, 'to be honest, I think there is something wrong with my drink. I was warming up before I took another sip of it.'

'Very wise,' said Gustav, 'to exercise one's hands before drinking. Mind if I try it?' He moved onto Penelope's couch.

'I really don't think you will like it at all,' said Penelope. She handed it to him. He took a sip.

'Why that's absolutely vile!' said Gustav. He coughed. 'What is even in that?'

'Quinine,' said Penelope.

'I should say so,' said Gustav. 'Plus rum? That is a disgrace to the art of drinking.'

'The good thing is, though, you will not get malaria,' said Penelope.

'Exceedingly smart,' said Gustav. 'One always must be prepared for the demmed mosquitos and a revolt in the mines, as my grandfather used to say. You aren't by any chance in my Counting People section, are you?'

'I don't know,' said Penelope. 'Or at least, I don't think so. I don't remember.'

'Do you have Jared?' asked Gustav.

'Yes,' said Penelope.

'See? I knew it. I knew I recognized you from somewhere,' said Gustav. 'Why haven't I seen you around before? Do you go to the S— much?'

'No,' said Penelope. 'This is my first time.'

'Who brought you here?'

'My roommate Emma. We came to meet her friend Bitty. I am in a play with both of them.'

'You are in that awful production of *Caligula*? Oh, you can't be serious!'

'I play a guard,' said Penelope.

'*Caligula*! Oh that is too humorous,' said Gustav, laughing. 'The one with two Caligulas.'

'I sort of got roped into it,' said Penelope. 'The director –'

'Oh my God,' said Gustav. 'That horrid little man. My father knew him for some odd reason and so I went to a play of his once. The demmed thing made no sense. It was a foreign play, but he had translated it, and, my God, it sounded like a machine had translated it and done quite a bad job, even for a machine.'

'That's what I think too!' said Penelope. She felt oddly triumphant.

'You see, I was almost roped into being in that play. Bitty is a rather good friend of mine. But last time I was in a play, I starred as Baby Jesus, and you can only go downhill from there. I made it a policy to do no more drama unless I reprise the role I originated.'

'That seems fair,' said Penelope.

Gustav looked at Penelope appraisingly. 'Are you having a good time here?' he asked.

'Oh, sure,' said Penelope.

'Really? I feel I can make the safe assumption that you are

not having a very good time. From the thumb twiddling. And the reading as well. Have you danced yet?' asked Gustav.

'No,' said Penelope.

'Do you want to?' asked Gustav.

'Maybe. I am a pretty bad dancer,' said Penelope.

'You're in luck because I am an excellent dancer,' said Gustav. 'I will lead you around the floor by your hind legs.'

'That sounds more like a race,' said Penelope.

'Penelope! There you are,' said Emma from across the room. She had come back. Bitty was nowhere to be seen. Emma strode over to Gustav and Penelope, arms outstretched. 'And you've found Gustav!'

'Oh, hello, Emma,' said Gustav stiffly. He stood up.

'Gustav!' said Emma, hugging him. 'Did you have fun in Abu Dhabi?'

'Quite,' said Gustav. 'How charming to see you.'

'Ha ha,' laughed Emma. 'So are you nearing a final decision in the punch process?'

'That is what they say. I took a couple of punches to Tanzania the other weekend. Flew them around in the old helicopter. Seemed as if they enjoyed it. I always had the sneaking suspicion that some of them wore hairpieces.'

'Who did you take?' asked Emma.

'All the ones I was worried wore hairpieces. Helicopter's the real test. Certainly, we can't have that kind of element in the club.'

'A baldness element?' asked Penelope.

'Oh, yes, Penelope. That sort of thing can be quite subversive if left unchecked.'

'What?' said Emma. She did her hooting laugh, this time in a high, piercing register that blocked out the sounds of the piano and all ambient conversation. 'Anyway, Penelope, I need you to come down and dance with me!' said Emma. 'You can't just stay up here.' She took Penelope by the hand and pulled her off the couch. Then she tried to twirl her, which Penelope didn't understand until much too late.

'Come on,' said Emma in a testy way.

'OK,' said Penelope. She did not want to dance with Emma instead of Gustav, but handling these sorts of situations was, like many things, not her strong point.

'I must get another drink anyway,' said Gustav. He waved at Penelope and sauntered off toward the mahogany room. Penelope had to work hard to hide how disappointed she was.

Emma grabbed Penelope by the hand and led her down the stairs.

'That is so weird that you were talking to Gustav,' said Emma.

'Was it?' said Penelope.

'What did you guys talk about?' asked Emma.

'Nothing really,' said Penelope.

'That's so funny. I always have the best conversations with him.'

They were outside the billiards room and dancing area. It was still crowded with people dancing. In fact, the number seemed to have increased tremendously since Penelope last walked by.

'Come on, Penelope,' said Emma, 'I always go near the pool table.'

Emma walked into the room and stationed herself in front of the pool table. Penelope stood next to her. After Emma was situated, she started thrusting herself against the pool table without moving any of her limbs. This soon attracted the attention of a dainty brunet man wearing a silver bracelet, who approached Emma and started gyrating into the front of her thigh. Penelope moved to the other side of the pool table to give them room. Eventually, after her eyes adjusted to the strobe light, she realized she was standing near Evan, who looked utterly miserable. She decided to approach him.

'Hi, Evan,' said Penelope.

'Hi,' said Evan. He was staring at Emma.

'How has your night been?' asked Penelope.

'OK,' said Evan. He was sweating a little, on his forehead and under his arms.

'Do you want to dance?' asked Penelope.

'Uh,' said Evan. 'Sure, I guess.'

Penelope grabbed Evan around the neck and started to dance with him. Evan stood ramrod straight and barely moved. He was not much taller than Penelope but somehow she had to crane her neck to make eye contact with him, which is a bother if you are doing complicated moves. She decided to introduce conversation to the dance.

'So do you like dancing to this beeping sound?' asked Penelope.

'Ha ha,' laughed Evan, whose eyes were scanning the room continually. 'It's OK.'

'What kind of music do you like?' asked Penelope.

'I don't know,' said Evan. 'I guess I don't really listen to music.'

'Cool,' said Penelope. Evan saw someone in the distance and waved to them. Penelope abandoned the idea of conversation and concentrated on complicated moves.

'Hey,' said Evan after the song changed, finally, to Michael Jackson. 'Slow down. You keep stepping on my foot.'

'Oh, sorry,' said Penelope. Penelope was trying to accomplish her famous crotch-grab-spin when she realized that Gustav was dancing right near her. He was with Bitty. Gustav was a very old-fashioned dancer, and Bitty was very uncoordinated. They were both drinking whiskey in large glasses full of ice. Penelope watched Emma unceremoniously abandon her dance partner and scamper over to Bitty and Gustav. Then they all started talking in a corner where the music presumably wasn't as loud.

Bitty kept tipping backward and Gustav kept having to catch her.

'So, Evan,' said Penelope. 'Is that Gustav dating anyone?'

'I don't know,' said Evan. 'That guy is a weirdo. Stop going so fast.'

'OK, OK,' said Penelope.

'I have to get a drink,' said Evan. He removed Penelope's hands from around his neck rather abruptly and left.

This, Penelope felt, was a good excuse as any to leave the dance floor. However, when she tried to make her exit, Gustav motioned her over to his group.

'Ah, there you are,' said Gustav when Penelope got within earshot. 'You must really, really like Michael Jackson.'

'I like Janet better,' said Penelope.

'Do you think our DJ is remiss? To be honest, I didn't really like the look of him. Rather small yet wearing a huge hat. No sense of proportion,' said Gustav.

'Penelope, the S— flew this DJ in from, where was it, Gustav, Belize?' asked Emma.

'Yes, or somewhere in that godforsaken swamp that is South America,' said Gustav.

'Aren't you from South America?' asked Emma.

'That is why I can say that with authority,' said Gustav.

'I think this DJ is fantastic,' said Bitty. 'Really, just fantastic!' She fell backward again. This time, she leaned against a wall and closed her eyes.

'Penelope,' said Gustav, stroking his chin. 'Although I have only met you just now, I am very impressed by your dancing skills. Can you do that moonwalk again, in this corner?'

'Actually, Penelope,' said Emma, 'we really should go. I am super-tired and I have to get up early tomorrow to write a paper. I'm sorry, guys. Gustav, are you coming to Harvard-Yale?'

'Yes, believe so. Have to get my bearskin dry-cleaned, of

course. Are you sure you ladies have to go right at this moment? I am almost positive I could convince Jesus to play Michael Jackson again, if that is what it takes.'

'No,' said Emma. 'We really have to go. But I hope we will see you soon!'

'It was nice meeting you, Penelope. Emma. Always a pleasure,' said Gustav. 'Bitty, darling, wake up! The wall is not a bed!'

'So did you have fun?' asked Emma halfway through the walk back from the party.

'Oh, yes,' said Penelope. Penelope was not one to get carried away on the wings of fancy, but in a short time, she had come to the conclusion that Gustav was the funniest, most interesting, most agreeable man she had ever met. She could not believe that he had talked to her. She could not believe that she had had the strength to answer any of his questions. 'I had a fine time.'

'I'm so glad you got to meet Gustav,' said Emma. 'He and I are really close, and it always makes me happy when some of my friends meet others of my friends.'

'How do you know him?' asked Penelope.

'I met him the first week of school. But I had heard of him before that. His family is extremely famous.'

'Oh, really?'

'They are originally German royalty. But then they went to Argentina after World War II. Gustav told me it was because they needed to hide out for some reason. But then they started some business. And now his dad does something with Formula One cars!'

'Why do you think they did needed to hide out after World War II?' asked Penelope in a nervous voice.

'Oh God, I don't know. How should I know?'

'I thought he was British,' said Penelope.

'He went to school in England. All rich people do. But he's not British. He doesn't sound British to me at all. He sounds very German. I think it's because I have met a lot of Germans. I recognized it immediately.'

'Oh,' said Penelope.

'I always feel weird around Bitty when I am with Gustav, so I was glad you were there with me. It kind of cut the tension.'

'What tension?' asked Penelope.

'Well, Bitty and I are like really good friends, of course. And Gustav is kind of involved with her. They knew each other from before Harvard and I think they have been hooking up casually for like years. It's weird though, because the first week of school, I hung out with Gustav one-on-one for like a long time, and it's been weird ever since.'

'Why?' asked Penelope.

'Well, nothing happened. It was four in the morning and I was in his room and I was drunk. It was totally platonic. The thing is, we've always had some weird tension between us ever since. Did you notice it?'

'Not really,' said Penelope. 'But next time, I will look for it.'

'Are you sure?' said Emma. 'I feel like it's so obvious.'

'Well, let me think. I guess I did notice some tension.'

'You did?' asked Emma. 'When?'

'At points,' said Penelope.

'Yeah, I know. It's sort of ridiculous,' said Emma. They were back at Pennypacker and climbed the stairs to their room. Penelope did not feel like sharing this story with Ted and Catherine, so she went straight to bed.

8.

The Game

'So, I have been hearing through the grapevine that some of you are having problems with your e-mail,' said Jared. Everyone in the section gaped at him silently. Jared glared at Penelope. Penelope drew a face on her new notepad, which she bought for just this occasion.

'If you are having problems with your e-mail, that is no excuse not to do your work or honor your obligations. You need to go to computer services and get your server fixed if this is the case. In the meantime, I can print you out handouts if you come to my office hours. Is that clear?'

Everyone nodded.

'Good,' said Jared. 'We can finally get started in our discussion.'

Penelope stared at Gustav as she drew eyelashes on the face she was illustrating. This was the first time she had seen him since the party. He was wearing a chocolate-brown cardigan, tan suede boots, and very dark, very tight jeans. The night before, Penelope had had a dream about Gustav in which he took her up in a helicopter and tried to make out with her, at which point she realized she was in a car seat made of lead. Even though there was a chain saw lying on the floor of the helicopter, it was useless in the face of the car seat's restraints. Suddenly, the helicopter took a rapid dive and the car seat tumbled out of the helicopter. She woke up just as she was about to hit the ground. It was hard to say what that meant. It depended on whether you thought dreams predicted the future or told you about your subconscious self. Penelope was feeling more and more like she was in the former camp.

The class was interminable. Today the discussion consisted of an extended question-and-answer session about the upcoming quiz. Everyone loved these kinds of sections, it seemed, as there was much active participation and shouted questions.

Penelope spent the entire class wondering whether to talk to Gustav when the class was over. Should she acknowledge that they knew each other? Or should she pretend that she had forgotten that they met? It was difficult to know.

As the class was filing out, Penelope had just reached the decision to ignore Gustav when he called out to her.

'Hey, Penelope is it?' said Gustav. He was a little behind her and jogged slightly to catch up with her as she was heading down the stairs.

'Oh, hi,' said Penelope.

'I thought it was you. Did you have fun the other night?'

'Oh, yeah. It was fun,' said Penelope. 'I was glad I got to moonwalk at some point.'

'As was I,' said Gustav. 'Are you going to the Barker Center?'

'Yeah, I have another section, actually.'

'Oh, woe is you,' said Gustav. 'What's yours for?'

'Images of Shakespeare,' said Penelope.

'I never really understood what that was,' said Gustav.

'It's self-explanatory,' said Penelope. 'What's your section for?'

'Oh, I don't have a section,' said Gustav. Was he just walking her to the Barker Center for no reason except her company? This was a stressful thought that made her unable to talk. Luckily Gustav was able to rise to the task of explaining his conduct and fixing on a subject.

'My dorm's just this way. Are you going to Harvard-Yale?'

'I don't know,' said Penelope. 'What is it exactly?'

'It's a football game.'

'Oh, that,' said Penelope. 'Everyone who I talk to keeps saying they have too much work to go.'

'Why, that's just ridiculous!' said Gustav. 'What kind of Jehovah's Witnesses are you talking to now? Excuse me, of course, if I insulted your religion.'

'The people in Pennypacker,' said Penelope.

'That is what your problem is. I have never even known anyone who lived in that wretched dorm. The housing isn't as random as they say. My father told me that much. Pennypacker is above the radio station, isn't it?'

'Yes,' said Penelope.

'Are you worried about ham waves?'

'Of course,' said Penelope. 'But I have a helmet.'

'Well, I hope it's steel plated,' said Gustav.

'It's for rollerblading,' said Penelope. 'And I gave it to my roommate when she was training our cat to do an obstacle course.'

'Why would she need a helmet if her cat was the one doing the obstacle course?' asked Gustav.

Penelope was just about to answer when she saw Ted. He was standing in front of the Barker Center, arms crossed. Ted and Penelope had this section together, and when they weren't avoiding each other, they waited for each other outside the Barker Center and walked into class together. Penelope had forgotten that they were not avoiding each other anymore. She sort of wished they were still avoiding each other, now that she thought about it.

'I have to go to class,' said Penelope bluntly to Gustav. The closer she got to Ted, the more she realized that his stance was exactly that of Yul Brynner in *The King and I*. It was a disturbing revelation.

'I have to go as well actually,' said Gustav, looking at his pocket watch, which was looped in the folds of his cardigan. 'But you should come to Harvard-Yale. The S— is having some sort of a tailgate afterward, I think. Of course, it will be a small affair. I wouldn't bring the teeming mob if you know what I mean.' Gustav looked at Ted, who, to Penelope's chagrin, was waving at her now as if they were bosom buddies. 'Bouncers and all that. Let me get your number and I can text you if anything actually materializes.'

'OK,' said Penelope. She mumbled her number in shock. 'Maybe I should learn the rules of football.'

'Darling,' said Gustav, 'batting around an olive-shaped rugby ball in a contest for pituitary supremacy is not football. I'll see you soon, I hope. Oh, hello there,' said Gustav to Ted.

'Hi,' said Ted.

'Bye, Penelope,' said Gustav. He took a sharp right and walked in the direction of the upper-class houses.

'Bye,' said Penelope to Gustav's fading figure. She and Ted went up the stairs.

'Who was that guy?' asked Ted.

'Oh, he's just this guy I know,' said Penelope.

They opened the door to the section. The class was assembled around a table. Ted and Penelope walked to the back of the table and sat down next to each other. The TF gave them an exasperated look. She was a short, round little woman who looked far older than she probably was. She wore a burnt orange cropped roll-neck sweater and clogs every day regardless of weather.

'Melissa was saying that this image of Shakespeare looks bloated,' said the TF, whose name was also Melissa and who therefore favored student Melissa in a shameless manner. 'What do you all think about that?'

There was silence.

'Bloated? I don't think we can start just throwing a word like that around without problematizing it a little,' scoffed a tiny boy in a herringbone vest. He was especially contrary when he wore the vest, Penelope had noticed.

Everyone disagreed. When the section ended, Ted and Penelope filed out of the classroom.

'Hey,' said Ted. 'Do you want to get a cup of coffee in the Barker Center café? We can do our homework in there.'

'OK,' said Penelope. She had a bad feeling about this. Hanging out with Ted in a group was one thing, but she had not really hung out one-on-one with him since the incident. She wondered what he wanted to talk to her about.

The café was on the first floor in a glass rotunda. It sold organic coffee and old sushi and was always very cold or really hot because of the windows. It might have been Penelope's least favorite place on campus, aside from the radio station. Ted threw his backpack, which was royal blue, on a table near the entrance.

'I really hate that kid in the vest,' said Ted, sitting down at the table.

'He is kind of mean,' said Penelope, also sitting down.

'I just don't understand rolling your eyes while other people are talking, or, for that matter, banging your hand on the table when you yourself are talking,' said Ted.

'He reminds me of William Jennings Bryan,' said Penelope.

'Yeah,' said Ted doubtfully. 'Do you want any coffee?'

'I might,' said Penelope.

'I'll get it,' said Ted. Before Penelope could really say any-thing, Ted had already sprinted to the coffee line. He came back a few minutes later coffee in hand.

'You like yours with just cream, right?' asked Ted, putting one of the coffees down in front of Penelope.

'Yeah,' said Penelope.

'I thought I remembered that,' said Ted. Then he looked at Penelope in a serious and pained manner that could not but strike fear in her heart.

'Actually, Penelope,' Ted said, 'I was really hoping we could talk.'

'Oh.'

'About the other night.'

'Really? OK.'

'What do you think about it?' said Ted.

'What do I think about it,' said Penelope. What did Penelope think about it? She had been trying to figure that out herself. At the time, the experience wavered from unpleasant to pleasant at parts. In the contemporary moment, it was firmly unpleasant.

'I don't know,' said Penelope.

'Do you think it was a mistake?' asked Ted.

'Sure,' said Penelope.

'Me too,' said Ted quickly. 'I was really drunk and everything. I think we both acted weirdly.'

'Hmm,' said Penelope. In her mind, they had not both acted weirdly. Only one person had acted weirdly. Another person was the hapless victim of the other's formless advances. 'Plus you are with Catherine.'

'Yes,' said Ted. 'I am. So that is good.'

'Yeah,' said Penelope.

'I think we can be friends now,' said Ted more self-confidently. 'You and me. It was too weird before with everything so undefined. I just had to take a stand and define it. I was just acting like an idiot.'

'That's OK,' said Penelope.

'We can even hang out now, I think,' said Ted. He ran his hands through his bangs, but they stayed put, as if shellacked to his forehead with Roman cement. 'I have been trying to hang out with you and Catherine and stuff. That was fun the other night. You and Catherine are such good friends so, I mean, we can all definitely still hang out. We don't have to tell her or anything.'

'Uh-huh,' said Penelope. She discerned the reason for the talk now and she was a little insulted by it. She would never have told Catherine anything. It was rather offensive that Ted thought she would. Penelope took out her notebook, put it on the table, and pretended to write in it, to communicate her displeasure at this intimation.

'You know, we should probably do homework,' said Ted, smiling ignorantly. He took out his textbook to read. Penelope felt that her displeasure had not been communicated very effectively.

'I think I'm going to Harvard-Yale. Definitely,' she said after about ten minutes of fake reading.

'Really?' said Ted, marking his place in his book. 'Are people going?'

'Yeah,' said Penelope. 'People are definitely going. I think only people in Pennypacker are not going.'

'So that European guy is going?' asked Ted.

'I don't know,' said Penelope. 'Maybe he is.'

'Are you dating him or something?'

'No!' said Penelope. 'Not even a little.'

'He did call you "darling,"' said Ted.

'I think he just does that to everyone he knows,' said Penelope. Privately she did not think this.

'OK, darling,' said Ted, which was not funny, but Ted started laughing anyway, which was right when Catherine snuck up behind him and covered his eyes with her hands.

'Surprise!' she said loudly. Penelope was the most surprised. She almost jumped out of her chair. She did not hear or see Catherine approach. Despite her glands and boxy shoes, the woman was as silent as the grave.

'Hey!' said Ted. He looked slightly abashed.

'What are you guys doing here?' asked Catherine, hugging Ted around the neck in a hold that could have been interpreted as a half nelson by those with less generous minds.

'We just wanted to get a cup of coffee after section,' said Ted.

'How fun!' said Catherine, pulling up a chair and setting herself down at the table.

Ted seemed to decide that the best way to handle this interruption was to soldier on with the original conversation. This was not how Penelope would have handled it.

'I'll tell you one thing, Penelope,' said Ted, 'it really pisses me off that European guys can't handle that football means something different in America than it does in Europe. That is the most tired thing ever. Like of course it's not the same sport. It's so annoying. I bet that that guy never played a game of soccer in his entire life.'

'Who are you talking about?' asked Catherine.

'This friend of Penelope's,' said Ted.

'What friend? Penelope, you never said you had a friend!'

'Well, I don't really,' mumbled Penelope.

'Who is he?'

'He's this really weird British guy that acts super old-fashioned. Is he British, Penelope? He sort of sounds like he's British, but he also kind of doesn't.'

'He is a citizen of the world,' said Penelope.

'That is so cute!' said Catherine. 'That you have a friend.'

'They are going to Harvard-Yale together,' said Ted.

'No, we aren't,' said Penelope.

'I didn't know people were going to Harvard-Yale,' said Ted. 'Maybe we should go too.'

'I don't know, Ted,' said Catherine. 'What about all our work?'

'Yeah!' said Penelope.

'We can do it another time,' said Ted. 'Let's go on a double date with Penelope's friend.' Catherine smiled, hit Ted on the arm, and placed a large, disgusting kiss on his lips.

Penelope privately wondered at her bad luck.

'Bad news,' Henry Wills-Mather intoned like a bass bell. The cast was just starting to get into places for Act 4, Scene 1. This was one of the few times in the play that Penelope was offstage. She was glad of the respite. In this scene, both Caligulas were to be clad in matching bloody tutus and dancing ballet to the recorded sound of barking dogs. It was not one of Penelope's favorites.

'Gather 'round, everybody,' said Henry Wills-Mather. He motioned everyone to sit on the front of the stage. The cast sat down obediently. Henry Wills-Mather stood on a chair in the front row. He stared into the distance sadly. Then he spoke.

'Craig dropped out of our dear little production.'

A collective groan went through the assembled cast members. Penelope was trying to think of who Craig was. She believed he had a line in Act 4, Scene 1, but she was not sure about that. Perhaps he was a senator. It was hard to tell what was happening really.

Henry Wills-Mather cleared his throat.

'I just want you all to know that what we are doing here is important. It may not seem like it is. It may seem like we are just a small theater company, trying to do the best job we can with a notoriously difficult text. But, in fact, we are doing something important. We are doing something terrifically important. We are staking a claim for independence in a world full of soulless conglomerates. Because this is a dangerous time in experimental theater. A very dangerous time. Thirty years ago, people didn't need spineless iterations of Disney musicals in order to keep Broadway afloat. They wanted real shows that engaged with the very real political climate of the time. Now people want to see Shrek onstage. A huge, lumbering Shrek yelling at Princess Fiona onstage.'

Henry Wills-Mather looked almost as if he was about to cry. Penelope wondered why Craig dropped out of the play. It was probably because of homework. Penelope couldn't really imagine it was for any other reason. Her hazy memories of Craig did not indicate a revolutionary spirit.

When Henry Wills-Mather recovered himself, he spoke again.

'I'm afraid we are looking for a replacement for Craig. Emma is on it, of course, but until then, I want one of you to take over Craig's role, just for the time being. We are running Act Four, Scene One today. Who is offstage in this scene?'

Penelope raised her hand to mid-height. Five other people, including Catherine, did as well.

'Good,' said Henry Wills-Mather, pointing to Penelope. 'You can take over Craig's lines.'

'No, that's OK,' said Penelope.

'Just temporarily,' said Henry Wills-Mather.

'I am just getting over this ear infection,' said Penelope.

'This really isn't a very big deal,' said Henry Wills-Mather.

'OK,' said Penelope.

'It really is temporary,' said Henry Wills-Mather apologetically. 'You'll just be reading a senator's lines. Let's start from the beginning of the scene.'

Catherine was looking at Penelope in a surprised and not necessarily pleasant way. Sometimes Penelope wondered if Catherine suspected something about the dead fish incident. If so, she was doing a great job of keeping Penelope psychologically on guard. It was the move of a classically trained detective.

If only they could all stop being friends with one another. When Penelope thought about it, it seemed that all of them, even Glasses and Nikil, hated hanging out with the others, and yet all of them kept doing it. Penelope wondered what she could do to extricate herself from this situation and nothing occurred to her. She wished for the thousandth time she could get out of going to Harvard-Yale with Ted and Catherine. What if they insisted on this double date with Gustav, which had started, like one of those horrible jokes, to become less and less hypothetical as time wore on? She had already used up the parade excuse and the ear infection excuse, and she couldn't think of any more excuses.

Penelope was roused from this flurry of anxiety when she felt something gently biting at her ankles. It was Raymond and he was doing it in a friendly way. Lan was standing a little behind him. She was wearing a T-shirt that said HELP FIGHT CHRONIC FATIGUE: IT IS REAL in Gothic lettering and had been watching the progress of Henry Wills-Mather's speech with her arms crossed.

'Hey, Lan,' Penelope whispered. She motioned for Lan to come closer to her. Lan reluctantly did. 'Are you here to start lighting design?'

'No,' said Lan.

'It's good that you brought Raymond,' said Penelope. 'I bet he loves plays.'

Lan started rolling a cigarette. Raymond kept biting at Penelope's ankles but in a slightly less friendly way.

'Are you really taking over for Craig?' asked Lan, tucking her cigarette behind her ear.

'How long have you been standing there?' asked Penelope.

'They will never find a replacement this late. I bet you will have to take over for him permanently,' said Lan.

'I hope not,' said Penelope.

'I hope so,' said Lan.

'Places!' said Henry Wills-Mather. Penelope opened her script and started reading Craig's lines. There were more of them than she expected.

The day of the Harvard-Yale football game dawned bright and clear and much too quickly for Penelope's liking. By this point, she was actively dreading it. The possibility that she would see Gustav was exciting on the face of it but mostly nerve-racking. It was horrible thinking about prospective conversations and what she could possibly do to screw them up. As Penelope fixed her hair in the bathroom, she seriously toyed with the idea of getting on a bus and going home early for Thanksgiving. Her mother, she knew, would be pleased.

Emma woke up as Penelope was coming back from the bathroom.

'Hey, what time is it?' she asked drowsily, her head peeping out from her covers. Emma slept with a keratin treatment in her hair, which made her look like she was wearing a nun's habit in the morning.

'It's like nine-ish,' said Penelope.

'Oh, shit,' said Emma.

'What?'

'I have to get to this mimosa breakfast at the Pudding. Shit! I am so so late. Oh God. You have to get out of here. I have to change.'

'OK,' said Penelope. She quickly went into the common room.

Lan was setting up rows of red cups on the floor. She was wearing a blue shirt that exclaimed I WENT TO NEW HAVEN AND ALL I GOT WAS SHOT! Raymond, who was sitting on the futon, was wearing the same shirt in a smaller size.

'Hey, Lan,' said Penelope. 'Are you going to the game?'

'No,' said Lan, who did not look up.

'Are you having people over here?' asked Penelope.

'No. I am not,' said Lan.

'OK,' said Penelope. 'But then what are you doing with all those cups? Why are you putting them on the floor?'

'Felt like it. Plus I am having a party here,' said Lan. 'Are you leaving soon?'

'Um, I think so,' said Penelope.

'Nice,' said Lan.

Penelope put on her coat and left.

In one of her weak moments, Penelope had promised Ted and Catherine that she would meet them in Ted's room before the game. Glasses and Nikil were having a pregame there at ten in the morning. Penelope knocked on the door in a resigned manner.

Glasses answered the door.

'Oh, hey, Penelope,' said Glasses. He smirked, perhaps at the remembrance of a certain incident. 'Have you come to our pregame?'

'I guess so,' said Penelope.

'Awesome,' said Glasses.

Nikil and Ted were sitting on the futon with a bottle of whiskey between them. Ted looked extremely inebriated. His eyes were bloodshot, and he was slunk so low on the futon that only his head was propped up. Catherine was sitting cross-legged on the floor, her head lying against Ted's shin. She was wearing a Harvard sweatshirt and a Harvard hat with a white pom-pom on it. Jason was lying facedown on the floor a couple of feet away. It seemed everyone had been drinking for quite a long time.

Ted tried to look slightly more lively when he saw Penelope. It was a futile effort.

'Hey!' said Ted.

'Oh, hi,' said Penelope.

'Do you want a shot?' Glasses asked Penelope.

'No thanks,' said Penelope.

'Why? I have had six shots this morning,' said Glasses.

'That's nuts,' said Ted groggily.

'Not to mention the peppermint schnapps,' said Glasses. 'That means I've had seven shots.'

Penelope hovered silently near the coffee table while everyone else had a mumbly conversation about football and alcohol. She looked around her. The room was messy. It had beer cans lying discarded next to the trash can, for example; but it was messy in a more normal, less existential way than Penelope's room, it seemed to her. This room had posters on the walls and books stacked on shelves. Penelope's suite had cigarette butts all over the floor and cat hair in the bathroom. Penelope would try to clean it occasionally, but her efforts were like sad jokes.

'I'm sort of glad I'm not going to the game,' said Nikil.

'You aren't?' asked Penelope.

'No,' said Nikil. 'We both have something for EC 10 on Monday and need to study this morning. We figured we could drink, but we couldn't go to the game. That's a lot of time. I need to keep my A average up. I bet none of the bastards at the Crimson Business Board had an A in EC 10. A straight A! That was such a political piece of bullshit –'

'Well, I think we should go to the pregame,' blurted out Ted.

'Aren't we at the pregame?' asked Penelope.

'I mean, I think we should go to the game,' said Ted. He stood up. Catherine stood up too.

'Do you guys want a shot before you go?' said Glasses in a leering tone that Penelope did not think was appropriate.

'No thanks,' said Penelope.

'I'll have one,' said Ted.

'Me too!' said Catherine. 'Although whiskey is so gross!'

Ted and Catherine took shots quickly.

'Ouch, that burned,' said Ted. He zipped his coat and walked toward the door. Catherine and Penelope followed him.

'Bye, guys,' said Penelope. She looked at her phone. Gustav had not texted yet.

'I could not stand another second of that,' said Ted, a bit too loudly, as they walked down the stairs. 'I've been listening to Nikil whine about that Crimson thing for the last eight weeks. When will he get over it?'

'Maybe never,' said Penelope. 'He is probably like Joe Kennedy.'

'It's really sad,' said Catherine. 'It's just really sad.'

It was a brilliantly sunny, frigid day. Ted, Penelope, and Catherine walked down Massachusetts Avenue and over a stone bridge that ran across the Charles River. On the other side of the river was the Harvard football stadium, a late Victorian replica of the Coliseum that was both imposing and wholly devoid of irony. When they finally arrived at the entrance to the field, there were cops stationed there checking to see whether the students had alcohol in their possession. Ted was forced to throw out the beers he had stowed in his coat almost immediately.

Inside, the field was overrun with people, none of whom Penelope had seen before, even though they were ostensibly her classmates. There were several U-Hauls parked on the grass. It was hard to decide what the U-Hauls were doing or why they were there. Many of them had grills set up but were not serving food. Some of them had empty bottles of alcohol strewn near them, but no actual alcohol was being served. One or two were playing music and people were dancing in front of them, but Penelope had a morbid hatred of dancing when it was light out. If Penelope had a daytime wedding, for example, she would eliminate dancing from the order of the event. It had no place.

'What time do you think people got here?' asked Penelope.

'No idea,' said Ted.

'This looks so fun!' said Catherine, dancing in place.

'Do you think there is any food here?' said Penelope.

'I don't see any,' said Ted.

'I want to dance!' said Catherine. She started grinding up against Ted aggressively. Ted started dancing too. Penelope understood why he had never really danced in front of her previously.

'I think I might just go into the game,' said Penelope.

'Are you sure?' asked Ted.

'We'll meet you in there!' said Catherine. She took Ted by the sweatshirt and led him to the dancing U-Haul.

Penelope was suffused with relief. If Gustav called her now, she would be unencumbered.

By the time Penelope took her seat, so far away from the field that she was alone in her own section, the crowd was already enjoying the halftime show. It was World War I themed, said the announcer into a loudspeaker. At the climax, a red papier-mâché plane representing Harvard flew into a blue papier-mâché Yale bulldog.

The game resumed. Penelope did not know anything about football, so she people-watched. The crowd was generally old and clad in fur coats. There were current students at the game too, but they seemed to be a constantly fluctuating, less vocal maroon number, like a small, sad, consumptive sister to the robust alumni of yore. At one point, a male Harvard cheerleader launched himself into the crowd to attack a male Yale cheerleader. This was the point when Ted and Catherine found Penelope. Penelope saw them striding up the steps to her section and felt that she now knew the exact feeling associated with the expression 'living on borrowed time.' Gustav still hadn't texted.

'There you are,' said Ted. 'It took forever to find you! Why did you sit all the way up here?'

'Did you see that guy just attack the Yale cheerleader?' said Catherine, wide-eyed.

'Yeah,' asked Penelope. 'I didn't really understand that. Do you know who is winning?'

'It was crazy,' said Catherine.

Ted and Catherine sat down next to Penelope. It seemed that despite the police crackdown, they had been drinking since daytime dancing at the U-Haul. Catherine immediately fell asleep with her head on Ted's lap. Ted's bangs were down, and he had a dried patch of ketchup next to his lip that he seemed unaware of.

'So this is fun,' said Ted. Catherine started to snore loudly.

'I guess,' said Penelope. She checked her phone. No word from Gustav.

'Why do you keep checking your phone? Are you waiting for that European guy to call you?'

'No,' said Penelope. 'He said he would text me.'

'And he hasn't yet?' said Ted.

'No,' said Penelope.

'If he really wanted to hang out with you,' said Ted in a malicious tone that Penelope did not appreciate, 'he would text you to watch the game with him. With us! So we can all go on the double date. I think he is blowing you off.'

'Maybe you are right,' said Penelope. Penelope had thought

of many scenarios associated with Gustav, but the one she hadn't anticipated was that he wouldn't call or text her at all. Once confronted with the truth, she felt a mixture of relief and disappointment. The whole situation with Ted, however, seemed far more intolerable if this was to be an accepted fact.

It seemed as if the game was in its final minutes forever. It was very close because each side kept fumbling the ball and throwing incomplete passes at each other.

'The weird thing about bad football is the heightened suspense,' said Penelope during the third overtime. Ted and Catherine were both sleeping and didn't respond.

After the game was over, Penelope roused Ted and Catherine and all three of them walked back toward Pennypacker. It was starting to get dark.

'Well, what do you want to do now?' asked Ted.

'I think everybody is studying tonight,' said Catherine in a slurred voice.

'You wouldn't think that would be the case,' said Penelope, 'considering this is supposedly the most celebratory school-sponsored event of the year.'

'We could go to my room, I guess, and watch a movie,' said Ted.

'That's fine,' said Penelope. Just then, Penelope got a text. It was from Gustav. It read as follows:

'Terribly sorry to have missed you today. Wasn't able to stay for the festivities myself. Skiing in Japan for foreseeable future and Mum sent the jet early. Drinks when we get back? xx'

Penelope laughed with happiness.

'Why are you laughing?' asked Ted.

'Oh, no reason,' said Penelope.

'Did you get a text from that guy?' asked Ted.

'No,' said Penelope. Ted grabbed the phone from her and read the text.

'He's probably at the S— right now and that's a lie.'

'I think he's in Japan,' said Penelope.

'You don't have any reason for thinking that,' said Ted.

'I don't know,' said Penelope. 'But I think you should just put Catherine to bed. She can't watch a movie. She is drooling on your sweatshirt.'

Two days after Harvard-Yale, Penelope took the bus home to celebrate Thanksgiving. She was happy to leave school. Recently, Raymond had started leaping into the shower while Penelope was washing her hair and watching her steadily until she was finished. Formerly, Penelope had thought cats were afraid of the water.

Penelope returned to school on Sunday and dutifully waited for Gustav to call her. He didn't. Two weeks after Thanksgiving break, Penelope had still not heard from him. Penelope never mentioned it to anyone, but this made her feel very bad. Every time her mother called her to talk, she was momentarily excited because she thought it was Gustav. Every time Ted and Catherine texted her to go to dinner, she always briefly thought Gustav was calling her to go clubbing. Ted asked her about Gustav all the time. He seemed to take great triumph in being right about him, like the narrator in *Tess of the d'Urbervilles*.

Penelope thought about asking Emma or Lan about Gustav, but it seemed like a bad idea. Lan probably didn't know Gustav and would definitely hate him if she ever met him. Penelope didn't think Emma would be very congenial to the idea that she and Gustav had a date and, instinctively, never mentioned he had texted her at all.

The only comfort Penelope had was that Gustav might not be back yet from Thanksgiving, although the longer she was back at school, the more unlikely this seemed, considering they were about to go on vacation again for Christmas in a couple of weeks. She had two Counting People sections after break and Gustav did not show up to either of them; he was not the most assiduous student. It was unfortunate he did not attend the section, considering that they had a very important final project for the class coming up, the country report, and Jared gave a lot of notes about it that Penelope did not write down.

The country report was the centerpiece of Counting People and the main portion of the course grade. Its mere mention made Jared voluble. It involved graphs and Excel spreadsheets as well as written content that analyzed the census data of the particular country on which one was doing one's report. Penelope had the sense that people had been working on their reports for weeks. She had not started hers yet, but she had picked her country. She had selected Luxembourg, as the capital of Luxembourg is also Luxembourg.

The problem with Luxembourg was that it had very little census data. Penelope figured this out about Luxembourg the day before the country report was due. She relayed this fact to everyone at dinner.

'I looked in all the databases,' said Penelope, drinking some chocolate milk for emphasis. 'I really think the census in Luxembourg is not very thorough. I should complain to their chamber of commerce.'

'You should have never picked Luxembourg. You should have picked a country more important to the world than Luxembourg,' said Nikil.

'I would have picked Brazil,' said Catherine. 'That country is so interesting.'

'Or do a country that needs more attention. Luxembourg is a pretty shallow, Western-centric thing to pick. Why don't you pick a country with real problems and issues?' said Glasses.

'I don't think these country reports help countries. Isn't it cool that Luxembourg's capital is Luxembourg?' said Penelope.

'Do you have Excel on your computer?' asked Ted.

'No,' said Penelope.

'You have to go to the computer lab then, to do the graphs there. Do you know where the computer lab is?'

'No,' said Penelope.

'It's in the basement of the Science Center,' said Nikil, disgusted.

'OK,' said Penelope. 'I have a lot of trouble with imagining graphs visually in my mind. This may be kind of hard for me.'

'Oh, don't be silly!' said Ted. 'Graphing things in Excel is one of the easiest things you will ever do. It's way easier than writing an Images of Shakespeare paper, and you can write those in like two hours.'

'Oh, shut,' said Penelope. 'Do you think that Luxembourg has so little census data because it is hard to keep track of the population amidst all the forest that is there?'

No one said anything in reply and Penelope drank the rest of her chocolate milk.

After dinner, Penelope walked over to the computer lab. After an hour of reading Wikipedia entries about Luxembourg, Penelope opened up Excel to start her project in earnest. *This isn't so bad,* she thought as she entered the data for the graph she was creating about Luxembourg's changing birth rate. *It is just putting a number into a box.* She pressed the button to graph the data sheet and a pie chart appeared. *That's odd,* thought Penelope. *I wanted a line graph.* When she went back to her spreadsheet all her data was erased. *Guess I have to do that again,* she said to herself and shrugged.

Over the next four hours, Penelope became increasingly frantic. At three in the morning, she started crying after she accidentally erased her line graph about birth cohorts for the third time. She had completed one graph out of twelve successfully and the report was due at noon the next day. She went out to the soda dispenser and got another Diet Coke.

She was alone in the computer lab save for one extremely thin boy in a massive red T-shirt, who was playing a computer game that involved chatting to other people through a headset. Periodically, this boy would look at her and shake his head. Then he would go back to his game. Penelope wanted to rip his hair out.

Penelope settled herself in her seat again. *I can do this!* she thought. She cracked her knuckles. She readjusted herself in her seat. She put all of Luxembourg's death rates in one row and all the years that the death rates were measured in in another row. She pressed the graph button. A black square appeared on the computer screen.

'Oh no!' yelled Penelope, who then dissolved into actual tears. Red T-shirt glared at her.

'Are you really crying?' he asked Penelope.

'Yes!' said Penelope.

'What are you doing?'

'A graph of Luxembourg,' said Penelope.

'I bet that's really easy,' said Red T-shirt.

'No,' said Penelope. 'It's really hard.' Red T-shirt was not listening to her anymore. He was trash-talking his Internet compatriots.

'Penelope,' said a voice from the corridor. 'Is that you?' It was Gustav.

Penelope turned around. 'Yes,' she said. She tried to wipe her face, but she had a feeling she had made herself look worse.

'Well, what are you doing here at the witching hour?' He strode into the room. Gustav was very tan and was wearing what seemed to be snow pants with shackles made out of nylon wrapped around them. He sat down at the computer next to her and peered into her face. Penelope hoped it didn't look too horrendous.

'I should ask you the same question,' said Penelope. She hiccoughed.

'Well, I am here because I just got back from Japan about two hours ago and have to do this demmed country report. Don't have Excel on my computer. Jared's been rather intractable as well. Wouldn't give me an extension despite my pleading and a bishop's letter.'

'Well, that is what I am doing,' said Penelope, 'and it is really hard.'

'What country are you doing?'

'Luxembourg.'

Gustav guffawed.

'The long-neglected topic,' he said. He had grown a slight beard during his trip to Japan.

'Which one are you doing?'

'Inner Mongolia. Or Outer Mongolia, whichever one is an actual country,' said Gustav.

'Do you have all the census data?' asked Penelope.

'Looked it up on the plane. Exceedingly boring country. No one has children anymore, yet archers abound.'

'Well, good luck graphing it,' said Penelope.

'Oh. Graphing? This shouldn't be hard at all. It's merely putting numbers in a box.'

'That is what I thought,' said Penelope in a monotone. She turned back to her computer. Both she and Gustav graphed silently for ten minutes.

'Why, that's odd,' said Gustav. 'Just erased my whole graph by accident. How did that happen? I guess I should start over.'

Gustav kept graphing.

'I say,' said Gustav, 'what kind of program is this? I didn't want a pie chart of any kind. Penelope, why did it give me a pie chart?'

'Hold on,' said Penelope. 'I may have actually figured something out.'

'Finally!' said Red T-shirt.

'The boy is rather a pill,' said Gustav.

'You guys are pills!' yelled Red T-shirt.

'OK,' said Penelope. She walked over to Gustav's computer station. 'I think this is what you do, so it doesn't erase everything all the time.'

'Oh, dear God, by Jove, you've got it! How did you figure that out?'

'Trial and error,' said Penelope.

'Also, you cried for like ever,' said Red T-shirt.

'What game are you playing?' said Gustav.

'*Myth II: Soulblighter,*' said the kid.

'Well, then, you have no business ridiculing this fine lady.'

'Whatever,' said Red T-shirt.

'Thank you, Penelope,' said Gustav. 'You have shown me the truth of graphing.'

'You're welcome,' said Penelope, who resumed her seat.

At 6:30 in the morning, Penelope finished her final graph. She had had three Red Bulls over the course of the night and she was wearing the worst bra possible. Gustav preserved his good looks well into the morning hours. The computer lab was, perhaps, the site of the most continuous self-recriminations Penelope had ever endured. She decided to take a brief nap.

'Darling, you can't sleep with your head against the computer screen,' said Gustav. 'I'm afraid you will permanently ruin your posture.'

'How long have I been like that?' asked Penelope.

'About an hour or so,' said Gustav. 'Didn't want to wake you initially, but your positioning seemed to become more and more uncomfortable as time marched on. Plus, according to my calculations, you only have about four hours to complete the written portion of the country report.'

'Is it already eight?' asked Penelope, suddenly sitting upright.

'Yes,' said Gustav. 'I myself just finished the graphing portion of the thing and am now going to get myself a cup of coffee. I will be back.' He strode out of the room without a jacket.

Gustav came back about half an hour later with several coffees and a large white bag. He sat down in front of his computer and set the bag down on the table between him and Penelope.

'Here, ma'am, is a coffee for you.'

'Thank you so much!' said Penelope.

'I got four coffees, because stupidly I did not ask how you liked yours. Also, considering we must write until noon today, we will probably drink all of them no matter how they are prepared.'

'I love coffee of any kind, really,' said Penelope.

'How far are you in your treatment of Luxembourg?'

'Not very far. I might introduce a forestry section to take up space.'

'Excellent idea.'

'I definitely think it will be my most entertaining section,' said Penelope.

'I am sure that Jared will appreciate it. And now to work,' said Gustav, who cracked his neck dramatically.

Penelope sipped her coffee.

Three hours passed. Penelope wrote as quickly as she ever had in her life. As time passed, she realized that each sentence she wrote had started to contain longer and longer words and make less and less sense in the logical context of the report.

'Do you think "the amelioration and amalgamation of various disparate elements has made Luxembourg what it is today" actually makes sense as a sentence?' asked Penelope.

'I wouldn't say that it exactly "makes sense," but I would say that the alliteration is very nice,' said Gustav.

'I did think that was good,' said Penelope. 'And I am also on my third coffee.'

'Good girl,' said Gustav, typing madly.

When it was ten minutes before noon, Penelope finally finished spell-checking her report. It wasn't good, but it did have all the required parts, plus a unique comparison between the forests of Luxembourg and Belgium.

'OK,' she said. 'I am done. I am going to print it.'

'I'm going to print too,' said Gustav. Penelope got up from her computer and stationed herself next to the printer. After two minutes of staring into space, willing herself to stay awake, she looked down at the screen.

'It's out of paper,' said Penelope. She frantically opened and closed the paper drawer. 'Oh, shoot! This can't really be happening! How is it possible that we are out of paper?'

'Not to worry,' said Gustav.

He ran out the door and leaped up several stairs. Penelope started sweating a little. It was 11:55.

Gustav came back three minutes later with a swath of loose-leaf paper.

'Here,' he said, handing it to Penelope. 'Load it into one of the trays.'

Penelope did. 'Where did you find this paper?' asked Penelope.

'I stole it from the other computer lab upstairs,' said Gustav.

'That was good thinking,' said Penelope.

'Well, I pride myself on quick reflexes,' said Gustav. By the time they finished printed out their country reports, it was 12:01.

'Hurry,' said Gustav. 'We have to run to his box. It's on the third floor, and we are already late. I am sure he is standing there, mentally categorizing us as delinquents. He would probably put us on a boat to Australia without a second thought.'

When they got upstairs, Jared was indeed standing outside his box. Penelope looked at the clock. It was 12:05.

'Just in time, guys,' said Jared. 'At 12:07, I was going to stop accepting country reports and you would have automatically got a failing grade, or at least a full-letter markdown, so congratulations, because you avoided that. I look forward to reading these. I really do. I hope you two learned a lot. I feel like I'm going to learn a lot.'

'Yeah,' said Penelope. 'I learned a lot about forestry. Maybe I want to go into it as a career.'

'What?' said Jared.

'Oh, nothing,' said Gustav. 'She's just delirious.' He kicked her in the shin.

'I hope you both didn't pull an all-nighter. You guys should have been working on this steadily since you got the assignment.'

'Of course we didn't pull an all-nighter,' said Gustav.

'Have you gotten your e-mail fixed?' Jared asked Penelope.

'Almost. I have been really busy,' said Penelope. 'I am in this play.'

'What play?' asked Jared.

'*Caligula*,' said Penelope.

'Oh my God. I love *Caligula*,' said Jared. 'It's my favorite play.'

'This production is very experimental,' said Penelope.

'I love experimental theater. Do you have a big part?'

'It's very small,' said Penelope. 'I am just a guard, and I am reading a senator's part until they find a replacement.'

'I look forward to seeing it,' said Jared.

Penelope hoped this was an empty threat.

'We really should be going,' said Gustav.

Penelope waved at Jared.

'Bye,' she said.

They walked down the stairs.

'Darling, I know, intimately, how truly tired you are, but you must try to keep it together in front of authority figures. Let me walk you back to Pennypacker.'

'Really? You don't have to,' said Penelope. 'Where do you live?'

'In Adams House. It's on my way, really. Plus, I have a duty to you, as a fellow soldier in the trenches.'

'Thanks,' said Penelope.

They walked for a while. It was searing cold and very gray. It had snowed two nights before, but it hadn't snowed very much and rained soon afterward, so the remainder of the snow had frozen and now lay rather dirtily and unevenly all over the Yard. Penelope, as was her custom, was wearing illogical shoes for the occasion.

'Ah, the beauties of nature,' said Gustav.

'I hate nature,' said Penelope. Her feet were freezing.

'What a charming sentiment! It does run in opposition to your fascination with forestry, but I am sure most things do. Penelope, can I ask you a question? What are you going to do today?'

'Well,' said Penelope. 'Maybe I will sleep.'

'That is a given. But after that. What is a typical day in the life?'

'OK. After I sleep, I will wake up. Maybe I will watch a DVD.'

'Watch a DVD? What DVD?'

'It varies,' said Penelope.

'I think you should become more involved in extracurricular activities,' said Gustav.

'That is what my mother says,' said Penelope.

They were at the door of Pennypacker. Some of the kids who worked at the radio station were talking on the path nearby. They were all wearing stupid hats, and, momentarily, Penelope felt embarrassed. Gustav turned toward her.

'Well, I should be off. Have to sleep and everything. Might even study. The semester is drawing to a close.'

'OK,' said Penelope.

'I think you should get a drink with me tonight,' said Gustav.

'OK,' said Penelope.

'Didn't I invite you out for a drink before Thanksgiving?'

'Oh, you did?' said Penelope.

'I texted you about it. After Harvard-Yale.'

'Oh, really? I don't know,' said Penelope.

'You might have Alzheimer's. Curious. Meet me at ten p.m. at Daedalus? The second floor. You do know where that is, I trust.'

'I will Wikipedia it,' said Penelope.

'Such a resourceful girl! See you then.'

'Bye,' said Penelope. She walked up the stairs in a daze. She couldn't sleep at all when she got to her room.

Penelope felt that 'going to drinks' definitively qualified as a date. It was also a date of a foreign and mysterious kind. Penelope had never 'gotten a drink' before. She had gotten coffee once, with her boyfriend who had the lisp that only she could hear. That was not very romantic, as they talked about the Olympics the entire time, which was Penelope's least favorite televised event.

When Penelope was walking up to Daedalus later that evening, she got a call from Ted. She briefly considered letting it go to voice mail, but instead she picked it up.

'Hello,' said Ted. 'Do you want to come over? Mike and Nikil are playing a board game and I don't want to play. How did the country report go?'

'Oh, pretty well,' said Penelope. 'I had to stay up all night.'

'You did? That sucks! Did you sleep today?'

'A little,' said Penelope.

'You should tell me all about it when you get here.' Penelope could hear Catherine's voice in the background. 'Who is that?' she was asking.

'Oh, gee,' said Penelope. 'I really would but I can't tonight.'

'What, are you serious? You can't come over? That's ridiculous, you can always come over. You never do anything.'

'I do sometimes,' said Penelope.

'Why are you talking in that weird voice? Are you going out with that Argentinean guy?'

'Yes, in fact,' said Penelope. 'We are going to get a drink.'

'Well, he should know better than to take a freshman to a bar and get her drunk. You don't even have a fake. I think that's kind of ridiculous.'

'I don't think so,' said Penelope.

'Well, have a good time, if you can even get a drink at all,' said Ted.

'OK, I will.' Penelope closed her phone. She was in front of the bar.

Penelope was nervous now. Ted was always very discouraging when he discovered things about her romantic life. Nevertheless, she walked inside Daedalus. There was no one at the door checking for ID, which was lucky. The downstairs was taken up by a large wooden bar filled with an intimidating number of alcoholic beverages. A bartender eyed her suspiciously. Penelope hurried up the stairs to the second floor. She looked around. It seemed empty. She wondered if she had come to the right place.

'Penelope, darling,' Gustav yelled from behind her. 'Why, we thought you would never come!'

Penelope turned around. Gustav was sitting in a booth with three other people. Two of them were men and one of them was Bitty, whom Gustav had his arm around. One guy looked like a tiny version of a 1930s movie star. The other had a ruddy, bony face, long limbs like a rower, and tight blond curls. Penelope had a strong desire to pretend she hadn't seen them and walk out. She made her way backward slowly.

'Come over here! I hope you are not still exhausted!' said Gustav. Penelope could not escape now. She walked over to the booth, but there was no obvious room for her. The 1930s movie star got up and moved a spare chair to the head of the booth, as befitting the gallantry of the decade in which he was born. Penelope sat down.

'Where have you been, darling? I was just telling Bitty that I was about to invoke the law,' said Gustav.

'Oh. I thought you said ten o'clock,' said Penelope, who took off her jacket.

'Did I? I must have done. But you do forget these things after a couple of scotch and sodas. What do you want to drink?'

'Oh, I don't know. Maybe I will have a scotch and soda too?'

'I am sure that is the opposite of what you want. I will get you something else.'

'OK,' said Penelope.

Gustav got up from the table and ambled over to the bar. He was wearing a green velvet smoking jacket. The table resumed the conversation it must have been having before Penelope got there.

'Didn't you think the way those girls acted at the party on Friday was a little ridiculous? It pains me to say it of Bee girls, but I think they didn't have enough respect for our club, and it really offended me,' said Rower.

'What did they do?' said Bitty, righteously indignant. She was wearing a black turtleneck sweater with pearls over the neck of the sweater.

'They just acted a little too comfortable in the clubhouse. Do you know what I mean?'

'I do,' said Bitty. 'I know exactly what you mean.'

'You just can't just go up to the second floor and like sit on the furniture like that. It's someone's house,' said Tiny 1930s Movie Star, who was wearing a tiny suit jacket over a tiny polo shirt.

'It's your house!' said Bitty. 'Well, it's your clubhouse. That's very disappointing to hear of Bee girls. I will have to talk to them.'

'Thanks,' said the 1930s movie star.

Everyone was silent for a bit.

'What are you doing for break?' Bitty asked Rower.

'Unfortunately, I have to stay in the city. I am taking some meetings with people. Remember how I told you I was starting up that company that was a social networking site for slow-food enthusiasts? It's a little like Facebook but just for slow food. Well, I am meeting with Jamie Oliver and Lloyd Blankfein about it. They are very interested. I just kind of want to hear what they have to say.'

'That sounds fantastic!' said Bitty.

'I really think people like that with experience in business can have great ideas,' said Rower in a self-deprecatory way.

'I totally agree,' said Bitty.

Gustav came back. He was carrying a pink frothy drink, which he put down in front of Penelope.

'This contains two cups of grenadine as well as various other things. I am sure you will love it.' He sat back down next to Bitty in the booth.

'Thanks,' said Penelope. She sipped her drink through the

small straw you were supposed to use to stir it. 'This is the best drink I have ever had. I feel like I am doing something wrong when I make drinks. They never taste like this.'

'I know that this is true,' said Gustav. 'Because I have had drinks that you have made before, and they have tasted like poison. It is clear that alcohol makes no sense to you.'

'It just has such a strong flavor,' said Penelope. 'What do you put with it, except milk or something.'

'Alcohol has such a strong flavor?' said Tiny 1930s Movie Star.

'Yes,' said Penelope.

'How do you know Gustav?' he said to Penelope.

'We have a class together,' said Penelope. 'And my roommate knows him.'

'Who is your roommate?' asked Bitty.

'Emma Green?' said Penelope.

'Oh, Emma!' said Bitty. 'How is she?'

'Good,' said Penelope. 'You and I are also in a play together. I am in *Caligula* with you.'

'Oh, right,' said Bitty.

'Bitty, is that the play you are in?' said Rower. 'I'm really excited to see it.'

'Me too!' said Tiny 1930s Movie Star.

'Oh, thanks, guys,' said Bitty. 'I am really excited for it too. I think it is going to be so good. Don't you, Penelope?'

'What?' said Penelope.

'Henry Wills-Mather is such a genius,' said Bitty. 'It has the potential to be really amazing.'

'I have been hearing really great things,' said Rower. *From who?* wondered Penelope.

'Bitty darling,' said Gustav. 'It does sound rather nice. But for my part, I do think this two Caligulas idea sounds suspect. Why can't you be the only Caligula?'

'Gustav!' said Bitty. She punched him in the shoulder. 'It's

because Caligula is a man. I am just the female side of his con-
sciousness.'

'Bitty, I do wish that you would control your violence better,'
said Gustav. 'I worry that you are indulging in method acting.'
Bitty started to hit Gustav with both of her hands.

'Where are you from, originally?' asked Rower politely.

'Connecticut,' said Penelope.

'Did you go to Hotchkiss?'

'Um, no,' said Penelope.

'I'm trying to think of anyone you would know, that I know,
from Connecticut.'

'Who do you know from Connecticut?' said Penelope.

Rower looked at her apologetically and then turned back
toward the group.

'Gustav!' Bitty said loudly. 'Can you get me another drink?'

'OK,' said Gustav. 'My you are a demanding woman. But as
they say in adverts, those are the ones who are worth it.'

'You know what? I think I had better go,' said Penelope.

'Oh, no, Penelope,' said Gustav. 'Don't go! You only just got
here.'

'I know,' said Penelope. 'But it's a school night. And I think
this drink is really alcoholic.'

'It is rather,' said Gustav. 'I feel guilty about that. Do let me
walk you home.'

'But Gustav! What about my drink?' said Bitty.

'I just have to step out and walk Penelope home and then I
will come back and get it for you.'

Bitty shrugged. Gustav got up and followed Penelope down
the stairs and out of the bar.

'What a wonderful end to a trying day,' said Gustav. 'I am officially drunk. Did you have a good time?'

'Oh, sure,' said Penelope.

'Chad is a funny chap isn't he?'

'Who is Chad?' asked Penelope.

'The one in the pink shirt,' said Gustav. *The rower,* thought Penelope. She had not noticed any jokes.

Penelope walked silently beside Gustav. The smoking jacket was resplendent in the moonlight.

'How do you know Bitty?' asked Penelope.

'Bitty? Well, she and I go back forever. We went to the same summer camp for a while. Though perhaps I knew her before that. These things are very hard to say.'

'Oh, cool,' said Penelope. 'It must be fun to know people before you get here.'

'But Harvard is so small,' said Gustav. 'Who doesn't know people before they get here? Half of my class from school went here. And, of course, one friend breeds fifty or something. Whatever that expression is.' Penelope had never heard that expression and considered describing how untrue it was in her case, but then thought the better of it.

They had reached the front door of Pennypacker. Penelope couldn't believe she originally thought this was a date. In high school this was always happening to her. She routinely over-estimated the gravity of a romantic situation. It had landed her in some embarrassing scrapes too, like the time she thought she was going on a date with the basketball team captain when in fact she was going to manage the basketball team practice. It took her three semesters to extricate herself from that activity.

'Well, thanks for walking me home. Bye!' said Penelope, turning around and trying to get into her dorm as quickly as she possibly could.

'Wait one moment,' said Gustav, grabbing Penelope's hand. 'Where are you going so quickly?'

'Inside,' said Penelope.

'Why don't you stay here with me, while I smoke my pipe?' said Gustav. He sat down on the stoop in front of her building and took out his pipe. It was made out of ivory and looked very old.

'But what about Bitty's drink?' said Penelope, who was so shocked by the pipe's appearance that she sat down on the stoop.

'Old Bitty is a resourceful girl. She'll see to it that one of those men gets her a drink. You have to pacify her in the moment, that's all. I know from experience.'

'OK,' said Penelope. Gustav lit his pipe.

'So, Penelope,' he said, 'what do you do?'

'I go to school,' said Penelope.

Gustav chuckled. 'Oh, I don't mean that. I know that. I mean, I suppose, what defines you? What are your passions and activities?'

'I don't really have any,' said Penelope.

'Oh, that's just ridiculous. Everyone does something, especially at Harvard. What about in high school? What did you do for fun then?'

'I don't know,' said Penelope. 'I taught myself Morse code sometimes.'

'Why did you do that?' asked Gustav.

'Well,' said Penelope, 'what if I was ever kidnapped by spies?'

'True,' said Gustav. 'I was not thinking of that. You should teach me to say something.'

'OK,' said Penelope. 'What do you want to say?'

'I am trapped by some spies. All of them are extremely handsome. Perhaps I am experiencing Stockholm syndrome? Love, Gustav.'

'That is a good message,' said Penelope. 'OK, I will teach it to you. Let me get a stick so you can hear it better.'

Penelope got up to look for a stick. She found one near a small tree planted in the sidewalk. She brought it back to the stoop and started tapping Gustav's message onto the stair. Gustav looked incredulous.

'I have no idea whether you are right, but it seems you really are very good at this. Of course, you are going far too fast for me to actually absorb any of it. I fear I am hopeless at distinguishing any of the taps.'

'You are not,' said Penelope. 'I mean, even Thomas Edison was a telegraph operator.'

After Penelope was done tapping, she sat down next to Gustav on the stair. He chewed the end of his pipe. Then he put his pipe in his pocket slowly and thoughtfully, like a judge would.

'What a weird thing to do,' said Gustav. Then he grabbed Penelope, pulled her into him, and kissed her. His tongue was nothing like a dead fish. Penelope was almost afraid she was too in shock to kiss him back, or to be good at kissing. Then she stopped thinking of anything.

'Hey!' said Penelope after about thirty minutes.

'What?' said Gustav.

'I have to go inside,' said Penelope.

'Are you saying that because I sort of tried to unbutton your shirt just then? I couldn't really help it, I'm sorry. I just have this thing about Oxford shirts.'

'I mean, it wasn't that, exactly, although if you had taken my shirt off on this stoop that would have been bad, I think.'

'Quite right. The evils of hypothermia and all that.'

'Also, I mean, it's sort of embarrassing. What if someone saw us? We are just lucky no one has walked by yet on their way back from the library.'

'All very good points,' said Gustav. 'Which is why, perhaps, we should go back to your room and discuss them?'

'No,' said Penelope. 'You have to go back to the bar and buy Bitty a drink.'

'Oh, screw Bitty!' said Gustav, who tried to bite Penelope's neck. 'She is probably gone anyway.'

'I would feel guilty if you didn't go back and at least see,' said Penelope. She stood up.

'Can I see you again?' said Gustav.

'Sure,' said Penelope. 'Maybe we can get ice cream.'

'Ice cream in the winter? You do have an interesting constitution. I will call you about it and discuss it further, at some point in my life,' said Gustav. 'I will think of some other activity. You do not have any say in the matter, because you will only confuse the issue.'

'That sounds good,' said Penelope.

'Bye, Penelope,' said Gustav. He got up and left. She went inside Pennypacker.

Penelope felt like jumping up the stairs. She could not believe this night had happened. Gustav, the man who was the closest to Hercule Poirot she had ever known (and although Poirot was the ideal, Gustav was much more handsome by classical standards), had kissed her. Then he asked her out on a date! Suddenly, Penelope could not remember why exactly she had said good-bye to him at the door. It had something to do with fear, but she hoped it would be mistaken for strategy.

9.

'Romance in Nondomestic Surroundings'

'When you whip the piano with your belt,' said Henry Wills-Mather, 'I want you to really destroy it.'

'But it's a Steinway,' said the Caligula with the rattail.

'I don't care if it's a Steinway. What I care about is that you fully channel Caligula's destructive personality.'

'You're right,' the boy said with a sigh. He was wearing a belt on his head. Eventually his costume would consist entirely of strategically placed belts.

The cast was rehearsing Act 2, Scene 5, one of the most harrowing scenes in all of *Caligula*, particularly noteworthy, Penelope thought, because *Caligula* was a play chock-full of harrowing scenes. In this scene, Caligula killed a senator and then subsequently destroyed all the pianos in the room by beating them with belts. The latter stage direction was an invention of Henry Wills-Mather, who, when he saw there were two Steinway pianos sitting in the theater that could not be moved, said to the cast, 'The piano is a bourgeois convention. This is the theater of the absurd! The only thing to do is to destroy them with belts.' Then he stuck to this idea, which was the truly amazing part.

The rehearsal was sparsely populated. Only Penelope, Rattailed Caligula, and Lan, who was sitting in the lighting booth refusing to do any lighting, were in attendance. All the other cast members had made some excuse and were studying for final exams in the library.

Final exams at Harvard took up an extraordinary amount of time. All told, it took nearly a month and a half of constant testing to finish them. There were final projects before Christmas, a brief vacation between Christmas and New Year's, and final exams that lasted the entire month of January. In an extremely unpopular decision, Henry Wills-Mather insisted on having play practice throughout this period, causing most of the cast to not attend rehearsal in favor of studying. As a result, Penelope had been playing more and more parts. She was wondering if she would eventually have to star in a two-man show with Rattailed Caligula.

'Where is Bitty?' cried Henry Wills-Mather, apropos of very little. Bitty had missed the most rehearsals of anyone in January, but Penelope heard it wasn't because she was studying but because she was still on vacation in the Seychelles. Everyone remained silent in response to this question. Bitty was Henry Wills-Mather's favorite member of the cast, and whenever he was feeling querulous, he asked where she was. This could only be interpreted as a bad sign.

'Well, I would like her to be here to run this scene,' Henry Wills-Mather continued. 'I think it's very important for her to get the cues exactly right on how to hit the piano. You have to choreograph it.' *Why?* thought Penelope.

'OK,' said Henry Wills-Mather. 'Let's start from "Well, I see you have become intelligent."' Penelope and Rattailed Caligula got into place in the middle of the stage.

'Well, I see you have become intelligent,' said Rattailed Caligula as he pretended to nibble at an olive. 'Soldiers, I am pleased with you. Is not it, Helicon?'

'Sure! What an army!' said Penelope in a low voice, because Helicon was usually played by a man named Justin. 'But if you want my advice, they are now too smart, and they will not want to fight. If they are still increasing, the empire crumbles!'

'Perfect. We shall rest. Come, let us randomly,' said Rattailed Caligula.

'Stop, stop, stop,' yelled Henry Wills-Mather. He looked upset. 'Lan, what did I say about the black spotlight? I don't want it now. I want it in the third act!'

'I know,' yelled Lan from the lighting booth. 'You said that. But you are just so wrong.'

Currently, the black spotlight was hovering over the features of Rattailed Caligula. If Lan did one piece of lighting design during rehearsals, it consisted of shining a black spotlight in the face of Rattailed Caligula expressly at points when Henry Wills-Mather did not want it to shine. Henry Wills-Mather and Lan argued about the spotlight at least twice a rehearsal, and sometimes more.

'Can you just turn it off?' said Henry Wills-Mather.

'No,' said Lan.

'It's not until the third act that the spotlight can represent the black hole of Caligula's personality!' yelled Henry Wills-Mather, who ran up to the lighting booth to start fighting with Lan. Rattailed Caligula and Penelope sat down on the floor underneath one of the Steinways.

'Hey, Penelope,' said Rattailed Caligula. He took a book about extraterrestrials out of his backpack. It was hardbound and laminated and had a very colorful photo on the front.

'Oh, hey,' said Penelope. Penelope was a little afraid of Rattailed Caligula. One time she saw him wearing a floor-length cape to class. Every Sunday he played the bells in the Lowell bell tower. He had very strange but not necessarily bad taste in bell music. One Sunday, Penelope awoke to the Darth Vader theme played by bells. She imagined this was his doing.

'What is that book about?' asked Penelope.

'Aliens,' said Rattailed Caligula.

'Oh, cool,' said Penelope.

'Do you believe in UFOs?'

'Sure,' said Penelope.

Rattailed Caligula smiled but said nothing. He went back to reading his book. Penelope scraped the floor with her fingernail and got dirt under it.

To everyone's surprise, Bitty swanned in a couple of minutes later. She was wearing a coat that looked like a series of oatmeal-colored cashmere scarves stacked on top of one another and expensive-looking gray boots. She was drinking a latte. She looked very tan and well rested.

'Hi, guys,' said Bitty. Rattailed Caligula and Penelope stayed where they were under the Steinway.

'Hey, Bitty,' said Rattailed Caligula. He waved at her spastically. 'When did you get back?'

'Oh, me? I was back like two days ago. I would have come in sooner but my friend Gustav – do you know Gustav? Anyway, Gustav had a ridiculous party two days ago, and I have been so hungover.' She said the last clause in a whisper: 'I have been barely able to walk.'

'Bitty!' cried Henry Wills-Mather from the lighting booth. He seemed quite pleased. 'Is that you? Are you back from the wilderness?'

'Indeed! Although I can't stay for long! I just came to say hello.'

'We can run the pianos scene!' said Henry Wills-Mather, oblivious.

It had been three weeks since Gustav kissed Penelope and then told her he would contact her 'at some point in his life.' During the interim, Penelope had gone home briefly for Christmas, where her mother bought her a book about how to apply makeup as well as other instructional presents. After she came back, she rehearsed the play even when others did not and wrote two final papers. Not once had she heard from Gustav. At first Penelope was relatively sanguine about this. She figured Gustav went on some sort of epic vacation for the Christmas holiday and thought, his being a man of his word, he would contact her on his return to the continental United States. This new information from Bitty was very troubling. The fact that Gustav was not only back on campus but also having parties that he didn't invite her to seemed to her very bad signs.

And so, on the walk back from play practice, Penelope decided to call her mother for advice. In her past, Penelope's mother had been quite good with men. In the eighties, she had broken off four engagements in the space of a year, two of which hadn't even involved her.

'Hey, Penelope,' said her mother when she picked up on the third ring. 'I'm in Sam's Club!'

'How is it?' asked Penelope. She was outside Lamont Library. She made her way over to the front steps and sat down on them.

'Oh, it's really good,' said Penelope's mother. 'I am buying some industrial-sized waters.'

'That's awesome,' said Penelope. Two people walked into the library carrying toothbrushes because they were going to sleep there.

'When are you coming home again?' asked Penelope's mother. 'Have you made a bus reservation for the end of finals?'

'No,' said Penelope.

'Penelope, you have to do that. I bet the buses are all sold out.'

'I don't think that route to Hartford is usually a crowded thoroughfare,' said Penelope.

'A crowded thoroughfare?' said Penelope's mother. She sighed a long sigh. 'How are your finals going?'

'Oh, good,' said Penelope. 'I am just about to take an exam in this class called Counting People.'

'That sounds like a great class,' said Penelope's mother. 'What is it about?'

'Counting. And, so, well, actually, in the class there is this guy.'

'Oh, really? A guy! See I told you you would meet someone! You said to me that you would never meet anybody, but, of course, I knew that you would! Who is he?'

'He is just this guy named Gustav. He's really handsome.'

'Does he have long hair or something?' Penelope's mother loved men with long hair. She was always talking to Penelope about Fabio.

'Um, no, not really. I guess it is a little long. It's sort of chin length.'

'Hmm,' said Penelope's mother. 'Wow, Penelope! That's pretty exciting. But you don't sound that excited.'

'Well, it's kind of a hard situation. Because we went for drinks with a group of people, but then it kind of turned into a date. And then he said he would call me for a real date.'

'And has he called you?'

'No! And then he had a party the other night that he didn't invite me to it. I just found out today at play practice.'

'What a jerk!' said Penelope's mother. 'Well, don't invite him to the next party you have.'

'OK,' said Penelope. When Penelope wouldn't get invited to parties as a youth, which was often, this was always something her mother would say. Penelope imagined this sort of reciprocal revenge would be very satisfying if you were the type of person who had parties. The punishment really fit the crime, etc.

'But wait. Tell me more about this. How did he ask you on a date again?'

'He was just like, "I will call you."'

'How did you react to that? Did you say anything?'

'Yeah,' said Penelope.

'What did you say exactly?' said her mother. Penelope's mother often said that if she had to do it all over again, she would be a detective. Perhaps this was the original source of Penelope's respect for the profession. It was at times like these when Penelope realized how much her mother's natural skills could have lent themselves to this career choice. She was indefatigable as a questioner.

'I think he said, "Let's go out sometime," and I was like, "Sure, let's get ice cream." And then he said, "Ice cream in the winter?" and I really didn't know what to say then.'

'Huh,' said her mother. 'Well, I don't know, Penelope, I think I would text him or something. What is the harm? Ask him what he is doing tonight. He may have just been confused by that ice cream in the winter conversation.'

'What? No,' said Penelope.

'Penelope. You asked for my advice and that is what I think. I think you should call him. Or at the very least text him. Imagine if someone said that to you? You probably wouldn't know what to think.'

'I would know exactly what to think,' said Penelope.

'I really think you should text him. Anyway, I am at the checkout line, so I have to go, OK? But make your reservations for the bus home! Bye!' said Penelope's mother.

After Penelope's mother hung up, Penelope sat on the library steps for a while, even though it was cold. Was Penelope's mother right about this? She was usually right about things and Penelope was usually wrong. But Penelope also felt there were certain inalienable social facts about life at Harvard that she couldn't really communicate to her mother. If she tried to explain why Emma was producing the play, for example, her mother would never believe her. 'Why would producing a play make anyone like you?' she would say. Anyway, it was a lot to think about, and Penelope didn't really want to be alone, so she went to the library.

Penelope often went to the library when she wanted company, because that was where everyone else was, studying for their exams. She usually sat near the café and stared at people doing their homework. Today she was going to try to read a book about whether Shakespeare was really Francis Bacon, instead of just a man named Shakespeare. She had to write a paper about it.

Penelope sat down on an uncomfortable brown armchair in the café and tried to read her book. Apparently, Francis Bacon's life was the exact plot of *Love's Labour's Lost*, and that was why he was Shakespeare. Should she text Gustav? Suddenly, Penelope was filled with the conviction that there was absolutely no harm in texting at all. It was just something people normally did in their lives. If Gustav construed texting as rude and invasive, then he was the crazy one! It did behoove her to write something completely neutral, however, in case he did. So she texted him 'Hi.'

After five minutes, Penelope felt her phone buzzing. She had a new text. Her heart started to pound rapidly and she almost felt like she couldn't breathe. Then she calmed down, because she opened her phone and it was a text from Emma.

'Hi, Penelope,' it read. 'I was wondering if you were in our room and you could check and see if my book about political society is there. I thought I saw Lan put it in Raymond's crate the other day.'

Penelope did not reply to this, closed her phone, and regretted the choice of 'Hi' as a text. When she thought about it, it was probably not as neutral as previously supposed. Then her phone started to vibrate again. This was a text from Gustav.

'I am glad that you used the medium of text to communicate such greetings. What are you up to?'

Penelope texted her reply quickly:

'Oh, nothing. Am in the library reading about Francis Bacon. Do you think he is Shakespeare?'

To which Gustav replied immediately:

'Of course. Only a sir could produce anything of note in iambic pentameter. What are you doing later? Want to get dinner?'

This was more than Penelope could have hoped for and she dropped her phone on the ground. When she picked it up and put her battery back in, she texted:

'Oh, sure. Which dining hall?'

After this there was quite a long pause on Gustav's end. During this pause, Penelope went to the bathroom and put on more lipstick, in case Gustav was eventually revealed to be in the library. (This she highly doubted. She had never ever seen Gustav in the library once and everyone was always in the library. Still, it was good to be prepared.) She went back to her seat, took a highlighter, and highlighted parts of the life of Francis Bacon. Then she wondered why Gustav was taking so long. Maybe he was having a party he didn't invite her to. As she was thinking about this party, Gustav texted her again:

'Funny thing about the dining hall. Ate there once and got terrible indigestion.'

Penelope had no idea what this meant. Did this mean that

Gustav did not want to go to dinner at all? Should she respond? But what should she say? 'Hi'? Then there was some more vibrating and Penelope picked up her phone.

'Why don't we have dinner at my usual spot? The Charles Hotel, 8 o'clock. Terribly sorry to inconvenience you.'

Penelope could not believe it. She was going to go out with Gustav, on a date, to dinner. She gathered up all her belongings quickly. She had to go home and change.

Penelope did not know where the Charles Hotel was, so she was late when she finally got there. Wikipedia was so helpful in some matters and so unhelpful in others. She spotted Gustav right away because he was wearing a red silk ascot and also because there was no one else in the restaurant under the age of sixty.

'Hello, Penelope,' he said, and motioned her to his table, where he promptly stood up and tried to kiss her on both cheeks. Penelope had never had anyone do this to her before. She almost kissed Gustav on the nose because she was so confused.

'Did you have any problems getting here?' said Gustav after he sat back down. He took out his phone and put it on the table. It was an iPhone of the newest stripe.

'I was a little confused,' said Penelope.

'Did you come from the library? I myself have never been in any of the libraries here. I find murals extremely vulgar and all of them seem to have murals. Who cares about people carrying things? I've always been partial to paintings of Roman heads.'

'It's not so bad, really. People have started to sleep in the library and that gives it an atmosphere of fun.'

'People sleep in the library? I am sure you are making that up,' said Gustav. He seemed genuinely incredulous. It was not a humorous exaggeration to say he had never been to the library.

'It's true. People are sleeping in the library. They always do. Everyone brings a toothbrush.'

'A victory for oral hygiene, I'm sure. Which is, I imagine, a battle with many small victories and very few won wars.' Penelope nodded.

The waiter appeared as if out of nowhere. Gustav looked at Penelope expectantly.

'Do you know which wine you want?' he asked her.

'No,' said Penelope. 'I don't even know what wine is, really.'

'It's grapes, dear,' said Gustav. 'Do you know what food is? Do you have any preferences?'

'No,' said Penelope. 'Or, actually, anything without beets.'

'Fair enough,' said Gustav. Gustav then turned to the waiter and started ordering very rapidly in French, apparently for Penelope as well. The waiter did not understand French. The waiter kept asking Gustav to point to the items he was referring to and Gustav refused to do so. After about fifteen minutes of this, the waiter wrote something down on a notepad and trudged sadly away.

'I hope he got our order. I don't really understand waiters in America. Why don't they speak French? How can they be waiters?' said Gustav.

'I don't know,' said Penelope, who took a robust swig of her water. 'Do waiters speak French in Argentina?'

'Of course,' said Gustav. 'Anywhere the water isn't bad. Though to be fair, I rarely go back.'

'Really?'

'Yes,' said Gustav. 'Parents sent me away quite early, you know. I think I was four when I first went away to school.'

'Four? Really?' said Penelope. She felt a pang. Penelope had always wished desperately for boarding school.

'No, probably not,' said Gustav. 'Probably seven. That seems more normal.'

'Did you like it?' asked Penelope.

'Well, of course, it was rather fun to beat the younger boys with sticks. And, you know, there is nothing like playing some odd sport on the grounds. I suppose I did like it. Well, I didn't like it very much when I was younger, but it is easier to say you liked it the whole time.'

'I agree,' said Penelope. 'Taking a definite stance is an important thing to do. My mother always says that.'

'What a wise woman,' said Gustav.

'But why didn't you like it when you were younger?' asked Penelope.

'Well, children are really the worst when they are young. And I didn't have this accent or anything then, so I was always having to repeat everything. Once I got the hang of it, it was smashing though.'

'Children are the worst when they are young,' said Penelope. 'That is really true.'

'But, of course, my life has really been quite standard. What is it like growing up in Connecticut? Did you go to the prom? Were you always getting into sordid intrigues with local football heroes? Did you go to the prom pregnant by a football hero?'

'Only someone cool could do something like that,' said Penelope.

The food came. Penelope carefully picked the beets out of her salad as Gustav explained to her why some wines are different from other wines.

'Fascinating,' said Penelope when Gustav finished.

'That was a very depressing utterance, Penelope. It was so hollow. No woman has ever so roundly rejected my wine talk.'

'No,' said Penelope, 'it was very interesting. Now I really know something about the role nunneries played in all this.'

'You can't speak French either! What is this country?'

'A country that does not speak French,' said Penelope.

'Shocking. Well, I am duly ashamed and turn the conversation to you. What would you rather talk about?'

'Oh, I don't know,' said Penelope. 'Have you ever solved any crimes?'

'Crimes? Hmm. That is an excellent question. Let me think. Well, once all of Mummy's jewels were stolen off this yacht we chartered in the Aegean. Of course, there were several people who could have taken them, including a very nefarious-looking butler who we hired for just the occasion. None of the regular staff got on with him; he sort of lurked around and all that.'

'Yes,' said Penelope.

'Then, of course, the thief was revealed to be poor Uncle Albert, who had stowed away in some sort of unoccupied steamer cabin and was living entirely off of empty potato chip bags. He just stole them because they were shiny. He's touched, you see. His mother is also his sister or something, before they knew that was bad.'

'I thought they always knew that was bad,' said Penelope.

'Maybe they were cousins. But I am pretty sure they were sisters.'

'So were you instrumental to solving this purported crime?' said Penelope.

'Well, no,' said Gustav. 'I was working on turning entirely orange, as was the style at the time.'

'To me that sounds as if you were actually doing research,' said Penelope. 'Sometimes in detective novels, the detective just lies around all the time, but inwardly he is thinking, and thinking very hard.'

'Perhaps you are right, you know. This has always been my cross. Although it seems I do not have a thought in my head, I am, in reality, thinking constantly about crimes and how to solve them.'

'I thought as much,' said Penelope. 'Because I too have that burden.'

Gustav motioned for the check and paid it.

'Let's go, shall we?' said Gustav.

'OK,' said Penelope. They left the restaurant. Penelope realized that she had never met a more like-minded individual in her entire life. She hated ordering her own food. Even the wine portion of the date she could forgive.

'Oh, look where we are,' said Gustav.

'This is not my dorm,' said Penelope.

'No,' said Gustav. 'It is my dorm.' They were outside of Adams House, by far the most elaborate dorm on the Harvard campus. The housing at Harvard did not become random until 1994. Before that, all the upper-class houses at Harvard were privately funded and sorted by type. For example, the athletes lived in one dorm, the WASPs in another, and the rattailed Caligulas of the world in quite another. When alumni gave back to Harvard in those olden days, they would often give to their particular house. As a result, some houses with historically rich associations greatly outstripped other houses in amenities. Gustav lived in a house with an entryway guarded by a marble balustrade and a stone lion. At one point his dorm had had a swimming pool in the basement.

'I guess I just forgot to pay attention,' said Penelope.

'I'm terribly sorry,' said Gustav. He put his hand lightly on Penelope's neck. 'I should be more aware of these things.'

'Oh, that's OK,' said Penelope.

'Do you want to go up to my room and watch a movie?' said Gustav, tapping his finger on the top of her spine.

'Oh, uh, sure,' said Penelope in a faint kind of voice. 'Do you have any?'

'Movies? Well, I remembered how you said I should get more DVDs, which was, I might add, a very reasonable suggestion. So, over Christmas break, I purchased many different DVDs. At this point, I believe I have assembled a full library of every movie every person could ever want to see. At least come up and look. I got a new bookshelf for them.'

'Well, OK,' said Penelope. She tried to breathe normally. Were they going to have sex? Was that what people did at this juncture? Were they actually going to watch a movie? That was a possibility too.

Penelope went inside Gustav's entryway, which was lined entirely in mahogany and featured many cavernous fireplaces set into the walls. Gustav's rooms were in a wing of their own. They walked down a long hall to get to them.

'Do you have all this to yourself?' said Penelope once she was actually inside Gustav's suite. The main room was an imposing Beaux-Arts parlor with twelve-foot ceilings and elaborate crown molding. Gustav had furnished it with a gigantic leather couch and a large Napoleonic-seeming desk. Yet, despite the hulking pieces of furniture, the room was very spare. The only wall decoration consisted of old maps. Penelope sat down on the couch.

'Yes,' said Gustav. 'My mother called the school and told them that I had never been vaccinated for anything and was probably carrying loads of tropical diseases. I have never had to share a room in my entire life for this very reason. Lovely woman. I'm about as primed for disease as an Indian, but it has its perks.'

'Wow,' said Penelope. She tried to look at a map on the wall to steady herself. In it, the Netherlands owned quite a bit of the world. 'Well, uh, what movies can we watch.'

'I'm so glad you asked,' said Gustav. He walked over to a short bookcase next to the couch Penelope was sitting on.

'Well, let me see here,' he said, and got on his knees to read the titles. 'We have *Marathon Man, Notorious, The Boys from Brazil*, of course, *Face/Off* . . .'

'Let's go with *Face/Off*,' said Penelope quickly.

'I don't know what this indicates about your tastes,' said Gustav, who was getting *Face/Off* out of its case and putting it in the DVD player. His TV was very large and mounted on the wall like a picture.

The movie started.

'I always wished this could happen in real life,' said Gustav, who put his arm around Penelope once he settled himself back on the couch. 'It seems so fun.'

'That you could literally take your face off?' asked Penelope.

'When you say it like that it sounds like far more of a ridiculous proposition.' Gustav drew her tighter under his arm and lightly kissed the top of her ear. Then he kissed her on her cheek right next to her mouth. And then he kissed her mouth.

Penelope and Gustav made out through the entirety of *Face/Off*. Penelope viewed this experience as a tutorial in the Art of Love. The first time she made out with Gustav, she was too shocked to take note of anything he was doing or anything she could be doing back to him. This time, she paid close attention to technical niceties. For example, Gustav knew exactly where her face should go and subtly indicated this.

During the movie, Gustav successfully removed Penelope's shirt, both of her shoes, and one of her earrings. He put them neatly on the end table next to the couch. When the movie was over, Gustav threw Penelope over his shoulder and carried her the ten steps to his bedroom, where he then laid her on his bed. Gustav's bed was much larger than the normal extra-long cot that everybody else slept on. It also had many pillows of various sizes strewn all over it. Penelope became petrifyingly nervous when he laid her on it. Making out on the couch seemed normal, even fun once you got the hang of it. But this required much more in terms of skill level were she not to be found out as a fraud.

'Is this a feather bed?' asked Penelope from her prone position. Gustav was standing up beside the bed, taking off his shirt. He was not one of those 'rip your clothes off' types that Penelope had heard about. He removed clothing in a very orderly manner.

'I think so,' said Gustav. 'It's very comfortable.'

'Is it made of real feathers?' said Penelope.

'I imagine it is,' said Gustav. 'Are you OK?'

'Yes,' said Penelope. She was worried that her arms were paralyzed. She could just have been nervous, but what if she was getting polio? That would be bad, as Gustav probably wasn't vaccinated for it.

'Penelope, I must ask you a question,' said Gustav. He lay down next to Penelope on the bed and pulled her into him. Penelope's arms remained stubbornly at her sides like a penguin's. Gustav took Penelope's arms and put them around his neck, and smiled what seemed to be a reassuring smile. At this point, Penelope made a pact with herself: This evening, she wasn't going to do anything she didn't yet know how to do, so as not to expose herself to censure or ridicule; but she also wasn't going to be needlessly reticent in a way that made her stand out from other girls her age. Of course, this was a difficult arc to navigate. Her poverty of experience in the first place was very abysmal. But one can always be taught. That was the lesson of *The King and I*.

'What is your question?' asked Penelope in a more confident voice.

'Are you going to be contrary about your pants all evening?' asked Gustav.

*

Penelope woke up the next morning, still in Gustav's bed. It was 11:00 a.m. according to the wooden duck-shaped clock on the wall. She wondered if her breath smelled. That would be awful if it did. She tried to get up and soundlessly go to the bathroom to look for toothpaste when Gustav woke up.

'Oh, hello, you,' said Gustav. He tried to kiss Penelope. She was able to avert this by shoving her forehead in his face.

'Hello,' said Penelope.

'How are your trousers?'

'They are good,' said Penelope.

'I was worried they would wrinkle.'

'Oh, I don't think you needed to worry about that. They have spandex in them,' said Penelope.

'Weren't you hot?'

'A little,' said Penelope. 'They sort of itched me.'

'They really itched me,' said Gustav. 'I don't think any woman has ever slept in pants before in this bed.'

'Really,' said Penelope. 'That is fascinating.' This was something she needed to take note of. She thought keeping her pants on was a convenient and concrete nonnegotiable that allowed certain things but kept other things firmly out of the picture. Apparently, however, it was a weird thing to do.

'What do you have to do today?' asked Gustav. He raised himself up on one arm. Penelope was struck again by how abundant his chest hair was. She could barely look at it.

'I guess I am going to study,' said Penelope, blinking. 'I have to go to a study group later.'

'Do you have an exam?'

'Yeah,' said Penelope. 'Tomorrow'

'I know this sounds horribly ignorant, but what is a study group?' asked Gustav. 'I have never even heard of that.'

'It's a group of people who get together and study for an

exam. Usually everybody has a section of the curriculum that they are in charge of.'

'That sounds awful,' said Gustav. 'I am going to immediately forget that I have this important knowledge.' He succeeded in kissing Penelope this time, although she kept her mouth closed. His breath did not smell, weirdly.

Gustav pulled Penelope extremely close to his chest and started kissing her neck very softly. While he did this, he also inserted his index finger under the waistband of her pants. Just then, his cell phone started vibrating on his bedside table.

'Oh, shit,' said Gustav. 'Hold on.' He reached for his cell phone. Penelope immediately disentangled herself from Gustav's grasp and sat up.

'Yes, hello,' said Gustav into the phone. A woman was on the other end; Penelope could hear her. 'No, darling, I didn't forget.' At this, Gustav jumped off the bed and started to rapidly pull shoes out of his capacious closet. 'I will be there in ten minutes. So sorry to keep you waiting. See you soon.'

During this conversation, Penelope got off Gustav's bed and tried to find her shirt. When Gustav hung up with the mystery woman, he ascertained what Penelope was doing and said:

'I think it's in the common room still. Hold on, let me get it,' and sprinted out in that direction.

Penelope stood in the middle of Gustav's bedroom with her arms folded across her chest. She was wearing only pants and a bra. She was pretty cold. It looked very cold outside too. The sky was gray in a way that promised precipitation but would probably not deliver on it. Penelope could not decide how bad it was that Gustav was leaving her to have brunch with another woman. This was the hard thing about modern life and friendships. How bad were things anymore if everyone was friends all the time? Also, which one was the friend, the mystery woman or Penelope? Or were they both friends?

Gustav came back to the room with Penelope's shirt, earring, and shoes. He handed them to her.

'Terribly sorry about all this.'

'Oh, that's OK,' said Penelope. She put on her shirt as quickly as possible. Gustav tried to explain things while she got dressed.

'That was Bitty on the phone, you see. We used to have brunch together every Sunday, and I have been blowing her off terribly for the past three Sundays. This Friday, she made me promise to go to brunch with her or she would disown me.'

'Oh,' said Penelope, putting on her earring. 'Well, that's OK.'

'I am so sorry,' said Gustav apologetically. 'When can I see you again?'

'Oh, I don't know,' said Penelope. She was all dressed now. She walked quickly out of the bedroom. Gustav followed her.

'I am sure I will see you at the S— or something,' said Gustav. 'At some point.'

Penelope laughed a little at this.

'Sure,' she said. 'How will I get inside?'

'Well, maybe I can try to make it over to the library. I probably should try that place out.'

'OK,' said Penelope.

'Bye, darling,' said Gustav. He kissed her firmly on both cheeks. Penelope only slightly messed it up. Then he scampered off and Penelope walked back to Pennypacker.

Penelope trudged up Pennypacker's staircase, concluding what could have technically been termed a 'walk of shame' from Gustav's dorm. Penelope's mother had warned her about walks of shame. She said they were a bad thing to do. Somehow, Penelope thought they would be a more flagrant enterprise than they actually were. No one on the street even seemed to notice she was on one.

Penelope was hanging up her coat on a hook in the common room when she heard Emma yelling at someone inside their bedroom. She couldn't hear what Emma was saying exactly, the words were muffled, but she sounded upset. For a second, Penelope wondered whether Emma was mad at her for staying overnight at Gustav's and was screaming at someone random on the phone to express her frustration. How Emma would know about Penelope's date with Gustav would remain a mystery, but Penelope had a history of being inconveniently found out and did not question that such a mischance could occur. Unfortunately, Penelope needed to take a shower and her towel was in the bedroom. She decided to brave the scene and open the door.

'Dad! I am trying, OK? I am trying. You don't . . . Yes, I do want you to call him . . . Well, I am going to get an A-minus if you don't call him . . . Yes, I do think that's unfair . . . Dad, I have worked – Dad, I have worked, DAD!'

'Hi, Emma,' said Penelope softly. Emma did not acknowledge her. Penelope got her towel and rushed into the shower. When she came back from her shower to dry her hair, however, the conversation still wasn't finished.

'Yes, I know it isn't good enough for law school . . . Dad, I know that, you don't have to tell me that . . . I mean, obviously that's why I am freaking out . . . Yes . . . Yes . . . Dad, you don't know how hard I am trying, really . . . Maybe when you were in college it was easier . . . I am going to hang up on you, Dad. I really am. DAD! I am!'

Emma violently turned off her phone. Then she violently turned toward Penelope. Penelope almost dropped her hair dryer on the floor in fright.

'Where were you last night?' demanded Emma.

'Oh, nowhere,' said Penelope.

'How can you be nowhere? I don't get what you mean by that,' said Emma. Then she sighed and fell back on her bed.

'I am so sick of my dad,' said Emma.

'Why?' said Penelope.

'He's just being impossible. Plus, my TF for EC 10 is such an asshole. I think he hates me because I am pretty or something. I will fucking murder him if he keeps me out of Yale Law School.'

'Wow,' said Penelope. 'That is extreme.'

'Does a ninety, an eighty-nine, and a ninety-one sound like an A-minus to you?'

'Yes,' said Penelope.

'But not if you factor in classroom participation, which is ten percent of the grade,' said Emma.

'That's true,' said Penelope.

'Exactly! And that is what I said. I always come to class incredibly prepared. I talk almost the entire time. Yet he is insisting that I get an A-minus for the year. It's completely unfair and I have to stop it.'

'But, you know, an A-minus isn't that bad, really.'

'It's not good enough for law school! If I was planning on doing nothing with my life, then it would be fine.'

'But it's pretty early on, you know. I'm sure it doesn't matter much. You could even have fun all semester and it wouldn't matter.'

'I am having fun! I am having incredible fun! I am meeting incredible people and I am making the best friends of my life.'

'Oh, awesome,' said Penelope.

'All I am saying is that fun is not the problem. Ugh, I just need to go in and talk to my TF, that's all,' said Emma. She lay down on her bed again, facedown on her pillow. Penelope took it as a cue and went back into the common room to pick up some books from her desk. Lan was feeding Raymond sardines out of a red, rectangular can. She was wearing a T-shirt that read ARE YOU THERE, GOD? IT IS ME, LAN. on one side and PASADENA CHRISTIAN CAMP 1997 on the other side.

'Hi, Lan,' said Penelope.

'Did you go out with that European guy yesterday?' said Lan without looking up from Raymond.

'How do you know about that?' asked Penelope.

'I just do,' said Lan. 'Anyway, he is weird. He's like an international playboy, except really nerdy and a freak. I wouldn't take it personally.'

'Take what personally?' asked Penelope.

'Whatever you are taking personally,' said Lan.

'OK,' said Penelope. She didn't agree. Still, she felt a little better.

Penelope was half an hour late when she got to the library for her study group. Everyone was already assembled around a table in the library café working quietly, and they did not stop working quietly when Penelope entered the room. The study group consisted of Ted, the tiny guy in the herringbone vest, and Melissa. Penelope did not understand how this group was ever formed. It consisted only of her mortal enemies. However, these were things you seemed to put aside during exam period.

Penelope sat down next to Ted and took out her notebook. Ted waved to Penelope silently.

'Hey, Penelope,' whispered Ted.

'Oh, hey, Ted,' whispered Penelope.

'Glad you could make it. Where were you last night? Catherine and I stopped by your room on the way back from dinner, but you weren't there.'

'Oh, I don't know where I was. I was around I guess,' said Penelope. She had no idea why she was lying. But then, of course, what was the point of telling anyone? It was probably the last time she would see Gustav ever again, as 'Maybe I will see you at the S— sometime' was by far the lamest of any of his nonpromises to hang out. Even when Mae West said things like that, they were lies. Penelope knew she really should consider the whole thing done. She didn't even have to take it personally. Even though it had been the best date of her life, it also had some flaws, like French and his uncle the inbred. It was not perfect.

'Yeah, Lan said you had been in the library for a while or something,' said Ted.

'Um, I have a question. Can we all flip to page three of the study guide? Is that really a passable sample essay question? I think she wants a more technical approach,' said the man in the herringbone vest.

'I think it's fine,' said Ted.

The man in the herringbone vest noticed Penelope for the first time.

'Where were you?' he said. He was wearing a bow tie today as well. He looked like a soda jerk in a saloon.

'Oh, I was just taking a shower. I woke up kind of late.'

'Did you do your portion of the study guide?' he asked.

'Oh, yeah,' said Penelope. She had cut and pasted several pictures of Shakespeare's goatee into a Word document right before she left.

'Good,' said the man in the herringbone vest. 'Do you want to give it to us?'

'Here,' said Penelope. She passed out what she had done.

The man in the herringbone vest looked at Penelope's portion of the study guide and sighed. 'Well, let's go through the material from the beginning, I guess,' he said.

Examining the study guide from the beginning, Penelope was filled with a certain amount of malaise and depression. If she didn't have Gustav, then what did she have to hope for?

Academic success in her classes? Penelope could think about that up to a point but only up to a point. Extracurricular activities? The mere thought of *Caligula* made her want to jump out a window. Friends? The Ted and Catherine situation was like a bedroom farce without jokes. It was all depressing, although not as bad as possible, obviously.

At some point, the man in the vest broke the silence and gave an impassioned speech about the inadequacies of images without context.

'I think that guy is worse when he has his bow tie on,' said Penelope to Ted in an undertone.

'Oh, definitely,' said Ted.

'I don't think I had ever seen anyone in a bow tie before, before I went here. Now I see some people wearing them every day.'

'My father wears one,' said Ted.

'Oh,' said Penelope. That explained a lot.

'I actually have some of his old ones,' said Ted. 'Maybe I'll wear one one day. I think they are kind of funny, don't you? I wouldn't wear it seriously, of course, but in an ironic way.'

'How have exams been going?' asked Penelope.

'Well, exams, you know. It's been a lot of work. Hopefully next semester will be less insane.'

'Yeah, hopefully,' said Penelope.

'Do you want to get dinner tonight?' asked Ted. 'I feel like I haven't seen you in forever.'

'Sure,' said Penelope. Because what else was there to do? Nothing.

'Guys,' said the man in the vest, 'are you going to join this discussion? It's like five right now and we haven't even really attacked most of the material we need to attack.'

It was at this moment when Penelope looked over at the door and saw Gustav walk into the library. He was accompanied by

both Tiny 1930s Movie Star and Rower. They all looked very dis-
oriented and had a lot of trouble swiping their ID cards at the
card swipe near the entrance. Eventually, Gustav had to show
the security guard his passport. Penelope felt her stomach flip
over. She could not believe Gustav had come here, the library,
a place he hated on principle. Did he come here to see her?

In any case, Penelope felt the best thing to do was to make
no signal to Gustav that she had seen him at all. Instead, she
started poring over her study guide. Out of the corner of her
eye, she saw Rower, Tiny 1930s Movie Star, and Gustav sit
down at a table about twenty feet away. Rower took out his
laptop, which was silver and extremely slim, and laid it on the
table. Gustav put his feet up on a chair. She could not tell if he
had seen her and was pretending to ignore her, or had not seen
her and was just sitting twenty feet away because there was an
empty table. In all probability, it was the latter. Gustav did not
strike her as particularly neurotic.

'Who did Images of Shakespeare from the seventeenth cen-
tury?' asked the man in the herringbone vest.

'I did,' said Melissa in a small voice.

'This is exactly opposite of what the test will be on,' said the
man in the herringbone vest. 'How did you come up with
this?'

'Hey, Penelope,' said Ted, pointing obviously at Gustav. 'Isn't
that your friend?' Penelope had to stop herself from lunging at
Ted and shoving his hand to the floor.

'What are you referring to?' said Penelope, looking at her
study guide.

'Fancy seeing him in the library,' said Ted. 'You should say hi.'

'No,' said Penelope.

'Have you two kept in touch since you went out for drinks?'
asked Ted.

'Not really,' said Penelope, looking at Gustav to see if he

noticed the pointing. It seemed not. He was laughing at something and slapping his knee.

'Too bad,' said Ted.

'I am going to get a cup of coffee,' said Penelope. The coffee bar was only ten feet away from Gustav's table. Penelope wondered if Gustav would approach her as she waited for her drink. He did not. She got her cappuccino and returned to her seat.

'What took you so long? Did you talk to your boyfriend?' said Ted when she sat back down.

'No,' said Penelope. 'I ordered a cappuccino.'

'Why are you attracted to this guy again?' said Ted. 'I don't really get it. I am going to be honest.'

'Really?' said Penelope.

'Yeah,' said Ted. 'He seems like such a weirdo. But I am not a girl, I guess.'

'Maybe that is why,' said Penelope.

'Darling?' said a voice behind her. Penelope whipped around. Gustav was standing right behind her chair. He appeared even taller than usual.

'Oh, hello,' said Penelope. She wondered if he had heard Ted. Ted didn't seem too perturbed, if that was the case.

'I thought I saw you ordering a cappuccino. Why didn't you come and say hello?'

'Oh,' said Penelope. 'I don't know. I guess I didn't see you.'

'That's so curious,' said Gustav. 'Come here.' He grabbed her hand and pulled her up off her seat. Then he kissed her on both cheeks. Penelope responded adequately.

'This is my first time in the library,' said Gustav in a loud voice. 'And what a place it is. Do you think it rather smells in here?'

'Maybe,' said Penelope. She looked anew at the library café. At the next table, a girl was slowly pulling out clumps of her eyebrow as she wrote Arabic vocabulary words on flash cards. On a nearby stool, a guy was reading a book called *Empiricism Rising: Hume, Voltaire, and the War of Jenkins' Ear.* Penelope felt embarrassed. It was as if the entire library was somehow her responsibility and it was acting worse on purpose because she had put it on the spot.

'Is this your study group?' asked Gustav.

'Yes,' said Penelope quietly.

'Who are you?' barked the man in the herringbone vest. 'We are kind of working here.'

'Oh, terribly sorry, old chap. I am Gustav.'

'I'm Ted,' said Ted. He stood up and shook hands with Gustav.

'Ah, Ted,' said Gustav. 'Hello.'

'Hi,' said Ted. He smirked at Penelope.

'So, Ted,' said Gustav in a convivial way. 'How do you know Penelope?'

'We live in the same dorm,' said Ted.

'Oh, isn't that nice. Aren't they always the best chums, really?' said Gustav. He cleared his throat.

'I guess,' said Ted.

'Penelope, darling,' said Gustav. 'As much as I love it here, do you mind if we leave immediately? I'll take you out for pizza as a bribe.'

'Well,' said Penelope. It was true she was sick of the library. It was hard to take after a while. However, there was her pride to consider. She could not seem too eager to leave. 'I do have to study.'

'Do you see my friends over there?' said Gustav. He pointed to them. They were throwing pieces of wadded-up paper at each other. 'They need to study too. I think that is selfish. Who knows what may happen to me as I rove the streets looking for pizza? I do not. Come, you have to save me.'

'I'm sorry, guys,' said Penelope. 'I think I have to go now. But good luck with the study group!' She got up.

'Oh, whatever,' said the man in the herringbone vest. 'You were no help anyway.'

'I'm sure that's not true. Come on, dear,' said Gustav, who led Penelope out by her elbow as if she were an invalid.

When they got outside, Gustav breathed a long, very audible sigh of relief.

'Darling, never make me go inside that terrible, terrible building ever again.'

'OK, I won't,' said Penelope.

'I know now why my father said to me, right before I left for school, "Son. The only way to have a good time at Harvard is to never go into the libraries." How right he was. Such sound advice.'

They walked in the direction of the Square.

Gustav took Penelope to a wood-grilled pizza place with slate tables. It was not a restaurant frequented by students. There, he ordered a beer that tasted like charcoal and made Penelope drink it.

'That beer is extremely good for you, darling. Has loads of vitamins, which you need. You look pale. That library is like an infirmary. I could feel my jaundice flaring up.'

'Gee, thanks,' said Penelope. She took a sip and grimaced. 'Why did you go there anyway?'

'Oh, to see you of course,' said Gustav. 'Not sure if I would do it again though.'

'You did?' Penelope blushed.

'Of course, darling,' said Gustav. He patted her arm. 'I felt quite bad about our scene this morning. I thought I behaved like a bit of a cad. I should have at least waited until you were out of the room to answer the phone.'

'Oh, it's OK,' said Penelope. She felt a little like crying. She always felt like crying when someone apologized to her, however briefly, badly, or disingenuously.

'Of course, this has to be extremely casual, I'm absolutely horrid with anything more, but I would like to see a bit more of you,' said Gustav. 'You're very funny.'

'Thanks,' said Penelope.

'Would you want to see more of me?' asked Gustav.

'Sure,' said Penelope. Gustav laughed.

'What an answer!' he said. He laughed more.

10.

In Which Penelope Is Forced to Consider Her Living Arrangements

A couple of weeks later, after Penelope finished her finals and started a new semester, she was having dinner in Annenberg with Ted, Glasses, Nikil, Jason, and Catherine. They were not eating a very good meal. The main course was a boiled chicken breast. The sides included peas and corn.

'You were so wasted on Saturday,' said Glasses to Nikil while he cleaned his glasses on his turtleneck.

'I wasn't wasted,' said Nikil. 'I was drunk but I wasn't wasted. I knew everything that was happening.'

'You were totally wasted,' said Glasses. 'I know what you are like when you're wasted.'

Saturday there had been another pregame in Glasses and Nikil's room. The pregame was supposed to lead to an actual party in Quincy, but it didn't. Instead, Penelope, Ted, Glasses, Catherine, Jason, and Nikil drank until Nikil got quite drunk and started to cry because he and Glasses got into a

disagreement about why the Dow Jones was called that. Then
Nikil started to projectile vomit onto the shower curtain. That
was when Penelope got a text from Gustav, who was done with
his party and wanted to see her. She quickly left and went to
his room.

'I can't believe you left early, Penelope,' said Ted. 'You really
missed out. It was actually sort of fun.'

'It's true. After you left, it really became fun,' said Catherine.

'We had a dance party and everything,' said Ted. 'And you
blew it off for a booty call?'

'Ha ha ha,' laughed Catherine in a shrill way.

'You must really like this guy,' said Ted to Penelope – meanly,
she thought. 'What is the deal with you two now?'

'What do you mean by deal?' said Penelope, although she
knew what he meant. This was not the first time Ted had posed
such a question, but the public forum was a particularly vile
new development.

'Like, what is going on with that?' asked Ted,

'I really want to get more chicken,' said Penelope, who got up
from the table and left to get more chicken. When she came
back, the conversation had blessedly reverted to everyone's
favorite topic.

'Did you get your chem exam back yet?' Nikil asked Glasses.

'Yeah,' said Glasses.

'Oh, cool,' said Nikil. 'I got mine back too.' Nikil's tone of
voice indicated a certain degree of satisfaction with his per-
formance. Glasses's less so.

Penelope's own exams came off with varying degrees of success. She did quite well in Images of Shakespeare, for example,
and relatively badly in Counting People. Neither of these things
was particularly surprising. Jared said her country report was
'weirdly specific in all the wrong ways' and Penelope even
agreed with that. In any case, it was a new semester now, spring

was on the horizon, and there was no use crying over spilled milk.

'I am going to start tutoring that chem class next year,' said Nikil nonchalantly

'Nice,' said Glasses. 'You know, that's a good idea. I might start tutoring too. Just to pick up some extra money.'

Nikil made a little sound in the back of his throat.

'Well, I think it's one of those things where the professor picks you to be the tutor. At least that is what my professor did to me. You have to get above a certain grade on the final to be a tutor. Not everyone can do it.'

'Oh,' said Glasses.

'Can you believe it's almost next year?' wailed Catherine. 'This year has gone by so fast!'

'We still have a while to go,' said Ted. 'It's not over yet.'

'It's true,' said Penelope. 'We still have to perform *Caligula*.' Penelope had found recently that she could not think about the future without realizing she would have to perform *Caligula* in order to get to that future. Her one comfort was that barely anyone would see the production. The poster advertising the play was really very off-putting. Lan designed it this way on purpose, she had told Penelope.

'Plus, we still have to figure out blocking,' said Nikil.

'Oh God. I know!' said Glasses. Blocking, Penelope recently figured out, was the process by which freshmen got into an upper-class house for their sophomore year. All freshmen organized into groups of up to eight people called 'housing blocks' and put themselves in a housing lottery. The logic ran that that way, students could live with their friends in the same dorm. The majority of freshmen, not excepting Glasses and Nikil, were obsessed with what house they were going to get into. In order of conversational preeminence, it was right up there with exams.

'I have figured it out,' said Nikil. He pushed his tray out of the way and daintily laid his elbows on the table. 'I definitely have it figured out. I think, to get into Adams House, we should only block with five people.'

'I thought you said we could have all eight,' said Glasses.

'Yeah, you did,' said Ted. He, Nikil, Jason, and Glasses were all blocking together. This had been decided quite early on and Penelope often wondered how Ted felt about this arrangement. It never seemed that he liked Glasses or Jason very much. He actively hated Nikil. However, if he had other friends, Penelope had never seen them, and if a tree falls in the forest? It was very probable that he had no other options.

'No,' said Nikil. 'I looked at the floor plan last night and I did a little game theory. Five people is best.'

'But you said I could have my two friends from Model United Nations come and live with us!' said Glasses.

Nikil shrugged his shoulders.

'I don't know why I said that. I really should have run the probabilities beforehand. I guess I could say I was sorry that I didn't do them, but I didn't see a copy of the floor plans until yesterday.'

'But my friend had a brother who lived in Adams House!' said Glasses, agitated.

'Hmm,' said Nikil. Although the housing was random now, many students felt, through anecdotal evidence, that legacy still counted for something in these affairs. 'Well, maybe he can stay in. I guess we should kick out someone else.'

'I have been to Adams House,' added Penelope helpfully. It was where Gustav lived. 'It is really nice.'

'I know!' said Nikil sharply. 'That's why we want to get into it.'

'Cool,' said Penelope. Catherine had her eyes demurely cast down and was eating her peas. Penelope wondered whom she was living with. For her part, she had not really thought about blocking very much. She had been too much entangled with the throngs of romance. This conversation, however, was emphasizing to her why she really had to consider the subject. The due date was looming, and these things seemed to be deciding themselves, which was usually when Penelope absented herself from any decision-making process.

'One thing I know is I am so excited to go to *Caligula*,' said Ted in a malicious manner.

'Ha ha,' laughed Penelope mirthlessly.

'I love existentialism,' said Glasses sincerely.

All told, Penelope's second semester was going far better than her first. She was taking new classes and they were not very hard. Jared was not her TF anymore. She also sort of had a boyfriend, in a way. *Caligula* was approaching, but not until the end of the year. These were Penelope's thoughts on a positive day.

The Gustav situation was confusing though. Penelope had seen him several times since she had been back at school. They had even fallen into a certain kind of schedule with each other, which was exciting. Penelope could be reasonably sure she would see him once or twice a week. Once she saw him three times in one week, but that was because she was going to a Gilbert and Sullivan concert by herself and he was lost.

However, if Penelope was honest with herself, the reason she avoided Ted's questions about her relationship with Gustav was because she didn't know what the 'deal' between them was exactly. She couldn't really say they were in a relationship, since they didn't really go on dates, and their arrangement seemed far less official than boyfriend and girlfriend. She also couldn't say they were just friends, since Gustav mostly called her very late at night and she slept in his bed. It was an anxiety-provoking situation for the type of person who enjoyed a one-word answer.

In many ways, Penelope had been preparing her whole life for a grand romance. Everything about one suited her down to the ground: the surprise trips to Malta, the avowals of continual affection, the heated sparring over pets and mink coats and rivals. Penelope knew she could have a grand romance with Gustav, but for some reason, she felt like she was spending a worrisome amount of time in the period before the romance was to begin.

The problem was, it didn't feel like things were becoming less casual as time marched on, as one would usually expect. If anything, it felt like they were becoming more casual. Gustav never saw Penelope during the day. He never introduced her to his friends. They very rarely talked about anything very much or for a very sustained period, which suited Penelope fine but also did not seem to be natural. On the other hand, Gustav was unfailingly polite when they did hang out, initiated all of their social intercourse with aforementioned regularity, and seemed to like her.

Later that night, for example, Gustav invited Penelope over to his room at two in the morning. He had gone to a benefit that evening in Boston for a charity that provided BlackBerrys to subsistence farmers.

'It was really amazing, Penelope,' said Gustav, taking off his tuxedo shirt and laying it over a chair. 'You would be shocked how many people in the world don't even have BlackBerrys.'

'That is amazing,' said Penelope, who was lying on the bed.

'Boston is really so insipid though. The women all have terrible sloping shoulders. The food was too awful because it was ecologically sound. Still, that was to be expected.'

Gustav sat on the side of the bed, shirtless but still in pants.

Penelope wondered whether people wore undershirts in Argentina. It was hard to know.

'Anyway, darling,' said Gustav. 'How was your day?'

'Oh, fine,' said Penelope. 'Who did you block with when you were a freshman?'

'Oh, it's that time again, isn't it?' said Gustav.

'Yeah,' said Penelope. 'Or for the first time.'

'Do you know who you are going to live with?'

'Well, no,' said Penelope. 'I haven't decided really.'

'Living with people is overrated, I think. I don't live with anyone because I would probably die of rubella, but it has always worked out quite well, really.'

'It's too bad I was vaccinated,' said Penelope. She really meant this.

'I know, dear,' said Gustav. 'Not being vaccinated has saved me from most of the unpleasant things in life. I don't really know what I would have done if I were vaccinated, aside from living to a more advanced age.' He bent down and gave Penelope a long kiss on the mouth. Then he stood up, took his phone from his pocket, and put it on his desk.

'Of course, if you don't have vaccination as an excuse, it is rather embarrassing to be a floater,' said Gustav.

'A floater?'

'Someone no one wants to live with, darling. It is quite shameful. Means no one likes you. Ahh, here are my cuff links. I could feel them digging into my thigh.' Gustav took two gold cuff links from his other pocket and put them on his desk.

'You really shouldn't worry about that though,' said Gustav, laying himself on top of Penelope in a very agile way. He kissed her again. Then he slowly slid one of Penelope's bra straps off her shoulder and kissed her shoulder. 'Just ask your friends to block with them, and I am quite sure you will have it all sorted by the end of the week.'

Penelope nodded. This sounded like good advice to her. It was worrisome, this floater business, however.

'My goodness darling, you look very nice tonight,' said Gustav, who took his mouth away from Penelope's neck to look at her face in a friendly sort of way, like they were meeting for the first time. 'Is this a new bra?'

'I don't know,' said Penelope blankly. It wasn't.

'Black is a very subversive color,' said Gustav, 'except on nuns! I wonder when all this frustration will get boring,'

'Ha ha ha,' laughed Penelope. But she was nervous. So you see the trouble.

A week later, Penelope arrived ten minutes late to the required freshman-only expository writing seminar she was taking called Southern Writers Reconsidered or Southern Writers Revisited – Penelope had never caught which it was. And now she had lost the syllabus so she was never to know.

As Penelope took her seat, the professor, a portly man with Darwinian sideburns, cleared his throat with displeasure. The first day of class he had brought his primary school uniform into the classroom and hung it over the back of the door. It consisted of pantaloons and a small blazer. He brought it in to show that 'everyone had to start somewhere.' It was a metaphor for writing. Ever since then, he and Penelope had been enemies.

'How nice of you to join us,' said the professor to Penelope. It was hard to tell if this was sardonic.

'Oh, yes,' said Penelope. She sat as far away from the professor as possible. She really needed to start taking her showers at night.

'*All the King's Men*,' yelled the professor at the top of his voice, 'American history through the looking glass?'

The class looked at him, unmoved. They were assigned to

read only the first one hundred pages of *All the King's Men*. Because it was an expository writing class, they read only excerpts of books or parts of articles 'just to get a taste of them,' as the professor said. Southern books are all very long, however. Quite often, Penelope didn't get the best sense of what was happening in the plots.

Penelope stopped listening to the professor and occupied herself by looking at the other people in the class. She had hoped that a compulsory course would be a good place to meet people you did not know already. However, it ended up that she knew quite a lot of her fellow students already, at least by sight, which was disappointing. Jason was in this class too. Sometimes he glared at Penelope when the professor was talking.

'Your second paper is due in a week,' said the professor eventually. 'You can go.'

Penelope wandered out of Emerson Hall and cut across the Yard on the way back to Pennypacker. Jason walked a couple of steps ahead her. They never walked back together after Southern Writers Reconsidered/Revisited and never seemed to feel the lack of each other's company on the way back to the dorm. This time, however, Jason slowed down so he was walking almost next to her. Penelope worried briefly that someone had died.

'Hi, Penelope,' Jason said.

'Oh, hi, Jason,' said Penelope.

'I saw that guy who is supposed to be your boyfriend walking around with another girl. In the co-op,' said Jason breathlessly. It was the longest sentence Penelope had ever heard him utter.

'Oh,' said Penelope. 'OK. Really?'

'Yes!' said Jason.

'Well, that is OK,' said Penelope. It was probably Bitty. Penelope knew that she had to be a modern woman and not overreact to this news. Seeing Gustav with a woman didn't mean anything. Women were equals in society now and could be platonic comrades. That was the good and bad thing about the women's movement.

'Are you living with anyone?' asked Jason.

'No,' said Penelope. 'But I will find someone soon.'

'It is the worst to be a floater,' said Jason. He broke out into a run and ran all the way to Pennypacker.

Penelope decided she would take Gustav's advice and ask one of her friends to block with her instead of waiting around like a discarded Victorian companion for them to bring it up with her. It was not her first inclination to be the aggressor, but when had her first inclination ever been correct or appropriate? Besides, she didn't want to be a floater, and as time marched closer to the date that housing forms were due, it was becoming increasingly likely that if she didn't take some sort of initiative she would be.

Penelope was going to ask either Lan or Emma to block with her. They were her closest approximation to friends, and all told, living with them this year had not gone too badly. Penelope was an inclusive soul and would have preferred that they all block together, but recently the tensions between Lan and Emma had reached some sort of apotheosis, especially since Lan taught Raymond two dog tricks.

So accordingly, and later that week, Penelope seized upon Lan while she was walking to the bathroom. Lan was wearing a Pink Floyd T-shirt that had the words 'I am ambivalent about' written above the band logo in marker. Raymond was following behind her, carrying Emma's copy of *Democracy in America* in his mouth.

'Hey, Lan,' said Penelope. 'Can I talk to you for a second?'

'What?' said Lan. She stopped walking and looked at Penelope. It was a scary look, but Penelope continued.

'How are you?' asked Penelope.

'Fine,' said Lan.

'That's good.'

Lan shrugged.

'Wow. Can you believe *Caligula* is coming up so soon?' asked Penelope.

'No,' said Lan.

'I hope they find someone to play Craig's part,' said Penelope, more to herself than Lan. 'I thought they would have found somebody by now.'

'I knew they wouldn't,' said Lan. 'I said that.'

'I am troubled by some recent developments in the play,' continued Penelope quickly. 'For example, that play within a play they put in the third act. That wasn't in the original script. I don't get why it is a puppet show either.'

'That was my idea,' said Lan. She started walking toward her room.

Penelope took a deep breath. It was time to confront the real situation. This was very frightening. More frightening, even, than the imaginary scenario, which involved a slap.

'Do you know what you are doing for housing?' asked Penelope.

'Oh,' said Lan. 'I am moving to the co-op.'

'Oh?' said Penelope. 'What is that?'

'It's this place off campus where everybody cooks their own vegetarian food and lives together and rides bikes. It's disgusting.'

'Oh, really?' said Penelope. 'So you are not moving into one of the houses?'

'No,' said Lan.

'Why not?' asked Penelope. She was really disappointed. She had not realized how much she had counted on living with Lan. She had pictured the two of them celebrating Raymond's birthday and eating in silence for many years to come.

'It's just really hard to keep a cat secret,' said Lan. She said this almost apologetically.

'Oh,' said Penelope. 'I can see that.'

'Well, I am going to my room,' said Lan.

'OK,' said Penelope. And then Lan walked to her room.

Penelope sat in the common room by herself. She was stung and upset. Still, on further reflection, it was a foolhardy enterprise to ask Lan to live in the confines of the dorms for another year. Lan would have never had agreed to their strictures. She was an iconoclast. Penelope was not, however.

'So how do you like living in America?' said Penelope to Gustav. She was sitting on the couch in his common room and sipping a flute of champagne. It was three a.m. Gustav was preparing to hit a golf ball into a putting green he installed near his desk. Gustav was often silent when playing golf. Thus Penelope had ample time to think of a conversational topic.

'Oh, I suppose it's fine,' said Gustav, laughing. 'Haven't we discussed this?'

'Oh, I don't know,' said Penelope. 'I guess I forgot.' *What a dumb conversational topic,* thought Penelope. It was just sometimes when she was with Gustav she didn't know what to talk about. Before she would hang out with him, she would sometimes try to brainstorm things to discuss. Everything she brainstormed never went the way she thought it would.

'How do you like that champagne?' said Gustav, putting his golf club back in its case. 'I am not entirely pleased with it. Perhaps it's too dry.'

'Oh,' said Penelope. 'Sure!'

Gustav sat down on the couch next to Penelope. He took off his shoes, which were brown and had tassels and holes all over them in some sort of swirly design. He smiled. Penelope smiled at him.

'In some ways I find it adorable,' said Gustav, 'but you are much too agreeable, dear! I think it's time for you to develop tastes, and standards!'

'OK,' said Penelope.

Penelope had to wait several days before she approached Emma about living with her. There never seemed to be a right time to broach the subject. Despite being in the same play and living in the same room, Penelope didn't see Emma all that much. At play practice, Penelope was onstage, acting several parts. She was one of the puppeteers now, which was really complicated because at the last minute Henry Wills-Mather changed the puppets to marionettes, and Penelope had to watch YouTube videos to learn how to operate them, whereas Emma, in her capacity as producer, dealt with ticket stubs on a different floor. In addition, Emma had a very active social life and was constantly going to parties of one sort or another, which left little time for sincere talks.

It was while Emma was getting ready to go to one of these soirees that Penelope felt the time was right to discuss housing. Emma seemed to be in a good mood. She was looking at herself in a full-length mirror that was adhered to the back of the closet door. She was wearing some sort of large Lilly Pulitzer expanse that was knotted at the neck. Was it a sari?

Penelope sat down on her bed.

'Hi, Emma,' said Penelope.

'Oh, hey, Penelope,' said Emma. She took a compact off her bureau and started applying bronzing powder to her cheeks using a large, round brush.

'Where are you going?' asked Penelope.

'A garden party,' said Emma. 'At the Owl.'

'Oh, fun,' said Penelope.

'Yeah, I think it will be,' said Emma.

'Isn't it too cold to go in the garden?' asked Penelope.

'Oh, Penelope, it's an ironic garden party!' said Emma. She laughed decibels into the sky. 'Their real garden party is next month or something. Whatever. I have to leave early anyway.'

'Why?' asked Penelope.

Emma sighed.

'I am so swamped. Like ridiculously. Classes are ridiculous. I spent six hours in the library yesterday.'

'Wow.'

'I know,' said Emma. 'I am not even half done with my work.'

'Terrible,' said Penelope.

'Not to mention all the other stuff I have to do, what with the play coming up, and Model United Nations having a conference, and like six HSA meetings, plus *Current* elections.'

'That is a lot of stuff,' said Penelope.

'I am incredibly stressed,' said Emma. 'It is just too much for one person.'

This seemed to put Emma in a taciturn mood, which was too bad because she had just been laughing very loudly. Penelope wished she had not brought up the subject of work during such an important conversation, but had she? Homework was like a North Star that everything turned to.

Penelope took a deep breath. She figured she might as well just come out with it.

'Do you know what you are doing for housing?' she said. Emma made a loud sound, somewhere between a scream and a click.

'Well, that is what is stressing me out the most! I just feel so upset about it. My friend Beth asked me to block with her, which is fine, I guess; she is blocking with these kids who I sort

of know from different things. They need like four more people.
It's not like they are super-nerdy or anything, and I like Beth,
but it's kind of like whatever. But I think Bitty and Katrina
might want to block with me. In the past, when I've asked them
about it, they have sort of said they wanted to, but now I feel
like they might not anymore because from what I have heard,
their blocking group is kind of full and I might not get in. But
I also don't want to offend them? By making plans? So it's just
really freaking me out.'

'Oh, wow,' said Penelope. 'I mean, well, if you don't get into
that one, I was going to ask you, you know, if there is any space,
for me? In the other one. If I could block with you?'

Emma looked too shocked to speak. Luckily, her metropol-
itan breeding enabled her to recover.

'Oh, you know, I would love that, but I think both of the
other groups I want to get into are really already full. You gave
me no notice! I know I said before that there was space, but
now that I am thinking about it I really don't think there is. I
mean, I would love it, but I really don't think it's possible. I'm
sorry.'

'Oh, it's OK,' said Penelope. 'I totally understand.'

'Oh, good, because, you know, I am already feeling really,
really stressed out about this, and I just can't really add to it in
any way. It's way way too much to think about this right now.'

'OK,' said Penelope.

'I am glad you understand,' said Emma.

Penelope went out into the common room and started to
panic.

The next day, while en route to Dinosaurs, a new class Penelope
was taking about dinosaurs to satisfy a science B requirement,
she called her mother. She needed additional advice.

Penelope's mother picked up the phone with unprecedented alacrity. It sounded like she was in the car.

'Penelope!' said Penelope's mother.

'Oh, hi, Mom,' said Penelope.

'Where are you?' asked Penelope's mother.

'Walking to class,' said Penelope, kicking a pinecone out of her way.

'Oh, good! Make sure you turn off your phone when you get there.'

'OK,' said Penelope. 'But I keep it on silent.'

'You should turn it off. How are you?'

'I am all right,' said Penelope

'What are you doing about housing? Did you find anyone to live with yet?' asked Penelope's mother.

'No,' said Penelope.

'Have you asked people?' said Penelope's mother.

'I think so.'

'Is there anyone from the play?'

'No,' said Penelope.

'Is there anyone from your classes?'

'Not really,' said Penelope. She thought of Jason.

'How is that possible?' asked Penelope's mother in a despairing but ultimately rhetorical tone. It was a tone Penelope was familiar with.

'I don't know,' said Penelope. She was just coming to realize she really didn't have any friends here. She didn't know what it said about her. On the one hand, she was never particularly good at making friends, so why should this change now? On the other hand, wasn't college the one place where even freaks made friends? That was what everybody said.

'Oh, Penelope,' said her mother. She sounded rather sad.

'It's OK,' said Penelope.

'I know,' said Penelope's mother, 'you should just ask Lan and

Emma to live with you! I bet they are looking for people to live with! Don't be afraid to ask them. It's the perfect solution.'

'Oh,' said Penelope. 'Well, I already asked them and they said no.'

'What?' said Penelope's mother. 'Both Lan and Emma? They both said no?'

'Yes,' said Penelope.

'Why did they say no?'

'Well, they already had other plans.'

'Well, what if you said you would join in their plans?'

'I kind of did,' said Penelope, 'and they still said no.'

'That is crazy!' said Penelope's mother.

'I know,' said Penelope.

'Are you still dating that guy?' asked Penelope's mother.

'I guess so,' said Penelope. 'It's not really called dating anymore though.'

'Of course it is,' snapped Penelope's mother. 'Have you told him you have no one to live with?'

'Why would I tell him that?' asked Penelope.

'Because that is what people do! You should ask his advice! Maybe he has a friend you could live with. Or a younger sister.'

'What?' said Penelope. 'He doesn't have a younger sister.'

'You get what I mean,' said Penelope's mother. 'He knows people.'

'No,' said Penelope.

'You fucking asshole!' yelled Penelope's mother. 'This driving is actually really tough. I am going to have to go.'

'Oh, OK,' said Penelope.

'Don't worry about this,' said Penelope's mother. 'But why does stuff like this always happen to you?' And with that she hung up.

*

'I have no one to live with,' said Penelope to Gustav. It was three in the morning and they were walking down Mount Auburn Street together. Gustav had been at a Chinese New Year party at the S—. He had texted Penelope to meet him outside the party at two thirty. Penelope had been sitting on the stoop of a nearby bookstore in the extreme cold, waiting for him. Her feet were freezing. That was the reason for the fretful honesty.

'Do you, darling? That is splendid,' said Gustav. He patted Penelope on the back. He was wearing a red Mandarin-style jacket, thin black cotton pants, and a flat straw hat. Penelope was worried he was wearing racist eyeliner but didn't really want to look.

'Oh, but I said I didn't,' said Penelope.

'What, darling?' said Gustav. He wasn't paying attention to Penelope. He was texting something on his phone.

'How was the party?' asked Penelope.

'Oh, marvelous,' said Gustav, putting his phone in his pocket. 'We even had an inflatable Chinese man that we set up in the game room.'

'Wow,' said Penelope.

'Do you want to get anything to eat?' asked Gustav.

'I don't really know if you should wear that in a restaurant,' said Penelope.

Gustav laughed loudly.

'You are too funny, darling.' He put his arm around Penelope and steered her in the direction of his dorm. 'Well, we can just go home then. Why ever would I not wear this to a restaurant?'

Gustav's dorm was conveniently close to all the clubs. The walk there was very short.

'Really, I do love theme parties,' continued Gustav, holding the door of his dorm open for Penelope. 'They are so fun. I plan to host bunches of them, even when I am an adult!'

'Oh, really?' said Penelope as they walked up the stairs. 'That is interesting. What themes?'

'I went to one back in London that was called "The Worst Men in History." All my old chums from school were there. It was great fun.'

'Who did you go as?' asked Penelope. They were inside Gustav's room. Penelope sat on Gustav's bed. He had recently changed the sheets from a blue piped monogram to a green piped monogram.

'Oh, dear, I forget,' said Gustav, taking off his straw hat and laying it on his desk. 'Something German, I'm sure.'

'Oh,' said Penelope. 'I went to a party once here that was *Peter Pan* themed.'

'Well, isn't that odd,' said Gustav. He sat on the bed next to Penelope. He put his arm around her. 'Why would the theme be a book? Themes should really be aphorisms or holidays, like Chinese New Year.'

'It was a terrible party,' said Penelope.

'Penelope, Penelope, Penelope,' said Henry Wills-Mather. With each iteration of her name, his tone had become louder and more aggrieved. This was one of the first times Henry Wills-Mather had ever addressed Penelope directly. She did not feel distinguished by the notice.

'Penelope, just put down your marionette,' whispered Catherine, who was sitting right next to her, also holding a marionette. They were situated in the midsized marionette stage that Lan had designed for Act 3's puppet show. This stage alone was thought to cost upward of three thousand dollars, as Lan had employed the highest quality in marionette technology. Penelope put the marionette down. It clattered as it hit the floor.

'Penelope, do you know why I stopped you?' asked Henry Wills-Mather.

'Uh,' said Penelope.

'I stopped you because – what does your marionette look like?'

'My marionette?' asked Penelope.

'Yes,' said Henry Wills-Mather. He looked at her expectantly.

'Well, I think this is supposed to represent Caligula.'

'Exactly!' said Henry Wills-Mather as if he had scored some point of contention. 'And what does it look like now?'

'I don't know,' said Penelope.

'It just looks too much like a marionette, Penelope. It's incredibly stiff. I need it to mimic the fluidities of human motion as much as possible while, at the same time, ironically referencing the artificiality of theater itself. Do you get what I am saying?'

Penelope nodded.

'You're just very stiff,' said Henry Wills-Mather, taking his black turtleneck by the collar and loosening it with his finger as if it were a cravat. 'It's just very puppetlike, it's very orthodox, it's very puppet show, puppet show. Oh God.' He sat on a chair in the audience section and put his head in his hands.

Henry Wills-Mather was really starting to lose it, according to everyone. As the day of the play grew nearer, he would fly into unaccountable rages and misplace his car keys over and over (they were always in the piano). To a certain extent, Penelope understood this. The play was only a couple of weeks away. It was insanely over budget because of the marionettes. Very few people knew their lines, and they had still not found a replacement for Craig.

'Where's Bitty?' asked Henry Wills-Mather in a strangled voice. 'Where is she?'

'Emma said she would be here soon,' said Rattailed Caligula. He was sitting underneath the piano doing a problem set.

'Goddamn it, how can we teach the puppeteers how to mimic her movements if she is not here?'

'I don't know,' said Rattailed Caligula, not looking up.

'He didn't say anything about my marionette, did he?' whispered Catherine in a worried manner.

'No,' said Penelope.

'Good,' said Catherine. 'I didn't think he did. I was just making sure.'

'OK,' said Penelope. 'I'm going to go to the bathroom.'

Catherine made her marionette wave good-bye to Penelope, and Penelope waved good-bye back to the marionette. She had been warmer than usual since she had realized Penelope was dating someone. Penelope admired Catherine's certainty about this fact.

Penelope walked out of the theater and toward the bathroom, which was in the basement. Just as she was about to turn down the stairs, she heard a familiar voice emanating from the courtyard outside. She paused and listened.

'Bitty, dear, I have things to do and people to see. I can't always be walking you everywhere just because you say so in some kind of wheedling voice.'

'Oh, Gustav,' said Bitty. 'I can't walk here by myself. Besides, I just need to go inside and make an appearance, then we can leave and get a drink before that party at the PC.'

'Ten minutes,' said Gustav.

'Not even!' said Bitty.

At this point, Penelope made a spur-of-the-moment decision. Instead of continuing down the stairs and going to the bathroom, she decided to go outside and 'accidentally' run into Gustav and Bitty. This was perhaps motivated by natural curiosity, although normally Penelope was rather deficient in that. In any case, she walked toward the door to the courtyard and opened it. Unfortunately, this was just the moment when Gustav and Bitty were coming inside, which resulted in all of them colliding in the door frame. Penelope walked right into the middle of Gustav's chest. She was worried she kissed it accidentally.

'Oh, sorry,' said Penelope without looking up. Her new plan was to pretend that although she had just run into Gustav (literally), she hadn't seen him because she was looking at the ground at the time. She was going to continue out the door when Gustav stopped her by grabbing her arm.

'Penelope, darling, what on earth are you doing here?' said Gustav. He seemed genuinely surprised to see her. 'Why are you going outside with just a T-shirt on?'

'Oh, I have to get something,' muttered Penelope vaguely.

'Well, at least put your coat on before you get it,' said Gustav. 'It's rather a tundra out there.'

'OK,' said Penelope.

Gustav was wearing a pale gray coat with a shearling collar and cuffs. Bitty was also wearing a shearling coat and a Russian-style hat. They looked like matching KGB agents. Gustav took Penelope by the arm and led her into the lobby. He, she, and Bitty stood in a triangle. Penelope stifled an embarrassed laugh.

This was when she realized that natural curiosity, so revered in some societies, had led her to a terrible social impasse. Although she and Gustav were practically dating (dating, hooking up, friends?), protocol for these daylight situations was as yet unclear. Since that time in the library, she had not seen him when the sun was out. If you ran into such a person by accident, how were you supposed to act? Like you loved them? Like you hated them? Like you didn't know them at all?

'How do you two know each other?' asked Bitty. She looked at Penelope in an inquisitive way. 'I know I've seen you before. You look so familiar to me! What's your name? I am horrible with names.'

'Penelope,' said Penelope.

'Oh, Bitty,' said Gustav. 'You know Penelope. She is a great friend of mine. You have met her before, dear. We all went to drinks together.'

'And I am in this play with you,' said Penelope.

'Oh, right right,' said Bitty. 'You do look familiar!'

'Oh, great,' said Penelope.

Bitty laughed. 'Well, I was just going to pop in for a second. Say hello to Henry.'

'Awesome,' said Penelope. 'We were just in marionette practice.'

'Marionette practice?' asked Gustav. He raised his eyebrow at Penelope.

'They put a marionette show in the middle of Act Three,' said Penelope.

'Oh my God. Are you a marionette operator?' he asked Penelope.

'Of course,' said Penelope.

'It's my favorite part of the play,' said Bitty.

'I wonder what it is like,' said Penelope.

Just then, Emma came running down stairs. Penelope was very glad to see her. Emma looked very agitated, however. She was wearing rain boots and a cable-knit sweater in the same shade of violent pink.

'Bitty, Henry Wills-Mather has been looking for you everywhere!'

'Oh, really?' said Bitty.

'He is like freaking out. Hi, Gustav!'

'Hello there, Emma,' said Gustav, bowing slightly.

'Oh,' said Bitty. 'Well, I can only be here for a second. I am going to that PC thing tonight. I was just going to say hello. I told Gustav this was going to be brief.'

'You actually didn't tell me about it at all,' said Gustav. 'I thought we were going to the party in an intensely roundabout way.'

'Are you going to the PC thing?' asked Bitty.

'Oh, uh, I don't know. I hadn't really thought about it,' said Emma. Penelope knew Emma wasn't invited to the PC thing. She had complained about it extensively to Penelope while crying. Penelope had had to look up almost everything she said on Wikipedia, which was exhausting.

'Well, I don't know if I am on the list,' said Emma. 'Gustav, are you coming to see the play?'

'Oh,' said Gustav. He smiled at Penelope in a knowing way. 'I mean, I suppose I have to. When is it again?'

'Friday, Saturday, and Sunday the second weekend in April,' said Emma.

'My Lord!' said Gustav. 'So many nights to choose from. Saturday, I have to go to the arboretum during the day, but other than –'

'Oh!' said Bitty. She clapped her hands excitedly. 'I have always wanted to go to the arboretum!'

'Me too!' said Emma.

'What is an arboretum?' asked Penelope.

'An arboretum, darling, is a collection of trees,' said Gustav. 'I have no great truck in the thing myself, but Harvard has one, and my family supports it rather extensively. Once a year or so, I go out there and check how everything is doing. You would hate it because of your stance on nature.'

'An arboretum is such a good cause,' said Bitty solemnly. 'It is so important for forestry.'

'Well, it's privately endowed,' said Gustav. 'But we do help everything stay tip-top. You should see the state of other arboretums. None of them has wheelbarrows decorated with a crest. Or a twenty-four-hour hotline for plant identification.'

Emma laughed. 'Gustav! There is no way we have wheelbarrows like that!'

'Oh, darling,' said Gustav, 'how very little you know.'

'Wait,' said Bitty, grabbing hold of Gustav's arm. 'When are you going again?'

'Saturday,' said Gustav. 'During the day.'

'I'm free during the day,' said Bitty excitedly. 'We only have to be here at night. I should go with you. Or me and Emma should.'

'Yeah!' said Emma. It might have been the happiest Penelope had ever seen her.

'It will be so fun,' said Bitty.

'Well,' said Gustav doubtfully, 'I do want company.'

'Oh, good!' said Bitty. 'We have to get back in time for our call. It's at six.'

'That shouldn't be a problem,' said Gustav. 'Arboretums are terrible at night. You half expect Ichabod Crane to leap out and ask you to dinner.'

'That is my worst nightmare,' said Penelope.

Gustav looked at Penelope like he had just noticed her again. It was curious, Penelope thought, how he seemed to visibly forget people. Not in a mean way, of course. Every time he realized they were there again he seemed to like them, which was more than you could say for most people.

'Oh, Penelope! You must come too! All three of you should come,' Gustav said in a jovial voice. Penelope felt a burst of relief course through her body. She had had no idea she was even tense. Nor did she really want to go to an arborctum, necessarily.

'Yay! That sounds fantastic! I just love being outside in the spring. I wish my dog was here,' said Bitty. 'I'm just going to run and say hello to Henry for a second. Don't leave!' she said to Gustav, punching him in the shoulder. Then she sauntered into the theater.

Gustav, Penelope, and Emma were left in the lobby. Gustav smiled at the girls but said nothing. He put his gloves back on finger by finger. Penelope and Emma watched him do this in silence. After he had his gloves entirely on, he said in a chipper voice:

'Well, I think I will get going.'

'Gustav, you can't!' said Emma. 'You can't leave Bitty!' She started laughing, but she also seemed legitimately nervous.

'You're just going to leave her?' asked Penelope.

'I'm just rather worried she is going to take hours,' said Gustav, looking at his watch. 'And I really do have to get to this party. I have to recite a limerick at dinner. Emma, you'll take her to the party, won't you? I will let them know at the door, in case they forgot to put you on the list.'

'Oh, sure,' said Emma, flushing with pleasure. 'I mean, ha ha.'

'Good to see you, Penelope, darling,' said Gustav. He patted her arm. 'I may call you after the party. You look quite adorable in that marionette costume. Please wear that little hat later. I have a great idea for what to do with it.' And with that, Gustav walked quickly out of the theater.

Penelope did not know what to think about the foregoing scene. Obviously, it was disturbing and exhilarating in equal measure. One thing she was glad of was that she looked good in her marionette costume. For a long time she had been unsure about it.

Unfortunately, before she was able to ponder this fully, she was greeted with another trial. Emma was staring at her malignantly.

'Penelope, what was that?' she said.

'What was what?' said Penelope.

'That. When he said he would call you. Why would he ever call you?'

'I don't know,' said Penelope.

'I didn't even know you hung out with him.'

'I don't really that much,' said Penelope.

'You hang out with him? How do you even know him?'

'Well, I met him at that party,' said Penelope. 'And then we took a class together and stuff.'

'That's weird,' said Emma.

'Yeah,' said Penelope.

'Are you hooking up with him or something?' Emma asked.

'Um, well, I guess so,' said Penelope. All the muscles stiffened in Emma's face. A vein near her chin became especially prominent. It was amazing, thought Penelope, how much her physical reactions mirrored her actual emotions. She would make a terrible politician.

'What? I didn't know that!' said Emma. 'Why didn't you tell me that?'

'Oh well,' said Penelope, searching desperately for something to say, 'I don't know. I just didn't.'

'How long has this been going on?' asked Emma.

'Not that long,' said Penelope.

Penelope and Emma were still standing in the middle of the lobby. Due to Penelope's ill-advised bout of Boy Scout morality, Emma went over to the stairwell and sat down on the stairs. Penelope followed her and stood near her but not with her, like a blimp hovering over a public event. Emma looked up at Penelope with sad eyes.

'It just feels like you have been lying to me. Like one of my best friends here has been lying to me.'

'I . . . I wasn't lying to you,' Penelope stammered.

'You lied by omission,' said Emma.

'I just didn't think it was that important.'

'Penelope, I consider you one of my best friends. How could you not have told me this? I feel so hurt. I tell you everything!'

'I know,' said Penelope.

'I also think it is really mean to Bitty,' said Emma. 'Like really incredibly mean to Bitty.'

'What? Mean to Bitty?' said Penelope. She felt her stomach drop. 'How is she involved in this?'

'Oh my God, Penelope. She dated Gustav before. And I don't even know what is going on with them now. I just think this is like ridiculously insensitive.'

'I'm sorry,' said Penelope. 'I mean, nothing is really going on. It is very casual.'

'Ugh,' said Emma. 'I can't even talk about this. I sort of feel bad for you because Gustav is an awful person and ridiculously mean to girls. He leads everyone on. He is a terrible boyfriend. And he probably only likes you because you act like you like him. You are a ridiculous flirt.'

'I am?' said Penelope.

'But I can't believe you lied to my face, so actually, I don't even feel bad! I am going back to practice.' Emma, true to her word, got up, turned on her heel, and went running back into the theater. Penelope left then, because they didn't need the marionette operators anymore.

The next day, Penelope was sitting in the dining hall, having breakfast and mulling over yesterday's events. Emma had refused to speak to her all evening. Gustav had texted her at four a.m. and told her he was too tired from limericks to see her. And now she was eating breakfast alone. It had all been very depressing.

Just then, Penelope saw Catherine come into the dining hall through the back door, near the marble statues. She looked agitated. Her eyes were red rimmed and she was wearing some kind of bathrobe. After scanning the room briefly, Catherine saw Penelope and started sprinting toward her table, her bathrobe barely doing its office.

'Oh, Penelope,' said Catherine. 'Thank God you're here.' Catherine sat down next to Penelope. A bulbous tear fell tragically down her cheek. Pretty soon she was crying.

'What?' said Penelope. 'What is the matter?'

'Oh my God!' sobbed Catherine. 'Oh my God!'

'What?' said Penelope.

'I was trying to find you everywhere. Lan said you were at the dining hall. I just came here. Thank God you're here.'

'What is the matter?' said Penelope.

'Oh God,' said Catherine. She rubbed her face with her hands and took a deep breath. 'It's about blocking.'

'Oh,' said Penelope. She had been so preoccupied by her fight with Emma and her brush with Gustav that she had forgotten, momentarily, about blocking groups. She had to declare herself officially as a floater soon.

'So anyway, I was going to live with these other girls. Emmeline and them? You know those girls. There were like four of us who were going to block together. We were totally set on it. We talked about it and everything.'

'Right,' said Penelope. She had not known this but it was not very surprising.

'I mean, I have been really busy and stressed out by the play and everything so I haven't been checking in about it every second. I thought it was just understood. I didn't think it was going to be this big deal. So then, last night after the cast party, I went back to Emmeline's room to get something and all of them were huddled around a piece of paper and kind of whispering. So I was like, "What's up, guys?" And they were like, "We have to talk to you. We don't think we can fit you into our blocking group." And I was like, "What?" and they were like, "We're sorry." And I was like, "Well, when were you going to tell me any of this?" and they were like, "Tonight. Because we are going to turn our sheet in early."'

Catherine threw her head onto the table and started sobbing again.

'Do you know why they did that?' asked Penelope.

'No,' said Catherine. 'I think they want to allow boys into the group or something. I literally don't even know why. They were like my really good friends.'

'That is horrible,' said Penelope.

'I know,' said Catherine. She wiped her eyes again. 'It's so bad.'

'That really is bad,' said Penelope.

'I just can't believe it,' said Catherine. 'I don't know why people would suddenly just turn on you like that.'

'I know,' said Penelope. This was making her even more depressed. 'Human beings are a mystery. I don't understand how to make friends. Or what makes anyone like anyone.'

'I usually have no problem making friends at all,' said Catherine. 'This is all new, what is happening to me. In school, I was super-popular. But girls have always hated me. I have always been more of a guys girl.'

'Yeah,' said Penelope.

'Girls have always been jealous of me for some reason. I don't know why.'

'Oh,' said Penelope.

'That is what is so hard,' said Catherine.

'Well,' said Penelope, 'what are you going to do now? Can you block with Ted?'

'I mean, I had talked about blocking with Ted originally, because I love all those guys to death, and they are my real friends, not those girls. But it was going to throw off all the game theory or something.'

Penelope nodded.

'Anyway,' said Catherine. She used a napkin that had been left on the table to wipe her eyes.

'Well, what are you doing for housing?' asked Catherine.

'Nothing,' said Penelope. 'I couldn't find anyone to live with.'

'Yeah, I thought so,' said Catherine.

'It's OK,' said Penelope. 'I don't really mind.'

'Well, do you want to live together?' asked Catherine. 'I mean, now that this has happened, we can.'

'What?' said Penelope.

'Yeah,' said Catherine. 'I don't have anyone else to live with.'

'OK, sure!' said Penelope.

'OK, good,' said Catherine. 'Because I really don't want to be a floater too. And you are friends with Ted and I'm dating Ted, obviously, so we have that in common. We have a lot of the same friends.'

'That is true,' said Penelope.

'Well,' said Catherine. She smiled at Penelope in a morose sort of way. 'That is settled. That's really why I was trying to find you. I think we might get a good room. Just two people. We could probably get a nice double.'

'OK,' said Penelope.

'Awesome,' said Catherine. Suddenly, her eyes seemed to become arrested on something in the distance. 'Wait, I just saw Ted come in. Did you see him?'

'Oh,' said Penelope, turning around to see where she was looking, 'no, I didn't.'

'I am just going to go say hi to him,' said Catherine. 'I'll leave you to your breakfast.'

'Oh, OK,' said Penelope. 'You don't have to. I'm almost done.'

'No,' said Catherine. 'It's OK. Stay here.'

'Well, OK,' said Penelope. 'Bye, then.'

'Bye,' said Catherine. She went running off in the direction of where she saw Ted come in. Penelope still didn't see him.

Well, at least one thing is settled, thought Penelope.

II.

In Which There Is Hardship

Springtime in Massachusetts is depressing for those who embrace a progressive view of history and experience. It does not gradually develop as spring is supposed to. Instead, the crocuses bloom and the grass grows, but the foliage is independent from the weather, which gets colder and colder and sadder and sadder until June, when one day it becomes brutishly hot without warning. There is no traditional logic attached. Certain days in May can be more cutting than any in December. It was fitting, then, that the first people who chose to settle there were mentally suspect.

So, although it was technically spring, it seemed colder than ever when Penelope hurried past Widener Library. It was raining a little, but the rain was turning into ice just before it hit the ground. The sky was slate gray. The bark on the trees was sopping wet. It was hard to imagine the climate ever warming up sufficiently again.

'Penelope! Wait up!' yelled Ted. Penelope stopped and turned around. Ted was running up to meet her. She blew into her hands to keep them warm as she waited for him.

'Hi,' said Ted when he finally caught up with her. His face was blotched red from the exertion of running. His bangs were curled up in little balls because of the humidity. All and all, he looked more becoming than his usual self.

'Hello!' said Penelope.

'I was in Widener, and I saw you out the window,' said Ted. He bent over, put his hands on his knees, and exhaled deeply. 'I was worried I wasn't going to catch you.'

'Good thing you did,' said Penelope. 'I was just walking to the Quad Library by myself.'

'Why do you have to go all the way out there?' asked Ted. The Quad Library was a Swedish-looking building on the old girls' campus. No one went out there unless they had to.

'I have to get a copy of *Look Homeward, Angel* and Lamont was all out. I have to read a hundred pages of it.'

'Why not the whole thing?' asked Ted.

'I don't know,' said Penelope.

'Well, I'll walk with you a little,' said Ted. 'I have to drop something off at the registrar's.'

'OK,' said Penelope. They started walking out of Harvard Yard and toward the theater on Brattle Street. Penelope put the hood of her coat up, because the rain had turned to sleet somewhere along the way and was now spitting in her face. It didn't really help.

'So how are you?' asked Ted. 'How is everything going?'

'Oh, you know,' said Penelope.

'How are classes?'

'Good.'

'Do you have a lot of work?' asked Ted.

'No,' said Penelope. 'But it's kind of hard to tell.'

'How do you mean?'

'Well, I haven't really been doing it. Because of the play.'

'Oh, the play!' said Ted. He laughed.

'Yes,' said Penelope.

'When is the end of the long national nightmare?' asked Ted.

'Tomorrow is the final dress rehearsal,' said Penelope. The cast of *Caligula* had been having dress rehearsals all week. Penelope could not tell how they were going. At least everyone had shown up for last night's rehearsal. Craig's replacement hadn't come. Penelope had given up on that.

'Are you excited for it?' asked Ted.

'I mean,' said Penelope, 'I don't think so.'

'You have to be a little bit nervous,' said Ted.

'Well,' said Penelope, 'I have been having some nightmares.'

'Good,' said Ted. 'So you're living with Catherine, I hear.'

'Yes,' said Penelope.

'That's so great,' said Ted. 'Are you living with your room-mates too? How are they?'

'Oh, I don't know,' said Penelope. Her face flushed. Interpersonally, things were actually rather tense in Pennypacker because Emma wasn't speaking to her. This wasn't so tiresome at rehearsal, but it was harder at home because they shared a room. If Emma was in the room when Penelope got there, she would sit there solidly, without speaking, while Penelope asked her questions. If Penelope went to use the bathroom as Emma was coming out of it, Emma would turn slightly away from her and pretend to see something across the room in order to avoid eye contact. Their group trip to the arboretum was in three days. Penelope hoped they could patch things up by then. If they didn't, it was going to be quite awkward. She tried not to think about it.

'Well, it's their loss,' said Ted, smiling. 'You are awesome.'

'Oh, thanks,' said Penelope. She was charmed in spite of

herself. She liked compliments and they were rarely bestowed on her. Gustav was complimentary but only in a way that sounded like an elaborate joke about compliments.

As Penelope walked beside Ted, she realized that she had not talked to him one-on-one in some time. Her mind involuntarily flitted to the time they made out on her futon. She had not thought about that episode in months. It had been obscured by all the making out she had been doing with Gustav in bed. When she thought about it now, it seemed vaguely humiliating. She felt like her presence in the story was the thing that made it especially embarrassing. If someone else had been in her place, she would have been more normal with Ted; they could have preserved a better friendship, or they would have chosen no friendship. She wouldn't have freaked out as much about Helen of Troy, or she would have freaked out more and gotten over it. Penelope always did things in the worst way.

'In some ways, I kind of envy you,' continued Ted.

'Why?'

'Well, whatever you do it must be better than living with Mike, Nikil, and Jason. They have been talking about game theory and its connection to the housing process for the past month. The pregames have really taken a turn for the worse.'

'Maybe you should make new friends,' said Penelope.

'Who else would I be friends with?' asked Ted.

'I don't know.'

'I literally do not know one person I would even want to be friends with.'

'You could live with me and Catherine?' said Penelope. Coed blocking groups were technically allowed. They were a sort of ornamental concession to liberalism, since you couldn't actually live in the same room as someone of the opposite sex.

'She wanted to do that,' said Ted. 'I thought it would be

weird. What if we break up? It would be so awkward to see her in the same house.'

'That's true,' said Penelope. 'But you probably won't break up.'

'We might break up this summer,' said Ted.

'Really?' Penelope was shocked. As hard as it had been for her in the beginning, she had now accepted Ted and Catherine as an inalienable fact.

'Yeah,' said Ted. 'I think I might get an internship in Washington. I can't really see how our thing is going to work. She's going back to California. It just doesn't make any sense.'

'Oh,' said Penelope. 'Well, you can do long distance?'

'We'll see,' said Ted grimly. 'But I would have to call her every day.'

'Oh,' said Penelope. 'Yeah.'

'What are you doing this summer?'

'I don't know,' said Penelope. 'I guess go home. Are people already deciding what they are going to do this summer? It is sleeting.'

'Oh, yeah, everyone is,' said Ted. 'Or at least everyone in my room. That's why I am going to the registrar's. I have to get my transcript for my intern application.'

'Oh, weird,' said Penelope. 'What are you applying for?'

'I am trying to be a Senate page.'

'You will be perfect for that,' said Penelope, thinking of the Roman Senate.

'Well, I think we have to separate here,' said Ted. They were in front of the library.

'Thanks for walking me,' said Penelope. She tried to wipe the sleet off her face with the back of her hand and failed.

'No problem. You know, you should apply to be a page in Washington too. It would be fun! It would be good to have a friend there.'

'Really?' asked Penelope.

'Yeah,' said Ted.

'I'll think about it,' said Penelope. 'But I don't even know how many senators there are.'

'Well, bye,' said Ted. He ran down the street. Penelope walked thoughtfully into the library. What did it all mean? She didn't care all that much, but she cared a little.

Sometime after this, Penelope was lying on her bed reading *Look Homeward, Angel* when Emma came into the room. Emma gave Penelope a look that could have peeled paint off a wall.

'Hi, Emma,' said Penelope.

Emma flung her purse onto her bed, turned around, and walked into the bathroom without speaking.

Early on in this feud, Penelope had hoped Emma would just somehow forget about their tiff about Gustav. However, it seemed Emma was going to keep this going no matter what, and in a way, Penelope found that admirable. But Penelope really wanted to go to the arboretum. She was gradually becoming certain that if she went, it would usher in a new era in her relationship with Gustav. It would be an era of peace and conventionality. Pretty soon he would start hanging out with her in the daytime regularly. So she really had to patch this up.

Penelope went out into the common room and found Emma sitting on the futon tearing used pages out of her notebook and clipping them into a binder. Penelope stood near the futon and looked at the ground. Emma was wearing a lime-green pashmina scarf around her neck. It was an indoor scarf, apparently. Penelope wondered about the scarf. Did it itch? That was not a good question, she thought.

'Listen, Emma,' said Penelope.

'I am trying to organize my notes,' said Emma.

'I just want to say I'm sorry,' said Penelope.

Emma looked up.

'Whatever,' said Emma. 'I am not mad.'

'What can I do?' said Penelope. 'I feel terrible.'

'I just can't believe you lied to me,' said Emma.

'I know,' said Penelope. 'I'm sorry.'

'People are always failing me, and they are always disappointing me.'

'That must be hard,' said Penelope.

'I had a friend in high school who lied to me about her boyfriend for an entire year. So it's even more hurtful.'

'Yes,' said Penelope.

'And for it to be Gustav. How could you do that to Bitty? Or me? I mean, we practically dated.'

'Oh. I didn't know that,' said Penelope.

'I told you before.'

'Oh, right,' said Penelope. She still didn't remember this, but it seemed futile to argue the point. 'Well, what can I do?'

'I think you need to stop seeing Gustav,' said Emma simply and articulately. 'It's just so bad. It's bad for you.'

'OK,' said Penelope.

'Good,' said Emma, who started clipping her notes into her binder again.

'Wait, really?' said Penelope.

'Yes,' said Emma.

'OK,' said Penelope.

Penelope walked back in her room. They had made up, it seemed. As she flopped onto her bed, she considered her philosophical stances. She tried to be agreeable most of the time and go with the flow, so if Emma really wanted her to stop seeing Gustav, then she supposed she would have to comply. At the same time, she really didn't want to do that. Maybe she could keep things a secret. Impulsively, Penelope picked up her cell

phone and texted Gustav the words 'Hello, what are you up to?'
Then she started reading her book again.

Two days later, Penelope woke up with a premonition of doom.
For a while, she lay in bed with her eyes open, mulling over her
current circumstances and trying to pinpoint the source of her
discomfort. Then she remembered that tomorrow was opening
night of *Caligula*. Yesterday's dress rehearsal had not been a
success. Rattailed Caligula fell into an accidental split during
the ballet. Bitty knew approximately one-third of her lines.

Intellectually, Penelope thought excessive guilt was self-
indulgent, but that did not stop her from the occasional
flagellating reflection. *Caligula* was a horrible destiny, but in
another way, what had she done to deserve such suffering? Why
did she even agree to be in this play? It was something about
being helpful, Penelope decided, the worst of all motivating fac-
tors.

Penelope got up and went to the bathroom to take a shower.
When she got out of the shower, she put on a pair of white
pants, a white sweater, and white socks to symbolize the sacri-
ficial nature of tomorrow's events. As she went into the
common room to get her coat and leave to go to class, Lan
came out of her bedroom to go to the bathroom. It was eleven
a.m., which was a relatively early emergence for Lan. She was
carrying Raymond under her arm like a book and was wearing
a yellow terry-cloth bathrobe over her T-shirt, so Penelope could
not see what was on it.

'Hi, Lan,' said Penelope. 'You're up early.'

'I couldn't sleep,' said Lan. She rubbed her eyes with the
back of her non-Raymond hand.

'Me neither,' said Penelope. 'I am worried about *Caligula*.'

'I'm not going.'

'But you do the lights!' said Penelope. 'You have to go!'

'No, I don't,' said Lan.

'Oh,' said Penelope.

'What is that outfit?' said Lan, looking at Penelope's pants.

'A white outfit,' said Penelope.

'If I do the lights for the play, then I am bringing Raymond to tomorrow's show. I hope you don't get allergies,' said Lan.

She walked into the bathroom and shut the door. Penelope left and started walking to her first class. Lan had never worried about her allergies before. Maybe they were becoming closer friends.

Penelope's first class was Southern Writers Reconsidered/ Revisited. Penelope arrived late. It was raining again, which was bad for her white outfit.

'Since we are only going to read the first forty pages of *The Sound and the Fury,*' said the professor, glaring at Penelope but blessedly not remonstrating her for tardiness, 'I might as well tell you what it is about.'

As the professor summarized the entire plot of *The Sound and the Fury,* Penelope sunk into a reverie about Gustav. Penelope had not heard from him since the limericks evening and it was starting to make her anxious. He never texted her back the other night. It had been only five days or so, so it was possible that Gustav was busy and therefore not available. Penelope was very busy too (she supposed), but it didn't really affect her availability. She was always available. That was the thing.

'And that's when he drops the flower on the ground,' said the professor. 'OK, so for next week, we are reading parts of *A Streetcar Named Desire.* Your assignment, for your response paper, is to go see a play this weekend. In your response paper,

I want you to discuss the differences between viewing a play and reading a play. They arc very different. Notice the staging. We are going to talk a lot about the literary quality in Williams's stage directions. In fact, the entire excerpt I am giving to you is stage directions.'

'What's playing this weekend?' asked one of the kids in the class.

'*Caligula*,' said the professor. 'My friend and former classmate here, Henry Wills-Mather, is directing it. I am sure he will do something absolutely fantastic with the text. He is extremely innovative.'

'I think there are other things playing too,' said Penelope without raising her hand. 'I think there is a dance show.'

'I don't want people to see a dance show. That is not a play,' said the professor testily.

'OK,' said Penelope.

'Class dismissed,' said the professor.

Ten people, thought Penelope as she walked slowly out of the classroom, dragging her foot behind her slightly, out of stress. *Ten extra people who were not originally going to go to* Caligula *were now going to go to* Caligula. Penelope was unsure the theater could even hold that many people. Maybe Henry Wills-Mather would use them as human props. She shuddered at the thought.

Penelope had a free hour between her Southern Writers class and her Dinosaurs section, so she went to get a coffee at the Barker Center. She was standing in a long line when something awful happened.

'Penelope, is that you?' It was Jared. He was in line behind her. He stepped obviously out of the line and sidled up beside her, perhaps to talk at length. Penelope felt a shooting pain in her foot. Maybe she was getting a clubfoot.

'Oh, hi, yes,' said Penelope, wincing.

'How are you, Penelope?' said Jared. 'How is this semester going?'

'Oh,' said Penelope. The line was moving very slowly. 'It's really cool.'

'I figured you must have been busy because you didn't come to the final office hours I had,' said Jared. 'We had Rice Krispies treats. I think the section really enjoyed themselves.'

'Well,' said Penelope. 'You are right! I was busy! You see, I am in this play.'

'Ahh, *Caligula*,' said Jared. 'I am going to that tomorrow!'

'You are?' said Penelope. 'Why?'

'Why not? I said I was going. You are still my proctee, after all. Perhaps I can get everyone in the dorm to go.'

'Can I have a coffee, please?' said Penelope in a strangled voice to the woman behind the counter.

'I'm very excited about it,' continued Jared. 'I love the idea of setting it in French Algeria. That's fucking brilliant.'

'Oh, yes,' said Penelope. The woman handed Penelope her coffee and Penelope slammed two dollars onto the counter with unnecessary vehemence. 'Well, I have to get to another class. Bye!'

'See you tomorrow night!' yelled Jared.

Penelope ran out of the building. She ran down the street and didn't stop running until she spilled coffee all over her white pants. She found a leaf on the ground and was trying to wipe the coffee off her pants with it when she got a call from her mother.

'Penelope!' said her mother.

'Mom!' said Penelope.

'I am so excited for the play!'

'You're coming?' asked Penelope.

'Of course I am coming! It is your theatrical debut!'

'I really don't think parents are allowed to come,' said Penelope.

'Penelope, that is ridiculous. Of course parents are allowed to come! I have never heard of something like this where parents wouldn't be able to come. That doesn't make any sense.'

'OK,' said Penelope.

'What is the play called again?' asked Penelope's mother.

'*Caligula*,' said Penelope.

'Oh, that's right,' said Penelope's mother. 'Is it a musical?'

'No,' said Penelope.

'Well, what's it about?'

'I don't really know,' said Penelope. 'It's an absurdist play, so it doesn't really make any sense. But that is on purpose. It's supposed to show how narrative doesn't mean anything in the modern age.'

'Oh,' said Penelope's mother. 'Well, that is depressing. Maybe I shouldn't bring your grandmother.'

'Yeah,' said Penelope.

'Or Father Bennigan.'

'Definitely not,' said Penelope.

Penelope wandered around for the rest of the day in a haze. She went to two more classes. She went to the library and opened up her laptop and stared at it. She was late for everything because of her clubfoot. Occasionally, she would feel a paroxysm of fear when she thought about the sheer number of people who were coming to the play. This would eventually subside into a mild sickness.

By dinnertime, Penelope was not particularly hungry, but she felt like she needed to at least show up at the dining hall and go through the motions of eating. She was putting pickles on a chicken patty sandwich when she ran into Glasses and Nikil. They were also making chicken patty sandwiches at the chicken patty sandwich-making station.

'Hey, Penelope,' said Nikil. 'Nice outfit.'

'Oh, thanks,' said Penelope. 'Do you want to sit together? I didn't come here with anyone.'

'No,' said Nikil. 'We are just taking these sandwiches to go. We have to do some studying tonight if we are going to see the play this weekend.'

'Oh,' said Penelope. 'What play? The dance show?'

'No,' said Nikil. 'I didn't know there was a dance show. Your play. *Caligula*.'

'Oh, why?' said Penelope too loudly. She couldn't help but feel there was a note of franticness in her voice. She didn't want it to be there, but she couldn't really help it.

'Because!' said Nikil, slightly annoyed. 'I love *Caligula*. It is one of my favorite plays.'

'Me too,' said Glasses. 'Plus, I am writing the review for the *Crimson*, so I get in for free.'

'Really?' said Penelope. 'But it's a Saturday night! Isn't there something else to do?'

'What else could there be?' said Nikil.

'A dance show,' said Penelope.

'Well, I have to do this,' said Glasses. 'It is my job.'

'Oh,' said Penelope.

'The quickest way to be president of the *Crimson* is through the arts board. It is so disorganized.'

'Oh, oh,' said Penelope. 'Right.'

'Well, we have to get going,' said Nikil. 'Anyway.'

Penelope did not bother eating dinner after that. She just sat staring into space until it was time to go to dress rehearsal.

12.

The Performance

It is funny how shock works. On the morning of the opening night of *Caligula*, Penelope did not feel the terror she felt the day before. She did not even feel the embarrassment. All she felt was sort of preoccupied, which was only partially *Caligula's* fault.

In addition to the fact that today was opening night, today was also the day she was supposed to accompany Gustav, Emma, and Bitty to the arboretum. However, things were not going as planned. When Penelope had woken up, Emma was not in her bed. Penelope had texted her, but she didn't reply. Then Penelope called her, but Emma did not pick up her phone. Now Penelope was sitting in the common room, waiting to see if Emma or Gustav would call her and ask her to meet them somewhere. So far this had not happened. Penelope was starting to feel quite nervous.

Penelope was still in the common room drinking coffee and waiting for Gustav to call her when Lan entered the room. She smelled intensely of paint. She was wearing a T-shirt that had the words MAJOR LEAGUE BORING written above a picture of a guy playing baseball.

'Hey, Lan,' said Penelope. 'How are you?'

'Terrible,' said Lan. 'Henry Wills-Mather won't let Raymond be one of the marionettes.'

'But he is not a puppet,' said Penelope. 'Have you seen Emma?'

'No,' said Lan. 'Why?'

'Oh, no reason,' said Penelope.

Lan grunted and stalked into the bathroom.

A couple of minutes later Ted leaped over the recycling bin and bounded into the common room. He was wearing green plaid pajama pants and his bangs were in full evidence.

'You are up early!' said Penelope jovially, because even this was better than waiting alone.

'It's one p.m. I already went to breakfast with Catherine,' said Ted. 'Oh my God, Penelope, are you excited for the play tonight?'

'Not really,' said Penelope.

'I know,' said Ted. He sat heavily on the futon. 'You have never been excited about it. Even when you were cast as a marionette operator.'

'It's true,' said Penelope glumly, thinking of Gustav and his love of marionette costumes.

'What's the matter?' said Ted. 'Are you OK? You look upset.'

'Oh, I'm fine,' said Penelope. 'It's just, well, have you seen Emma?'

'Oh, yeah,' said Ted. 'I saw her on the way back from Annenberg. She was getting into a seventies BMW with some other girl. It looked like they were going somewhere. Are you looking for her?'

'Well, kind of,' said Penelope. 'Emma, Gustav, and that girl and I were supposed to go to the arboretum together.'

'Oh, weird,' said Ted.

'But then, when I woke up to go, Emma was already gone and I have been texting her and stuff and she has not answered me. They probably went without me.' With this realization, an enervating depression settled in the middle of Penelope's chest. Nobody wanted her to go to the arboretum, really, anyway. She was kind of forcing herself on them.

'That's really whack,' said Ted. 'I'm sorry.'

'It's OK,' said Penelope.

'Did Gustav text you?'

'No,' said Penelope.

'What a dick. But that dude Gustav is so weird, so it doesn't surprise me.'

'No, he isn't,' said Penelope.

'Yes, he is, Penelope. God, he is terrible. Like, what the fuck is that accent? And what the fuck are those clothes? It also seems like his grandparents were Nazis, from everything you have told me.'

'No, it doesn't!' said Penelope hotly.

'And honestly, I don't think he treats you very well. Like, why didn't you ever see him during the day? Why the fuck was he always making you go to his room at two in the morning? His room? He never comes here! That's weird.'

'Well, he lives alone,' said Penelope. She was trembling a little. 'He hasn't been vaccinated.'

'Another really weird thing!' said Ted. He was getting agitated now.

'I think it's sort of nice. I wish my mother did it to me,' said Penelope.

'No, you don't, Penelope,' said Ted, almost yelling.

'Yes, I do,' said Penelope.

'You really don't get anything,' said Ted in a despairing way. He looked like he was going to say something else, but then his phone beeped. He looked at it.

'It's Catherine,' said Ted. 'She's in my room and she wants to know where I am.'

'Well, I guess you should go there,' said Penelope, 'and tell her where you are.'

'OK,' said Ted. He sighed. 'Have fun at your show tonight.'

'I will. Bye,' said Penelope. Ted walked out the door.

As soon as Ted was gone, Lan emerged from the bathroom. On the way to her room, she turned around and looked at Penelope. Then she said:

'Why would you want to go to an arboretum? They sound terrible.'

'I don't know,' said Penelope forlornly.

'What douche bags,' said Lan. 'And I mean that about everyone.' Then she walked into her bedroom and shut the door.

Penelope spent the rest of the day napping on the futon. She was not generally a day sleeper, but *Caligula* had made her narcolepsy come back. When she woke up, it was six p.m., just about in time for her call. She rushed to the theater without brushing her teeth.

When she got to the theater basement, everyone was putting on makeup. Emma was helping Bitty apply kohl to her eyelids. They were both wearing dirty Wellington boots, the type of boots that prepared, outdoorsy people would wear to an arboretum, to add insult to what Penelope was gradually feeling was a grievous injury.

Penelope slid next to Catherine at the makeup table. She had to add dirt to her face for her first scene as a guard.

'Hey, Penelope,' said Catherine. She was already half done with her dirt makeup.

'Hey, Catherine. Good job on your makeup,' said Penelope.

'Thanks,' said Catherine, dolloping dirt (brown eye shadow)

on her forehead. Dirt symbolized the collective guilt implied in Caligula's crime. 'I am so nervous.'

'Oh, really?' said Penelope. 'What are you nervous about?'

'The play!'

'Oh, right,' said Penelope. 'I am also nervous.'

'There are so many people here. I just went up to check like five minutes ago. I think I saw your mom in the audience. Or someone who looks like you. Is it possible that she could be with a priest?'

'Yes,' said Penelope.

'Oh, also,' said Catherine, 'they found a replacement for Craig finally.'

'Really?' said Penelope.

'Yeah,' said Catherine. 'It's that kid over there.' Catherine pointed to a boy sitting in the corner of the basement. He looked like Henry Wills-Mather if Henry Wills-Mather were nine years old and in the Vienna Boys' Choir. It seemed as if he had recently been crying.

'Why is he so young?' asked Penelope.

'It's Henry Wills-Mather's nephew,' said Catherine. 'He goes to school around here. Henry thinks it will be ironic if the Old Senator is actually played by someone young. Because it is an absurdist play.'

'Oh, yeah,' said Penelope. 'Good idea.'

'I think he is worried it's going to be embarrassing,' said Catherine matter-of-factly. 'That's why he keeps crying. But he's a little too young to find things embarrassing, don't you think?'

'I don't know,' said Penelope, looking at Bitty and Emma, who were laughing hysterically at something.

About ten minutes before the show, Henry Wills-Mather came down to the basement. He was wearing his usual turtleneck and jeans combination, with the addition of a black blazer for the occasion's sake.

'Gather 'round, everyone,' he said. Everyone gathered duti-fully in a circle.

'To sit in solemn silence in a dull, dark dock, / In a pestilen-tial prison, with a life-long lock, / Awaiting the sensation of a short, sharp shock, / From a cheap and chippy chopper on a big black block!' said Henry Wills-Mather. 'Repeat after me!'

Everyone repeated that several times.

'I think you all are ready to have a fantastic show,' said Henry Wills-Mather. 'We have an entirely full house.'

The cast cheered.

'Places in two,' said Henry Wills-Mather. Then he tramped up the stairs.

Penelope went back to her corner and gathered up her props (a gun, a spear, the Algerian flag) to bring upstairs. This was when Emma tapped her on the shoulder.

'Penelope!' said Emma.

'Oh, hi, Emma,' said Penelope.

'I was looking all over for you!' said Emma. 'Where were you?'

'In the bathroom,' said Penelope.

'I can't believe it. I just got your texts now! There is some-thing really wrong with my phone, I think.'

'OK,' said Penelope. 'Did you go to the arboretum?'

'Yeah,' said Emma. She looked at Penelope defiantly.

'Cool,' said Penelope. 'When did you go?'

'This morning,' said Emma. 'I figured you would text me if you wanted to go. And then I didn't even see these until just now!'

'It's OK,' said Penelope. Emma let out a relieved sigh and then smiled in a pitying way.

'It was really fun, actually. The arboretum itself was beauti-ful, and Gustav was so hilarious. He is dating this Swedish princess and he told us all stories about her. Apparently, she's really dumb but can cross-country ski or something?' She let out a deafening laugh.

'Wow,' said Penelope.

'It was just so funny.'

'That is,' said Penelope.

Emma wiped tears from her eyes.

'Gustav is actually here tonight, which is the funniest thing. Bitty and I made him come. He literally didn't even want to and we were like, "Gustav, you have to," because, honestly, Penelope, you would have died to hear these stories. He is just hilarious. He's like an old-fashioned playboy. The man must be dating like eight different girls.'

'The playboy of the Western world,' said Penelope, who was beginning to feel a little sick.

'What?' said Emma.

'I have to go to places,' said Penelope.

'Oh, OK,' said Emma. 'Have a good show.'

'Thanks,' said Penelope. She climbed the stairs to the stage and took her place behind the marionette theater. She actually had a good view of the audience from behind the curtain. When she saw them all, gathered there, her heart sank.

The auditorium was packed. Immediately Penelope spotted two kids from her Southern Writers Reconsidered/Revisited class sitting in the front row. Behind them, she saw Ted, who was sitting next to Glasses and Nikil. Ted looked nervous even though he was not in the play. Nikil was trying to talk to him and he was staring at the stage. Glasses was already writing things down on a notepad with a light-up pen. Jared was sitting cross-legged on the floor next to Adorno Eric. Who knew they were friends? Her mother was sitting contentedly in the corner next to Father Bennigan. Gustav was sitting in the very back. He was wearing a red cashmere sweater and a green hunting jacket, and his hair was rather long over his eyes. *Very outdoorsy,* thought Penelope. The lights went down then, and Penelope couldn't see Gustav anymore.

This is it, thought Penelope. *This is the moment where I run out of the theater.* She didn't, however.

The play started, as it always did, with a bunch of senators gossiping about Caligula. They talked about how Caligula was murdering people and how he might have been sleeping with his sister. Some had French accents and some did not. Some were pretending to sleep on the floor and some were not. This lasted for about ten minutes. Penelope watched it from backstage.

Eventually, both Caligulas walked onto the stage holding hands, Rattailed Caligula wearing his belt costume and Bitty wearing a very elegant black shift dress. This was Penelope's cue to enter stage right. It was interesting how fine this was when it actually happened. Onstage, she couldn't see anyone in the audience because the lights were too bright. She just held her spear impassively, like in rehearsal.

'I want the moon,' Rattailed Caligula said to the senators.

'What for?' said Helicon/Justin after an unaccountable pause. Justin still didn't know his lines all that well.

'Well ... This is one of the things I did not have,' said Bitty. She stared into the audience, breaking the fourth wall, as she was directed to do. Then she sat on the floor, which she wasn't supposed to do for another five minutes.

'Do you have it now?' asked Helicon, who looked confused.

'No,' said Rattailed Caligula, 'I could not get it. You must think I am crazy. But I'm not crazy. Things as they are do not seem satisfactory. So I need the moon, or happiness, or immortality.'

What a horrible play, thought Penelope. And it wasn't even horrible just because the lines didn't make any sense and the cast had to make up the words to the Algerian songs at the end. It was philosophically horrible. Penelope should have realized that earlier probably, but hindsight is twenty-twenty, as Father Bennigan used to say.

It was Caligula. Caligula was the worst. It was always about him and what he was doing and the things he wanted, like the moon. If anyone wanted to talk about anything else with him, he didn't care. He certainly never cared if he hurt anyone's feelings. That's why he was freely able to kill everyone's wives in front of them.

If Penelope put on a play, it would have been very different from this. There would have been fewer speeches in it and no dancing and no singing and no marching. It would have been about a plucky young heroine who always spoke her mind. It would start with a German named Hans driving a 1970s BMW up to a brick building that also housed a radio station.

'Come on, Patricia!' Hans would say from the car. Patricia would bound down the stairs of the brick building.

'Why are you driving a vintage car? I think that's incredibly pretentious! Get a new car,' Patricia would yell. She always spoke her mind.

'It's your friend Emily's. I told her not to come because I hate her,' Hans would say laughingly. 'You are uniformly charming!' Then they would drive away. That would be the end of the first act.

If Penelope was honest with herself though, she knew that people liked plays about Caligula. They sympathized with him more. The audience liked him even. People probably invited Caligula to arboretums and lunch. It was beginning to dawn on Penelope that she might never know the secret of how to do that. It was so depressing. She felt like bursting into tears.

What was the secret? How do you have friends? How do you make people want you around? Penelope always thought that if a person just said 'Hello!' and 'Cool' and 'Awesome' that everyone would like that person. But even that didn't guarantee anything. Maybe you were just the type of person that people liked well enough but not well enough to invite you to an arboretum. Then it was almost as if they didn't like you at all.

'Come, let us randomly,' said Rattailed Caligula. He and Bitty were just turning toward the door when Lan shone a black spotlight onto the stage. Then the audience spontaneously erupted in applause.

After the play, Penelope really wanted to leave the theater and never return. Unfortunately, as she was gathering up her stuff, she saw Gustav talking with Bitty and Emma in the lobby, blocking the only exit. He was holding several bouquets. Penelope decided it was better to take the bull by the horns, so she started walking toward them rapidly, hoping to imply she was on her way somewhere and could not talk. This did not work, as Gustav intercepted and grabbed her arm as she was reaching for the door. He took one of the bouquets he was holding and gave it to her. Penelope had no choice but to stop.

'Darling!' said Gustav. He put his arm around her. He had gotten her pink carnations. Bitty was holding a single orchid. 'I have been looking all over for you. You were wonderful in the play, simply wonderful.'

'Oh, thanks,' said Penelope, suddenly worried she was going to burst into tears. The violence of some of her emotions amazed her. She should just become a hermit and live up in Cornish, New Hampshire.

'We're going out to dinner, darling, to celebrate. Come have dinner with us.'

'Oh, Gustav,' said Emma, 'I'm sure she's tired.' Penelope noted with satisfaction that Emma was holding purple carnations.

'That's OK,' said Penelope. 'I don't need dinner. I'm not very hungry.'

'Oh, darling. At least come for the fun of it. I am going to buy all you girls a massive amount of drinks. You need it after this play. My God, that marionette show. I have never laughed harder in my life.' Gustav squeezed Penelope's shoulder. 'I haven't seen you in forever, dear.'

'I know,' said Penelope, wriggling away. 'It's too bad! But I have to go backstage and get my things. It will take too much time.'

'You can text us later and come meet us,' said Emma.

'But what about your phone?' asked Penelope. She had the satisfaction of seeing Emma look confused.

'Gustav,' said Bitty, 'we really need to go. We have to get to the Fly sometime before midnight!'

'Let me get them with you,' said Gustav to Penelope, apparently referring to her things.

'Oh, that's OK!' said Penelope.

Penelope started walking backstage very quickly. Gustav followed her. She had lied when she said her stuff was there, but now she had to follow through. Luckily, she found a plastic grocery bag on the floor by the makeup table. She started to fill it with all the communal makeup. Gustav sat down in a nearby chair, put his feet up on the makeup table, and stared at Penelope. It appeared he was going to wait until she was done with this. Penelope started to put the makeup in the plastic bag very slowly.

'I'm tired, darling.' Gustav sighed.

'Oh, really?' said Penelope.

'Yes,' said Gustav. 'I positively hate getting up early. Such an overrated virtue.'

'I didn't know it was a virtue,' said Penelope.

'Oh, of course it is, darling. Haven't you heard all those contemptible expressions concerning early rising?'

'No,' said Penelope.

'"The early bird catches the worm" and all that?'

'Oh, maybe,' said Penelope. 'Why were you up so early?'

'I was up early because I went to the arboretum. I have no great truck with the thing myself but Harvard has one, and my family supports it rather extensively. Once a year or so, I go out and check how everything is doing. You would hate it because of your stance on nature.'

Gustav laughed genially and it dawned on Penelope that she had been thinking about this trip to the arboretum in an entirely wrong way. While in her room and throughout the play, she had decided that this whole thing was a concerted snub, a directed effort to make her feel unwelcome. In actuality, Gustav had simply forgotten he had ever invited her to the arboretum at all. He just didn't care. He had even entirely forgotten their previous conversation. He had repeated himself exactly. Did he repeat himself all the time? It was something to note.

'That's cool,' said Penelope. A concerted snub is a concerted snub, after all. You read about them and they are dramatic, final, and personal. This was sort of worse.

'Emma and Bitty came. They didn't seem to have that good of a time. But they can't say I didn't warn them.'

'I have to go,' blurted out Penelope.

'Well, all right, dear,' said Gustav, surprised. He stood up. 'If you must go, you must go, I can't keep you. I did want to take you out, but I imagine you are so tired.' He patted Penelope on the head in an abstracted manner.

Penelope looked at Gustav. He looked so handsome. Like someone in Princess Grace's family. Maybe the whole problem was that she herself was never honest about her intentions. If perhaps she had said to Gustav, 'Gustav, let's see each other during the day,' he might have done it. If she had said something to Emma about going to the arboretum, she might have invited her. But she never said anything to anyone about anything.

'Gustav,' said Penelope, 'I have to ask you a question.'

'Shoot, darling,' said Gustav. He stretched and yawned.

'Why have we never hung out during the day, do you think?'

'Why, darling,' said Gustav, looking slightly taken aback, 'whatever do you mean? Of course we have.'

'Oh,' said Penelope.

'My, you are funny,' said Gustav.

'I just,' said Penelope. 'I don't know.'

'Darling,' said Gustav, 'are you upset about that? Is that why you didn't want to go to dinner?'

'No,' said Penelope. 'I don't know.'

Gustav rubbed his finger against his temple as if he had a migraine.

'You and I. We have a lot of fun together, of course. But you have no right to be upset or something, dear. We are just friends. I have things to do during the day.'

'OK,' said Penelope. That stung. Did he think that she thought they were dating? But, then of course, they weren't not dating. She was silent for a moment. 'Well, what is happening?'

Gustav let out an exasperated sigh. 'Whatever do you mean by that?'

'Are we really friends? I mean, I didn't think we were dating, but I don't know.'

'Oh, darling,' said Gustav. He ran his hand through his hair. 'Well, I don't know. I can't be in anything serious at the moment.'

'Oh, I didn't think it was really serious or anything,' said Penelope, who suddenly had a feeling in her stomach that occurs when you realize that your time enjoying composure is rapidly coming to a close.

'Darling,' said Gustav. He made a tsking noise. 'I never thought I'd have this sort of thing with you. You're not the dramatic type. It's a little bit bourgeois to expect a picket fence and a house in Scarsdale, don't you think?'

'But I am bourgeois. That is literally what I am in society,' said Penelope. 'I also never said anything about Scarsdale. So I don't think we can really keep this going.'

'All right, darling,' said Gustav. 'Although I don't really know what you mean by "this." We can still be friends, of course. I want to be.'

'I don't really think so,' said Penelope, her voice shaking. She was about to cry. 'I sort of always knew there was something wrong, the way you always used to see me at such weird times.'

'What?' said Gustav. 'The melodrama, my dear! It doesn't appeal to me.'

'Oh, OK,' said Penelope, and sprinted out of the backstage area and up the stairs to the exit.

Penelope sat down on a wide cement stair outside the theater. It was really cold out and very dark. A brick patio stretched from the stair to the street. Across the street was a vintage-looking drugstore and a vintage-looking grocery store and an American Apparel.

Penelope started crying. It had been ill advised to have that conversation with Gustav, she knew. Conversations like those were dumb. They only confirmed what you already knew.

'What a night,' said someone theatrically into the air. It was Henry Wills-Mather and he was stretching his hands widely toward the sky, like Lee Radziwill on a trip to India.

'Hi,' said Penelope quietly.

'Oh, who's there?' said Henry Wills-Mather looking around.

'It's me, Penelope,' said Penelope, still sitting on the stair. She huddled closer into her knees.

'Oh, Penelope,' said Henry Wills-Mather. 'Hello.' He looked at her without recognition. Then he sat down on the step next to her. Penelope was surprised. She thought by saying hi she would scare him away so she could cry in peace.

Henry Wills-Mather stared ruminatively in the direction of the vintage drugstore.

'Did you think we had a good show tonight?' asked Penelope for lack of a better topic.

'Yes,' said Henry Wills-Mather, 'I did. Of course, we are going to have to pay for the pianos. I didn't know that at first when we ordered you to destroy them, but now I do. Now I know. But it's OK.'

'Yeah,' said Penelope.

'The theater is a demanding mistress,' said Henry Wills-Mather.

'I could see that,' said Penelope

'I fell in love with her as a young boy,' said Henry Wills-Mather.

'Gross,' said someone. It was Lan. Penelope wondered how long she had been there. She was wearing a gray military jacket with huge pockets and she was smoking a cigarette. Raymond was lying on her foot.

'What did you think of tonight's show, Lan?' asked Henry Wills-Mather with an edge to his voice.

'I hated it,' said Lan.

'If you put the black spotlight on Caligula's face in the second act again, the play will devolve into meaningless tripe,' barked Henry Wills-Mather.

Lan smoked in silence. Raymond walked over to Penelope and sat near her leg. Penelope patted him and sneezed.

'When did you come out here, Lan?' asked Penelope.

'A while ago,' said Lan.

'Oh,' said Penelope.

'I hate that black spotlight,' said Henry Wills-Mather. 'I hate it. Don't you hate it, Penelope?'

'I don't hate it,' said Penelope.

13.

Penelope, or Virtue Rewarded

The months following the end of *Caligula* were an unhappy blur for Penelope. She had not realized how much structure the play had given her life until it was over. It had been a relief to be somewhere most afternoons, even if that place was inside a marionette stage. Now she had to resume wandering around alone. In many ways, it was the most upset Penelope had been in her short life.

Penelope was not a martyr, however. She tried to bolster herself as best she could. She bought a quote book from Amazon called *Disappointment: It Can Only Lead to Success?* It did not help her much, but she sometimes still read it. She read extracts to Catherine after they received their housing assignments and were placed in Mather House. Catherine was excessively disappointed. Mather House was the only dormitory made entirely of cement, but, as Penelope helpfully pointed out, it was not the only dormitory with orange floors.

"'The sudden disappointment of a hope leaves a scar which

the ultimate fulfillment of that hope never entirely removes,'" read Penelope to Catherine. They were sitting in Annenberg eating dinner. It had been a trying day. In the morning Catherine had a final, and in the afternoon she and Penelope toured Mather House with some other freshmen. Catherine had cried when she saw the cement dining room and the cement art gallery of student work.

'Who said that?' asked Catherine.

'Thomas Hardy,' said Penelope.

'Why are you reading that book to me again? That has nothing to do with anything,' Catherine wailed. 'We are in such an ugly dorm. Mather is the ugliest dorm!'

'OK,' said Penelope. She closed her book.

It was true that Mather was a very ugly dorm, but Penelope was not really disappointed by it. She liked Soviet architecture. And other things in her life were more disappointing. She had not seen Gustav since their conversation after *Caligula,* for example. Her classes too were winding up badly. Instead of a final exam for Southern Writers Reconsidered/Revisited, the class was forced to choose between writing an epic poem or a short story or a manifesto for a fake agrarian literary movement, all of which Penelope's principles inhibited her from doing.

What she had to keep in mind, Penelope reminded herself, was that she was not the only one experiencing trials. Others were also experiencing them. Nikil was upset because he hadn't gotten the summer internship he wanted and instead would have to stay at Harvard, working for the business that put refrigerators in dorms. Glasses was upset because he had gotten two internships and couldn't decide which one to take, because one was in Bulgaria at its national bank and another was in New York City at a think tank for libertarians, and it was hard to do both at the same time. Lan was deciding whether to let Raymond become an outdoor cat, just for the summer.

'At least Ted is in Dunster,' said Catherine gloomily. Dunster was next door to Mather. 'Even though I am glad he is close to us, I would not want to be in Dunster. Dunster is much prettier from the outside, but it has very small rooms. A murder happened there too. A horrible murder-suicide.' This cheered Catherine somewhat. She took a large bite of her turkey sandwich.

'Oh my God, Ted,' she said and sighed theatrically. 'It's been so weird recently. Did he tell you what happened?'

'No,' said Penelope. It would have been impossible for Ted to have told her what happened. Ted hadn't really spoken to Penelope since their fight before *Caligula*. Penelope didn't know if she was sad about it or not.

'That's true. Why would he?' said Catherine rhetorically. 'Anyway, I was talking to Brad about it.'

'Who is Brad?' asked Penelope.

'Oh, Brad? Brad was my sort of boyfriend from high school. We were in band together for four years and we always liked each other. Now we are just really good friends. I hadn't talked to him in like forever, and then last week he called me because he is home this summer and he wanted to hang out, but I was still here, obviously, because I have to take my finals. He is the most hilarious guy ever!'

'Oh, OK,' said Penelope. Sometimes she could not fathom the romantic pasts of her contemporaries. How were they already so robust?

'I think Ted and I are taking a break over the summer,' said Catherine abruptly.

'Oh, wow,' said Penelope. She was not too shocked as Ted had mentioned this as a possibility all those months ago, but still, it was moderately shocking. She composed her features.

'I know. The other night, we were just talking about this summer, and I asked him if we should stay together while he was in Washington and he said that maybe a break would be good and I was like, "I want to take a break.'"

'Oh,' said Penelope.

'I was really glad I said it.'

'Me too,' said Penelope. 'I don't think taking a break is a bad idea, if you want a break.'

'I really don't think Ted was saying we should take a break though,' snapped Catherine. 'But I think we just have to do it. We just have to take a break. Long distance is too hard. Maybe he feels insecure that I will get with Brad when I get home.' She started laughing crazily. 'But I am not going to get with Brad. I mean, that is just so ridiculous. Even though he's said really flirty things recently, that is just how he is.'

'OK,' said Penelope quickly.

'So anyway, that is what is happening,' said Catherine. 'We are just not going to be together over the summer, then when we get back to school, we will reevaluate everything.'

'Good idea,' said Penelope. She was surprised. This was all so much more painless than she could have imagined. When Penelope had considered what would happen when Ted and Catherine went on their inevitable break, for she was not so wholly absorbed with her own troubles that this did not occur to her, she always pictured a scene of Catherine wandering the halls of Pennypacker like Lady Macbeth, screaming until Penelope brought her to Health Services. She could not have allowed for the succor of Brad's affection. It led Penelope to wonder: Was it really true what her mother said? That men were like trolley cars and there was always another coming down the block? Could one man liking you make you forget that there was another man who didn't like you back? It was hard to know. That was not something Penelope had yet experienced.

*

Five days later, Penelope was walking back from the library. She had been studying for her Dinosaurs exam. The library, once the most crowded of social hubs, had been almost deserted. People were really leaving for the summer, it seemed. Glasses was gone. Nikil was leaving soon. Lan told Penelope she wasn't taking exams. Penelope's final exams were all clustered on the last day possible to have a test – Dinosaurs was her last exam before she went home.

However, when Penelope finally turned up the street to her dorm, she was greeted by an unexpected sight. Gustav was in front of Pennypacker. He was leaning against the stone railing. It was really him too. She could smell his pipe from where she was.

Penelope's stomach lurched. She wanted to hide somewhere, but there was no place to hide. There were no trees and no other dorms, only a very ugly wooden fence in the colonial style. In a state of panic, she turned a quarter to the right and pretended to be examining the fence. Maybe it was not structurally sound. She knocked on it.

'Ahh, Penelope,' yelled Gustav, waving to her. 'Hello! Come here, darling!'

'Hi! OK!' said Penelope in a strangely bright tone. She stopped knocking on the fence and walked toward Gustav.

'What were you doing with that fence, darling?' said Gustav.

'Oh, I don't know,' said Penelope.

'I hope it is structurally sound,' said Gustav.

'Me too,' said Penelope.

Gustav looked somewhat worse than she remembered. His face was puffy. His eyes were red rimmed. He was not wearing a suit jacket but instead a cashmere sweater and very expensive-looking tennis shoes. Looking at his ruined countenance (this was an overstatement), Penelope was seized with an unlikely hope. Could this change in his appearance be due to distress over their breakup? Had he recently been crying? Maybe he had come to her dorm for a rapprochement of some sort.

'I'm sure you can help me, darling,' said Gustav, putting his pipe in his pocket. 'Do you know where the library is? Is this it?'

'Oh,' said Penelope, with a sinking feeling. 'Well, this is my dorm.'

'Well, goddamn it!' said Gustav genially. 'Is every building around here some sort of totem to youths lost in war? Everywhere you look there is some sort of memorial plaque. It's impossible to tell the difference between a library and a dorm, for example.'

'Do you really not know where the library is?' asked Penelope in disbelief.

'Well, I know I went to the library once before,' said Gustav. She held her breath, but Gustav did not seem to have any particular nostalgia for Penelope associated with that memory. 'But I remember very little about it. These buildings all look so similar.'

'The library's on the other side of the Yard,' said Penelope.

'See, I knew you would know these sort of things,' said Gustav. He patted her on the shoulder. 'You look so pale and studious. Is this contraption you are wearing what they call a sweat suit?'

'I don't know,' said Penelope, feeling desolate. Why was she wearing a sweat suit? It was very uncharacteristic of her; she usually dressed better. 'Why are you going to the library?'

'I'm looking for a book, darling,' said Gustav. 'On financial theory.' He sighed heavily.

'I didn't know you liked that,' said Penelope.

'I don't, really,' said Gustav.

'Oh,' said Penelope.

'My God. What a rubbish day,' said Gustav. He rubbed his eyes with the back of his hand. 'My father's being a terrible pain. Called all the children for a stern talk. Well, really just me, actually. He rarely does things like that, but when he does, he talks for such an excessively long time. You see, I was supposed to go on another safari with Goldsmith this summer. I may have told you?'

'Oh,' said Penelope, who was starting to feel like she was in some sort of dream, where everyone was speaking English but no one understood it. 'I don't remember.'

'Yes, I was quite excited. You see, we were going to have the run of the park. It's much better when you have the park to yourself, you know. But today Dad called me and told me I have to do something rather more practical, whatever that means.'

'What does that mean?' asked Penelope.

'Oh, you!' said Gustav. He ruffled her hair. 'I am doing financial things in Hong Kong instead.'

'Oh, wow,' said Penelope.

'It's shit,' said Gustav vehemently.

'But Hong Kong, you know? That seems fun,' said Penelope.

'Oh, darling,' said Gustav. He sighed. 'Maybe the first five times. But after a while it just gets rather grating. All those lights all the time.'

'Oh,' said Penelope. 'That's bad. For light pollution.'

'It's so tiresome being a drone,' said Gustav passionately. 'You don't understand, but it is truly awful for me especially to sit behind a desk. I'm very restless. I love to travel. I wish I could do that for my career.'

'Me too,' added Penelope.

'Everyone here always assumes I don't have to get a job. But I do,' said Gustav. Were his eyes filling up with tears? Penelope shifted uncomfortably. 'I have to get a job.'

'Oh,' said Penelope. 'That is horrible. But not for a couple of years.'

'No,' said Gustav reflectively, 'I suppose not.'

'Have you been having a good couple of months otherwise?' asked Penelope.

'Oh, rather,' said Gustav distractedly.

Penelope looked at Gustav's miserable face and his red-rimmed eyes. This was probably the most earnest she had ever seen him. She had to admit it was not very becoming. The thing Penelope had always liked most about Gustav was her feeling that he never said what he really thought. College might have been a place where everyone took their plights seriously and used honesty like a mallet, but Gustav always preserved his sense of humor in adversity, like Patton. However, now he looked genuinely moved by the prospect of employment. The passing months must have robbed him of his best qualities. Penelope felt sad about the changes wrought by the vicissitudes of time.

Although perhaps it was not just the workings of time. It was more probable that Gustav was the same as he had always been, and she had fundamentally misunderstood him during the whole of their acquaintance. Was everything he said that she thought was a witty bon mot actually what he was really thinking? He probably really did want the Netherlands to take over the entire world, for example.

A small part of Penelope wondered whether Gustav's appearance at her dorm was some sort of apology – a gentleman's apology. You couldn't really be that confused about where the library was. You probably could, actually.

'I have to go,' said Penelope.

'You can't point me in the direction of the library?' said Gustav, recovering his cheerfulness slightly. 'You could guide me through the stacks like an invalid.'

'No,' said Penelope firmly. And then she went into her dorm.

*

Penelope closed the door behind her in a state of elation. She felt invigorated, like Joan of Arc before being burned at the stake. She had seen Gustav, but she had not cried, or screamed, or begged for him to return. She had been normal and he looked way worse than she remembered. It was a triumph in many ways.

When Penelope opened the door to her room, she was surprised to see that Emma was moving out of it. Her father was packing all her books into a large box. Her mother was sweeping the floor. Penelope looked at these oft-mentioned creatures with a certain amount of curiosity. Emma's father was short but had broad shoulders and prominent jowls like a bulldog's. He was wearing a green polo shirt and his hair, which was suspiciously black, was parted to the side. Emma's mother was very thin and had thin short hair that fluffed around her scalp like cotton candy on a stick. She was wearing capri pants and loafers.

'Dad!' said Emma. 'I think you are packing the books too heavily. They are all going to fall out.'

'Hi, Emma,' said Penelope. 'I guess you are moving out?'

'Yes,' said Emma uncomfortably. Since *Caligula,* Penelope and Emma really hadn't interacted very much. Emma was too busy with the end of the semester to be in the room, and Penelope didn't care. 'I finished all my exams this morning.'

'Oh, cool,' said Penelope. 'Hi, I'm Penelope,' she said in the direction of Emma's parents.

'Hello,' boomed Emma's father. He put the box of books down and strode over toward Penelope and shook her hand very firmly. Emma's mother also walked over but stayed a couple of feet behind him and didn't shake hands.

'So you're Emma's roommate?' asked Emma's father. 'What's your concentration?'

'Oh, I don't know yet?' said Penelope nervously. 'I really like this class that I am taking called Dinosaurs.'

'Do you want to go into paleontology?' asked Emma's father in an angry sort of way. 'There's no money in that. You can't be a professor anymore. There are no jobs.'

'No,' said Penelope. 'I mean, I don't really want to do that. I don't even like dinosaurs. I don't know why I said that.'

'Your roommate seems confused,' he said to Emma and Emma's mother. Emma's mother laughed softly. Emma's father still looked mad. 'You can't afford to be confused, Penelope.'

'I agree,' said Penelope.

'Emma's going to have to work incredibly hard to get into law school,' said her father, looking at Emma and nodding at her in a forbidding way.

'That's good,' said Penelope.

'Me, I goofed off the entire time in college. I drank and I partied, but I still went to a pretty damn good law school. Yale's a pretty damn good law school, I think.' Emma's father laughed and Penelope saw where Emma got her laugh from. 'Her brother graduated from Harvard in two years. And that kid was a screwup. Drank and partied just as much as me.' Emma's father laughed again. 'Emma, however, will have to work. She'll have to work really hard.'

'Dad,' said Emma, 'I know I will have to work hard. Do you think I do not know that I will have to work hard? I do! I know that!'

'David,' said Emma's mother softly.

'Do you need any help with the move?' asked Penelope.

'I think we're all set, Penelope,' snapped Emma.

'OK,' said Penelope. 'I'm going to go to the library!' Then she left quickly.

Penelope wandered down the stairs. She didn't really know where to go. She was still too jumpy from her Gustav encounter to go to the library, and she couldn't stay in her suite if Emma's father was going to keep laughing like that.

After a while, she found herself near Ted's room. She hadn't seen him for months. For some reason that she couldn't really explain, she knocked on his door.

Ted answered right away.

'Penelope! Hi!' He was wearing a polo shirt, cargo shorts, and a baseball cap, which obscured his bangs.

'Hi, Ted,' said Penelope. 'What are you doing?'

'Nothing,' said Ted. 'What are you doing?'

'I don't know,' said Penelope.

'Do you want to come in?'

'Sure,' said Penelope. She went inside and sat on Ted's futon. Ted sat down next to her. Their room was very dirty. It smelled of old Chinese food.

'Are your roommates all gone?' asked Penelope.

'Well, Mike left for Bulgaria yesterday. And Nikil's still here, but he hasn't left his room for like three days. He thinks going to the dining hall is a distraction from studying. He keeps ordering take-out Chinese food. Can you smell it? I can't stay here anymore. I'm so glad I'm leaving tomorrow.'

'You are leaving tomorrow?' asked Penelope.

'Yeah, I have my last exam in the morning.'

'Oh,' said Penelope. She felt a little disappointed.

'Do you have any more exams left?'

'A couple,' said Penelope.

'Wow,' said Ted. 'I can't believe you have to stay so long. That sucks. So many people are done already.'

'Lan is not taking exams,' said Penelope.

'Catherine left yesterday,' said Ted.

'I know,' said Penelope. Catherine had noisily bid her adieu the day before. In the course of their conversation, she had made Penelope promise to write her an e-mail every day of the summer and Penelope said OK. Now Penelope regretted that, but she was still probably going to do it.

Ted stared at the floor for a minute. 'Hey, do you want to go for a walk?' he said abruptly.

'Sure,' said Penelope. She got up from the futon.

'I just hate it here,' said Ted. 'It smells so weird. It's so dirty.'

'I know how you feel,' said Penelope.

It was very dark when they got outside but warmer than usual. Penelope took off her sweater. No one was around, not even the last weirdos pacing outside the library. The streets were entirely empty. She and Ted walked past several imitation Victorian streetlights toward the Charles River. When they got to the bank of the river, they sat down on a bench.

'It's a nice night,' said Ted.

'Yes,' said Penelope reflectively.

'Can you believe the year is almost over?' asked Ted. 'It seems like we just started a week ago.'

'Oh, I don't know,' said Penelope. 'In a way it seems like it's been a very long time to me. Like an eternity.'

'Really?' said Ted, moving closer to her on the bench. 'In a good way?'

'Is an eternity always pejorative?' said Penelope. She didn't know. 'Do you feel like you have been dating Catherine a long time?'

Ted looked sheepish.

'I mean, I guess I do,' said Ted. 'We're not dating anymore.'

'Oh, right,' said Penelope.

'Did you know we're taking a break this summer?' asked Ted.

'Oh?' said Penelope, trying hard to look like she knew nothing of Brad and his predilection for unintelligible practical jokes.

'Yeah,' said Ted. 'It's too hard with the long distance, you know?'

'I do know,' said Penelope.

'I do feel like I dated her for a long time,' said Ted. 'I can't believe we dated for as long as we did. I don't know why really.'

'"How many young hearts have revealed the fact, that what

they had been trained to imagine the highest earthly felicity, was but the beginning of care, disappointment, and sorrow, and often led to the extremity of mental and physical suffering,'" said Penelope.

'What?' said Ted.

'It's a quote from my quote book,' said Penelope.

'You have a quote book?' asked Ted.

'Yes,' said Penelope. 'It's all about disappointment. I bought it on Amazon. I think I'm going to throw it out.'

'OK,' said Ted. 'What happened with that guy you used to date? Are you still seeing him?'

'Oh,' said Penelope, pleased that he had remembered her troubles. 'I just saw him for the first time tonight in like two months. He has to get a job this summer. And he started crying about it.'

'What?' asked Ted.

'Yes,' said Penelope.

'That's so insane,' said Ted.

'It was insane,' said Penelope. She looked at Ted. Sometimes, after the Gustav split especially, Penelope cherished the fact that Ted had been extraordinarily mean to her and she had weathered the whole thing beautifully. But now she didn't know. Ted was pretty normal, really.

'I'm really glad we're talking,' said Ted. 'I was worried we wouldn't ever talk again.'

'Oh, no,' said Penelope.

'I've actually missed you, when we, you know, weren't talking,' said Ted, looking down at the ground.

'Oh, Ted,' said Penelope. She was touched. 'I missed you too.' This was true, she realized. She had missed him. He might have been her only real friend.

'Well,' said Ted shyly. 'You should come down to DC this summer.'

'OK,' said Penelope. She was pleased. 'I would like that. It's not that far away from Connecticut.'

On the day of her last exam, Penelope was pulling her posters off the wall of the common room when Lan came out of her bedroom carrying a large suitcase and a crate containing Raymond.

'Well, I'm leaving. I finished all my exams,' she said. She was wearing a mauve T-shirt that had ITALY printed on it. Below the letters there was a drawing of the boot of Italy.

'What? I thought you weren't doing exams,' said Penelope.

'I scheduled all my exams for today,' said Lan.

'What? How is that possible?' asked Penelope.

Raymond mewed inside his crate.

'Shut up,' said Lan to Raymond.

'How long did it take you?' asked Penelope.

'What?' said Lan.

'To do all of your exams in one day?'

'It was supposed to take me nine hours,' said Lan. 'It actually took me one hour.'

'Cool,' said Penelope.

'Well, bye,' said Lan. She started walking toward the door.

'Wait,' said Penelope. 'Where are you going?'

'The bus,' said Lan.

'OK,' said Penelope. 'Can I go with you?'

'No,' said Lan.

'I will carry Raymond's crate,' said Penelope.

'Fine,' said Lan. She gave the crate to Penelope. Penelope looked inside the crate and put her finger in one of the holes, but Raymond didn't notice. He was too busy chewing a small hole on page one hundred of *Democracy in America*.

'Did you say good-bye to Emma?' asked Penelope.

'Penelope, do you have a mental illness?' asked Lan.

'No,' said Penelope.

They walked down the stairs of Pennypacker and out the door toward the Square. It was really cold again, even though it was almost June. Penelope was wearing jeans.

'So where are you taking this bus?' asked Penelope.

Lan said nothing.

'What are you doing this summer?'

'Hopefully, teaching Raymond how to roll over,' said Lan. 'I decided he shouldn't be an outdoor cat.'

'I agree,' said Penelope.

'His IQ is too low,' said Lan. 'He would never survive.'

Soon they were at the bus stop.

'Well, Penelope,' said Lan once she put her bag down and sat down on a plastic bench inside a plastic waiting area, 'good-bye.'

'Good-bye,' said Penelope. 'Do you want me to wait with you?'

'No,' said Lan. 'My bus is coming in one minute.'

'OK,' said Penelope. 'I had a good time, you know, with you as my roommate. I think we had a lot in common.'

'It's hard to say,' said Lan. She patted Penelope's hand. Then Penelope walked back to the dorm. In an hour, her mother was coming to pick her up.

14.

The Review

**WEEKEND ARTS PREVIEW:
'CALIGULA' BATTLES BLEAK IDENTITY**

Innovative Production Revitalizes Famous
Existential Play

By Michael S. Martinez, Crimson Staff Writer
Published: Saturday, —, 23, 20—

The world has no meaning anymore. This is the main point of 'Caligula,' a 1944 play by Albert Camus that experienced an innovative revival last night at the Loeb Ex. From the heart-wrenching belt-whipping scene to an intimate marionette show, this production got to the heart of the theater of the absurd.

'Caligula' tells the story of Caligula, a real-life Roman emperor who slept with his sister and murdered many of his subjects and friends. Historians have explained that this behavior was due to syphilis or mental illness or lead poisoning. In the play, Caligula is trying to reach a state of freedom through his transgressive actions. He uses violence to be liberated from morality. In this way, Camus examines existential philosophy.

In this production, director Henry Wills-Mather ('77–'79) translated the play from the French himself. The result is the literal language of speech. Caligula is played in dual roles by Chris A. Gustaffson ('0–) and Elizabeth B. Congdon ('0–). Both give bravura performances, representing the two planes of Caligula's personality. The supporting players are equally good, including Catherine T. Johnson ('0–) and Trevor R. Wang ('0–). Everyone seems committed to bringing a difficult text to life. Also in the cast are Penelope D. O'Shaunessy ('0–) and Charles Wills-Mather, a local middle schooler enlisted to play the Old Senator in the production.

Wills-Mather is a director in New York City (see interview in this week's magazine), and he brings some really professional touches to the production. The light show in the middle of the intermission is particularly stunning, if slightly out of place.

All and all, 'Caligula' is an interesting night of theater.

Acknowledgments

This book was a phenomenal team effort and I can't thank you all enough for such incredible support during the process. I have to thank everyone at Lutyens and Rubinstein, my agency, for their invaluable input. I could not be part of a better group. Felicity Rubinstein and Sarah Lutyens have been the most tremendous help in every part of this process. I blush to think of how many conference calls I put these women through, and yet they bore the whole thing with characteristic grace and aplomb. Thank you so much, Daisy and Anna, for your incredibly informative e-mails. I especially have to thank my agent, Jane Finigan, who took me on after reading fifty rambling pages of *Penelope* and helped me shape the book, draft after draft, into the sheaf of papers you see today. She is the smartest, coolest, most elegant person I know. I trust her instincts more than I could possibly communicate and she has talked me off the ledge more times than I could count. I feel so lucky to have met her. Thank you, Jane!

I also have to thank David Forrer at Inkwell for taking me on. David's wit, intelligence, and ability to make even the most nervous person in the world feel at ease was such a great help to me. He would not stop until he got people to read this book, and I am grateful for all the hard work he put into selling this novel. He is the best!

I also have to thank my team at Virago, especially Ursula Doyle, who was so fantastic. Her edits of my language and sentence structure were truly brilliant, and she has an uncanny knack for changing just one word in a sentence and making it funnier, lighter, and more subtle.

My book found a great home at Vintage. Everyone has been so tremendously kind and welcoming, but I especially have to thank Jenny Jackson, my brilliant, *brilliant* editor, who had great instincts about this book and knew exactly what it needed. Jenny has such an innate sense of structure, pacing, and timing; she immeasurably improved *Penelope*. Plus, she's so incredibly funny herself. I knew if I made her laugh I was on to something.

I would like to thank my friends, many of whom have kindly regaled me with stories of their own wacky college experiences. Thank you so much for being there for me every step of the way. What would I do without all of you in my life? And thank you, Harvard, for giving me a truly great education.

Finally, my entire family has been amazing throughout. I would especially like to thank my mother, the best anyone could have, who even let me borrow her friend Liz's name for my own purposes; my siblings, William and Allison, for their incredible support and excellent dance skills; my father, for his kindness and encouragement; and my grandparents, without whom nothing would be possible.